THE
BULLET
SWALLOWER

A NOVEL

ELIZABETH
GONZALEZ
JAMES

SIMON & SCHUSTER

NEW YORK   LONDON   TORONTO   SYDNEY   NEW DELHI

1230 Avenue of the Americas
New York, NY 10020

First Simon & Schuster hardcover edition January 2024

SIMON & SCHUSTER and colophon are registered trademarks of Simon & Schuster, Inc.

Simon & Schuster: Celebrating 100 Years of Publishing in 2024

For information about special discounts for bulk purchases,
please contact Simon & Schuster Special Sales
at 1-866-506-1949 or .business@simonandschuster.com.

The Simon & Schuster Speakers Bureau can bring authors to your live event.
For more information or to book an event,
contact the Simon & Schuster Speakers Bureau
at 1-866-248-3049 or visit our website at .www.simonspeakers.com.

Interior design by Ruth Lee-Mui

Manufactured in the United States of America

1   3   5   7   9   10   8   6   4   2

Library of Congress Cataloging-in-Publication Data is available.

ISBN 978-1-6680-0932-1
ISBN 978-1-6680-0934-5 (ebook)

For Antonio and Antonio and Zeke

*"Poor Mexico, so far from God and
so close to the United States."*

*—General Porfirio Díaz,
Presidente de México,
1876–1880, 1884–1911*

THE
BULLET
SWALLOWER

PROLOGUE

Alferez Antonio Sonoro was born with gold in his eyes. The gold was sharp and it stung him so that he blinked uncontrollably and always carried a vial of salted water in his pocket. Of the four Sonoro brothers he was the only one thus signified, and his parents regarded it a blessing, incontestable proof of divine favor. Though he was the youngest, the servants carved his portion of meat first, even before his father's. His mother often knelt before him at night, delivering her prayers directly to her child, rather than to God.

The Sonoros lived in Dorado, a mining town established by their silk-clad forebears in the arid brushland fronting what the Texans called the Rio Grande, but which the Mexicans gave the more descriptive name Río Bravo del Norte. A flock of clay-colored buildings studded with wooden vigas and decorated with dahlias drowsing in white pots, Dorado sat quiet and erect across the water from the wilds of the province of Texas, a four-day journey upstream from where the river spooled emerald into the briny Gulf. Dorado, meaning "golden," was both a wish and a command— the earth there was split apart by the Sonoros and her bounty revealed. And they took lustily.

The pain in his eyes made Alferez Antonio unsympathetic. *If I can stand it,* he thought, *anyone can withstand anything.* And most people

1

believed he'd been born with gold in his loins as well for he lusted after more, more than he could spend, more than he could hold, more than could ever be dragged by the cartful from the belly of the earth.

When Alferez Antonio stood in the sunlight, the gold gleamed white and it was impossible for anyone to address him without averting their own gaze. Even his father, abandoning all pretense that he was master of his child, took to doffing his hat and holding it at his chest and looking at the ground one day when his teenage son stood at the entrance to the mother lode and demanded to know why only grown men worked in the mine.

"Surely there are small pieces that women and children could gather," Alferez Antonio said. He kicked dirt at a thin, clubfooted child who'd stepped timidly forward, one palm open in supplication. "We ride mares the same as colts. We slaughter the fattest kid goats and cook them in their own blood. Why is it different with these Carrizo mongrels?"

His father watched the bare backs of the Carrizo tribesmen as they shuffled single file into the maw. Eleven thousand years of careful cultivation of the ungenerous earth, and for all their toil they were now granted the license to squat on their own land. The Spanish outnumbered the Carrizos and had long ago forced them west away from the riverbanks, because their God said to replenish the earth and subdue it. Their God granted them dominion over every living thing that moved upon the earth.

The father turned his hat around in his hands as though he might find courage somewhere along the velvet trim. "When the mine is yours you may run it as you like," he said quietly. And with a tremor in his voice he added, "But I caution you against working the Carrizos too hard. They will bend only so far."

Alferez Antonio snorted. "When will it be mine?" And then, in a voice his father took to come not from the boy but from God, added, "You won't live forever."

"A lame horse can't run," the father whispered.

When the father died days later it was assumed throughout Dorado that Alferez Antonio had killed him. And like all news that is unpleasant and inevitable, the story was accepted, absorbed, and forgotten in one gulp.

Mine work was presented to the Carrizos as an opportunity for advancement. Imagine closing your fist around your own centavos every week! The mine spokesman jingled change in his pocket and leered at the women as he strolled in pointed boots past their thatched-roof jacales. Imagine your children liberated from the drudgery of tilling the fickle soil, imagine the freedom to earn a wage and contribute to your family. A job in the mine is a hand reaching out to you. Grasp that hand and be free. The people listened to the man's speech with one eye trained on the spokesman's cronies still seated on their horses, rifles pointing to Heaven. Those who did not voluntarily enlist were rounded up the first day, herded to the mine entrance, and forced down into the bowels by Alferez Antonio's private militia. It took only two days for the first fatality, a boy of five who was skittering along a ledge to bring a lantern to his father when his feet faltered and he plunged, the light illuminating his round face as he fell and fell, extinguishing on the rocks below.

Soon, explosions rattled the plaster saints in Dorado's church niches and sloshed water over the round rims of clay ollas. Alferez Antonio was tunneling deeper and wider. Before, the mine had been worked by three hundred—Alferez Antonio would have three thousand in his shafts, entire families outfitted down to the toddlers with hand drills and black powder.

The mine spit gold out of its mouth with such regularity it became known as El Fuente—the fountain. A bridge was hastily built across the river so shipments could travel north to San Antonio. Alferez Antonio oversaw construction of a new church in the center of Dorado, with the tallest bell tower north of Monterrey. He built himself a sprawling hacienda on the southern edge of town with white Roman columns and smaller adjacent structures for his brothers and their wives. He threw parties, served mountains of shrimp and shark fins he had packed in ice and floated up the Río Bravo on barges from the Gulf. Over the next ten years he took one wife and then another and another, parading them through the plaza on Sunday evenings in their gauzy regency gowns like three naiads. The people of Dorado swallowed their misgivings like bitter medicine topped with sugar—they danced at his parties, played faro in his cantinas until dawn, wore braided gold chains around their necks, and cleared their throats and changed the subject when the Carrizos loudly bore another of their dead through the streets, wailing and wringing their hands and clanging their bells.

But in his early thirties, Alferez Antonio's eyesight began to fail. The gold had slipped from the edges of his irises and was now invading his pupils, clouding his vision. The pain woke him at night and he'd stomp through the halls of his splendid home, glaring out the windows and between the columns at the dark fields and the dark mine beyond. Soon the workers were divided into shifts and the mercury furnaces burned all night, rivaling the moon for their radiance.

It was then that the Carrizos' dissent began to grow tendrils, spiraling out and clutching legs as the men worked with rags tied across their faces, leading horses around circular patios to agitate a foot-thick slurry of gold, mercury, salt, water, and copper sulfate. Two more girls dead, they whispered, and an old man. And everyone had the headaches, the weakness in their limbs. Mal aire, *bad air*. No, said another, it's the chemicals, and he pointed at a young roan pushing through the slurry with knocking knees. They managed to lead the horse out of the patio before it collapsed dead. An overseer pushed the men aside and split open the animal's stomach with one flick of his large knife. He reached in up to his elbow and extracted a bloody lump the size of a mango. He demanded water and, once it was rinsed, the gathered men recognized it as an amalgam of gold and mercury, warmed in the humid oven of the horse's stomach.

A strike was planned for the following week.

Alferez Antonio heard the whispers. His spies knew the location of every meeting. The day before the strike, a sultry June morning thick with impending rain, Alferez Antonio appeared before his workers and announced he was allowing them the day off, that they should rest with their families. Pickaxes were dropped, donkeys were left unloaded, and the Carrizos returned to their huts laughing and singing. *Why, brother?* the other Sonoros asked. *The Carrizos will grow indolent. Next they'll expect*

4

us to rub their calloused feet. Alferez Antonio laughed. *You're exactly right,* he said.

That night the Carrizo men were meeting in a cypress grove to list their demands. Alferez Antonio waited for his spies to ride back with word that the meeting was underway, and then he dispatched his men to the Carrizo shanties to round up all the women and children. *Drag them by their heels*, he said. *Every last one.*

There was a defunct vein and a series of stopes along the northern edge of the mine and they were deposited there, shoved at gunpoint down into the hole. When the Carrizo men returned to their huts, Alferez Antonio himself was waiting to tell them exactly where their wives and babies were.

Everyone in Dorado sat up in their beds at the screams of the Carrizo men as they tore through the brush to their families. The men stormed down into the warm earth, their families blinking up at them out of the blackness. Everyone spoke at once, everyone had a plan, and no one heard Alferez Antonio's men strike their matches, nor the hiss of the fuses. The explosion sealed the exit behind ten meters of rock and created a wave of dust and debris that blew the Carrizos deep underground and smothered the most fortunate.

Alferez Antonio swallowed the last drop of golden añejo in his glass and watched with satisfaction as the smoke from the explosion rose under the full moon. He was about to turn to his lieutenant and order the man to ride to Agualeguas in the morning and recruit a new corps of workers. Tell them, he was about to say, what happens to agitators in El Fuente. But as he opened his mouth the ground beneath him began to shake. The explosion on the north end had worked loose the supports along the western edge of the lode. Beams snapped. Tunnels caved. The moon was white as an egg and in its glow Alferez Antonio watched whole trees sink and disappear. The shaking grew more violent and was accompanied by great explosions as the methane gas trapped underground flooded and lit every artery. The new bridge collapsed into the turgid river that sloshed over its banks and dampened the homes fronting the water. In town the people left their beds and ran out into the streets and looked up at the new church steeple rocking side to side before falling to the ground and shattering. In Laredo, Texas, three days' journey by horse, the shaking rang the bell at San Agustín Church.

The moon disappeared behind smoke and dust. North of the mine, where the Río Bravo had peacefully carried silt and rainwater for millions of years, the explosion caused the river to split into two, to fork like lightning and then rejoin itself past Alferez Antonio's big white house, at the southernmost edge of the Sonoro lands. Within minutes Dorado became an island, as though the river had spread its legs and delivered the town, now long and liver-shaped, and as disconnected from Mexico as it was from the United States. The rocky bluffs of Texas rose undisturbed like a sleeping leviathan on the other side of the water. Dorado was a land without a country.

When the sun rose and Alferez Antonio could see what remained of El Fuente, he felt as though he'd slipped away somewhere else, had been plucked by giant fingers and deposited into a foreign land, so unrecognizable was the terrain that appeared in the purpling dawn. The mine hadn't simply collapsed—it was no longer there. A waterlogged crater five kilometers wide spread before him, a shallow hole that had swallowed every horse, every rock, every tree, every shovel, and left behind a barren depression as though crushed under an enormous boot heel. His eyes burned and his heart felt torn in two, for it wasn't his wives he loved or his children or even the gold. It was his power for which he now grieved. He knew he would never again be able to take unquestioningly. His freedom and his privilege were trapped underground with the Carrizos, buried under kilometers of strata. He envied them even as he hated and blamed them. Their dirt-stained hands had managed to reach up out of the ground and clutch tight to his ankles, fixing him forever to the spot like an old Russian story he once heard about a soldier who'd been dared to thrust his sword into a grave. He rode his horse through the Sonoro lands, which now comprised the bottom three-quarters of the island, to where the river reconverged. He watched the rushing water carry away the last of the trees that only yesterday had stood on dry land. *So it is*, he thought and he spat on the dirt. He had ruled the town and now he would rule an island. And he took some consolation in knowing his will had been strong enough to bend a river. His fury had remapped the earth.

But the townspeople were disgusted by what Alferez Antonio had done, not least because their maids and ranch hands had been cousins of the Carrizos, and had packed up their rosaries and their Sunday shoes and fled, claiming they couldn't hear themselves think for the whispers of the dead begging for a candle or a prayer. Children threw rocks at Alferez Antonio and his wives when he took them for a stroll. More than once he awoke to find cow's blood smeared on the white columns of his home. The Sonoro brothers fought: one brother's house was burned to the ground, another dropped dead into his caldo, and the third became convinced his wife favored Alferez Antonio and he strangled her with a curtain tie. Nephews and nieces washed up dead on the banks of the river.

Alferez Antonio continued to live in the white house, even after scorpions invaded the library, nesting in Cervantes and fighting atop the yellowed writings of Sahagún. He closed the rooms he did not need and his world shrank. One of the wives he buried in the garden after she choked on a fish bone, another ran away after a violin salesman, but the third stayed, dutifully producing children and grooming them for their eventual return to moneyed society. This wife died in childbirth on her fortieth birthday, a squirming baby girl at her breast. The child was named Perla, and perhaps owing to her hand in her mother's death, the girl grew up sickly and fearful, certain every sneeze portended doom.

Alferez Antonio was nearing sixty when his daughter Perla was born. His other children had grown and gone, but not before they'd dragged off as much of the family's dwindling fortune as they could carry. When Perla was a young girl, she could see the faded rectangles of paintings that had once cluttered the walls, dust outlines where once rested fauteuils and tufted ottomans, glass cabinets emptied of their Chinese figurines. At twenty she married a distant cousin who promised he could repair the cracks in the white walls and reclaim the books from the scorpions, though he always found excuses to be away from the house and meanwhile pigeons roosted in the bedrooms.

When Alferez Antonio awoke one morning crying that he could not see—the gold had finally pierced the nerves and blotted out the last lights of the visible world—Perla ran screaming through the brush that now surrounded the white house and into town for the doctor. But the old man died before she'd even closed the heavy oaken door of the main house, expiring with a cough and a whimper, his last thought just a single word repeating like one key struck again and again on a piano: *Mine*.

Perla hung black cloth over the mirrors, stopped the clocks, and refused to eat anything but bread and water for a month. That year, 1864, the year Napoleon III installed the Austrian archduke Ferdinand Maximilian into the Mexican presidency, Perla's son was born.

She named him Antonio Sonoro, her priceless child.

After Perla had banished the doctor, the maids, and her cousins from the room, afraid they would breathe impure air into her son's delicate lungs, she nursed her infant.

And watching her from a chair in the corner and jiggling his foot in angst and anticipation, unseen and unheard by the doctor, the maids, the cousins, and most of all Perla, sat Remedio.

Remedio had been to the house several times before to make a collection—a young man who had pleaded with him, a young woman who had sobbed, and an old man who had laughed and shaken his defiant fist in the direction he presumed to be Heaven.

Perla used her fingertips to brush black hair from the baby's forehead and Remedio got to his feet, no longer able to sit still. The only indication that he moved across the room was a slight disturbance in the uniformity of the air, his presence as easily blinked away as an eyelash.

"I don't understand," Remedio said aloud, standing behind the woman and staring down into the grass-green eyes of the newborn. "He's done nothing. He knows nothing. What if he lives his entire life virtuously?"

There was, of course, no answer.

Perla began to sing to her child. Antonio stopped suckling. He looked up at his mother, neither of them aware of the shadow behind her headboard, the edges of which vibrated slightly in agitation. Though the baby was scarcely ten minutes old, there in his mother's arms and bathed in the warmth of her love, he smiled.

Remedio walked around the room and tried again, though he knew his arguments were futile. "Look at him. How can someone so young be assigned such a fate? That's not justice—it's little better than chaos."

The baby began to cry and Perla put him on her shoulder and patted him gently on his back until his lids dropped. In another moment Perla was asleep as well, and Remedio thought the mother and child looked as still and posed as if Filippo Lippi himself had painted them onto the landscape of the bedchamber.

"I won't do it," Remedio said, taking one last look at the baby and putting on his hat. Men and women were marked for Hell every day by their own iniquitous hands, their misdeeds open around them and touching everything like a spreading tide. But this was the first time Remedio had ever been sent for a baby. "Strike me down if you will," he said, "but I won't do it."

He left the house through the front door and walked down the path that led to the Río Bravo. A day, a year, a lifetime—viewed from up high the movement of time held as little significance as the rotations of distant galaxies. He would return—he was duty bound for that much—but only he would decide when.

PART ONE

THE
IDIOT

ONE

Antonio Sonoro was on his fifth cup of pulque. The sour-sweet drink had finally mellowed the bandido to the point he could sit down at a table instead of leaning against the bar, could allow his eyes to drop into a hand of cards instead of surveying the room gathering men and their intentions into little piles through which he could sift. Men nodded at Antonio but kept a respectful distance. Fending off rival gangs when they'd come to Dorado to collect a bounty on his head had alone fixed Antonio in the public imagination as a killer on par with Billy the Kid. And skirmishing with the detested Mexican customs agents and federal police had earned him credibility as a man who took no shit. Thus he was largely left alone. Yet since he'd come into the cantina a small pile of gifts accrued at his feet—a basket of brown eggs, a small bundle of dried minnows, a dozen tallow candles yellowed and curved like old bones—thank-yous from a woman to whom Antonio had given a chicken, a man whom Antonio had hidden from the rurales, and a teenage girl with one child and another on the way into whose small hands Antonio slipped coins whenever he had them. These gifts he accepted with averted eyes and a grunt. Later he would leave them on the bar for the cantinero's mother.

And so even though he had little to fear inside his own local bar, the new bridge to Texas was close by and outsiders regularly drifted into town looking to buy guns, looking to sell guns, or looking for a place to hide as they'd been chased north by the rurales or south by the Texas Rangers. Antonio always spent the first hour in the cantina at the bar, his back to the drowsy cantinero, drinking cup after cup of pulque until the electric surges that ran through his legs quieted and his fingers loosened around the sides of his clay mug, until he could fill his lungs with slightly more air. That night he was invited to join a game of monte and, surveying the competition, he sat down.

He was playing with three ranch hands and a fourth man whom Antonio privately called the Idiot. The Idiot was sitting across the table from Antonio, so drunk a whitened line of drool ran down his chin. His shirt was streaked with vomit and Antonio pegged him as someone who'd lately come upon some money—not enough to get anywhere or do anything, but just enough to fund a couple weeks of whores and mezcal, to trace fingertips over the rim of freedom before being yanked back earthward. Antonio watched the Idiot slam his dirty fist upon the table when he lost and tried to peer under the skirt of the cantinero's aged mother as she slouched between tables, and he watched the other men narrow their eyes and tap their fingers near where they holstered their guns, and he amused himself guessing how long it would be until someone killed him.

The Idiot made lurid boasts—"I once had a Coahuilan girl with a wooden leg. Ay cabrón, her leg was wood but her coño wasn't!" He leaned forward to shout an order to the cantinero and spilled his mug over the arrayed cards—"Pah, you bastards didn't have nothing." At one point he attempted to jump up on his chair and demonstrate how he could ride a horse standing up—"Just like Buffalo Bill, pendejos!"

"I've been in Zacatecas," the Idiot said, and Antonio could see by the way the ranch hands met each other's eyes over their cards that they were no longer listening and were trying to decide when they would take him behind the cantina, rob him, and beat him blind. "The whites are taking everything that's not nailed down," the Idiot continued. "They looted the ruins at La Quemada. They took all the good mezcal—not a drop until you get to Monterrey! Every month they send out a train to New Orleans full of all kinds of shit." The Idiot cackled, flecking tobacco-brown spittle onto Antonio's cards, and Antonio was thankful he'd now lost count of his pulque, otherwise he'd be reaching for his pistol, too. "Let me tell you," the Idiot concluded, "the Americans want everything in Mexico except the Mexicans."

At that moment the Idiot caught a lucky hand and, in his excitement, he stood up to cheer and knocked the hat from the head of one of the ranch hands. A smile broke out across the ranch hand's face, happy as he finally had a reason to draw his weapon. A moment later blood streamed around the knife in the Idiot's stomach and washed under the table and across the Saltillo tiles to where Antonio sat smoking and thinking. He left red footprints behind him when he finally went home.

The next day Antonio rode to the nearest railroad stop and conferenced with the station agent until the man pissed himself and offered Antonio his silver pocket watch. For despite being the local badass, Antonio was just as poor as his neighbors, and his farm as drought-stricken as the next. He was in need of his next opportunity. They were in the sixth year of the drought. It hadn't rained in eight months and that had been little more than a sprinkle. Everyone everywhere needed more water, more food, more money. "Where is God?" was the refrain taken up all over town. And Antonio looked at the sallow stomachs and leaden eyes of his neighbors and he could answer honestly, *Not here.*

He rode back to Dorado that night with the good news that the train the Idiot spoke of did exist, a treasure-laden caravan delivering riches into the United States and beyond. The train would travel through Mexico, crossing the border well north of Dorado at Ciudád Porfirio Díaz, and was guarded along the way by a troop of federales that would stay with it as far as the Río Bravo. Hearing of the armed guards Antonio decided that robbing it while it was still in Mexico was impossible without a veritable small army that could outshoot the government men. After it left Mexico, the train wouldn't stop until it reached Houston, six hundred kilometers away. And it was there that Antonio decided he would make his play, while the train sat in the rail yard in Houston waiting to be decoupled, before its goods could be freighted on their way to New Orleans, Chicago, and wherever else lived Yankees with money.

As he rode home his head was full of calculations. He'd need men. To do it properly, twelve; to do it at all, no less than six. And his biggest challenge was going to be geography. It would take two weeks to reach Houston under ideal circumstances, no telling how long they might have to wait for the train once there, and far longer than two weeks to return, figuring the mules would at that point be laden with several hundred pounds of cargo apiece. To say they'd be conspicuous would be to say a coyote is conspicuous among newborn rabbits. Out of twelve men he could depend on three dying or getting waylaid, and he had to account for losing between thirty and fifty percent of the take, as stolen goods had a way of falling into ravines, drifting far off down a river, or simply vanishing when someone fell asleep or went behind a tree to take a leak. And of course he might never find the train. The station agent had been fairly certain it was the 339 engine on the Texas and New Orleans line, and his certainty had grown the deeper down his throat Antonio had stuck his pistol, but the human mind is a feeble thing for names and numbers, and Houston was a sprawling place. No telling how many rail yards there might be or how easily a gang of train robbers could blend in.

Antonio dealt mostly in cattle, rustling herds from Texas and driving them south, where they would board ships for Cuba, though he'd smuggled most everything across the river, from tequila going north to cotton going south, and guns going in every direction. But he didn't like venturing any deeper into the United States than Laredo. Antonio was wanted for cattle and horse theft, smuggling, fence cutting, murder, and a dozen other charges culled from the wanted posters of other bandidos and pinned to him under the legal statute of "they all look alike." And yet, the lust for treasure, for a gamble, for the breath-holding moment of rolling back the boxcar door and glimpsing what lay within, would not subside.

The agent had been unsure what exactly was on the train. He'd mentioned gold and Toltec masks, the cultural flotsam of centuries-dead savages. Gold jewelry would be tricky to unload. The last person who'd had gold in Dorado had been his own mother and she'd only inherited that meager sum. But Antonio savored a challenge. And the station agent had mentioned one item in particular that had made Antonio's palms go slick:

several crates of saddles from Hermosillo, the finest ever crafted. "If the bastard Cortés had ridden across the ocean on a horse," the station agent said, "his ass would have rested on one of those beauties."

It was the thought of Cortés and those saddles that tick-tocked around Antonio's brain back in Dorado, where he lived with his wife, Jesusa, his two children—Nicolás and the baby, Aura—and his younger brother, Hugo. He thought of the saddles as he drove his skinny mules, planting another season of crops that would die for lack of rain. It bounced between the mud walls of his jacal at night when Jesusa chided the two children to sleep and got into bed with her back turned to him, refusing his hands and kicking him away with her bony heels. The thought tugged at his pant legs as his feet shuffled down the worn path from their jacal—which was situated on the end of a long, downward slope on the southern edge of the Sonoro lands, facing Texas—to the river to collect water for the goats, a rut that traced a perfect circle from the jacal to the riverbank, the goat pen, and back to the house. *A man is at war with everything*, he thought, *even time itself*, which he increasingly suspected of moving not in a straight line but a spiral, so that he passed and passed again the same moments in his life: planting, drinking, fighting with Jesusa, children, goats, pallid corn, whores, cows, his double-barreled shotgun clattering against the wall every time he slammed the door of his house. He was just past thirty—he should not know already what his life would look like at sixty. He felt he'd lived every day already until he couldn't remember if he'd done something Monday or Sunday or a month before or a year. He'd been born three hundred years too late, he decided. He should have been on the ship with Hernán Cortés bearing a long sword with rubies in the hilt. He would have trampled the jungle in his suit of armor, shaking a clutch of animal heads at the temple priests and filling chests with enough gold to buy entrance to fifty Heavens. A man of his character shouldn't be subjected to the daily tyranny of domestic life any more than a jaguar should be expected to pull a plow. He needed to find that train as much for what it contained as for what it symbolized—something he couldn't yet articulate, but that comprised no less than his manhood, freedom, and divine right.

Hugo, on the other hand, bore well the mantle of home life. He'd come to live with Antonio and Jesusa and the two children in the little jacal when the roof finally collapsed on their grandfather's big white house. Chased penniless into the hot, hungry world, the very last of the Sonoros' money spent on his education in Monterrey, Hugo soon realized that his knowledge of ancient Greek and Catholic philosophy would not be parlayed into beef on the table, and that no woman in Dorado would ever marry a man possessing neither calluses nor hair. And so he joined Antonio and his family in the little shack, helping Jesusa gather eggs and mend holes, and teaching Nicolás his letters and arithmetic.

Antonio and Hugo had been brought up as brothers, though in actuality they shared no blood. Antonio was the last person alive who knew that his mother had accidentally killed a woman with her carriage and had been shamed by her maidservant into taking in the woman's baby boy. When he was young Antonio tolerated the child and, over time, came to have a fondness for him, the greatest proof of which was that he continued to let Hugo live under the lie that he was a Sonoro. What greater gift could he give him, Antonio thought, than a gilded name? But the fact that they were not brothers grew more and more apparent as they all squeezed into the tiny jacal, as confinement and desperation made the differences between the two men more stark.

A few weeks after he learned about the train, Antonio barged red-faced into the jacal and kicked the solitary table so hard, the table flipped up on its side and smacked him in the face. Hugo was sitting on the floor grinding corn on a metate and regarded Antonio with a barely suppressed smirk. "I believe something is bothering you," he said.

Antonio could see the suspicious outline of a book inside Hugo's shirt. "I'll throw that book in the fire if you don't get back to work," Antonio said. And then, because it was his house goddammit and he was still master of something, he added, "And then I'll throw you in."

Hugo slipped the book out of his shirt and put it on the floor and bent once again over the metate. "Maybe you're better off forgetting it. If no one will go with you, it seems like a bad omen."

Antonio chewed the inside of his cheek. He'd learned in the last week that his lust for the train was not shared. He'd approached every smuggler in Dorado and, to a man, everyone had said no. Too far, too dangerous, the rewards too uncertain. "Let the whites have those Indian masks," one old bandit had said. "They're cursed anyway." The man he'd visited that afternoon, a big brute with whom he'd once eaten worms and ants while hiding out from Apaches, had gone so far as to feign a sudden interest in farming. "I have to look out for my family," the man said. "Why not do the same?" Antonio had watched this man scratching a rusty hoe against the pale dirt like a chicken searching out forgotten corn, and he spit at his feet.

"I can still stand," Antonio had said. "Even if the rest of you bow."

The man waited until Antonio mounted his horse before he responded. "People are talking."

Antonio glared down at the man from beneath his hat.

"They say it's the Carrizos. That they're the ones stopping the rain."

In the unflagging sunlight Antonio's face was darkness.

"Ride to Texas if you want," the man had said, "but you'd better take your family, too."

Jesusa banged into the jacal with Aura strapped to her back with her bright red rebozo. Her face was drawn from heat and exhaustion and lack of water. She dropped a basket on the floor. Six small pale quince rolled out. "Barely enough for one jar," she said, looking with disgust at the sum total of the season's harvest. She pulled Aura out from behind her and shoved her at Antonio while she wordlessly gathered the quince and began preparing them for jam.

The baby was beginning to fuss and Antonio gave her his knuckle to suck.

"Look at my skirt," Jesusa said, and she shook two fistfuls of her drab brown dress. "It's dry. I went into the river to cool off and the water's not even up to my hem." The river had been dwindling all year. Soon it would dry completely, and no one knew when it would refill.

"We can dig another well," Antonio said. "Try another spot. I can go back to the big house. Look around and see if there's anything left to sell." He closed his mouth after that, for they both knew there were no spots left to try for wells, nor anything at the big white house but ghosts.

Hugo, with a remarkable talent for unwanted insights, said, "I was reading about a man in France who's been sending balloons up into clouds to see if he can stimulate them to produce rain. It's quite fascinating, see—"

Jesusa was muttering under her breath. Her dark eyebrows had gathered together and they presented as one black line running across her face in a way that made her look very young. Antonio watched his wife fume around, bringing spoons down with a clatter, upsetting a basket half filled with malformed potatoes. "Say it aloud, goddammit," he finally said. "There's no privacy in this place."

"Acres," Jesusa said louder and without looking up from her work, "and acres all the way to the sun and you let everything get overgrown like some fool peon and we're left with a little patch that can't grow worth nothing—"

"Yes, I've never heard this one before," Antonio said. "Please tell me how you thought you were marrying a wealthy patrón only to find out he had nothing."

"And how many times I used to pass the big white house when I was a little girl and how I believed we could just fix the holes in the roof—"

"A thousand apologies, princesa, for not wanting to raise our children in a house of ugly memories."

"Everyone said don't marry you. They said the ghosts of those dead Indians would chase me through my dreams, and God forgive me they were right—"

"I'm confused now. Is it the dead Indians who ruined your life, or me?"

"But you were funny and handsome. You used to sing—"

"I'm still handsome, chamaca—you better not forget it."

"My mother said she'd throw herself off the roof of the church—"

"Your mother never did keep a promise."

"Today in the quince trees when I went branch after branch and everything was dead and dried up I said, 'Why God?' I asked the Virgin Mother—"

"Hugo, did you know that I control the rain? I alone, Antonio Sonoro, am responsible for whether the clouds open or close. I tell you if I *could* I'd flood this hellhole. I'd send it to the bottom of a lake."

"And I'm scared, God help me, I'm so scared for the children. Our children and their children and—"

Hugo had long stopped pretending to grind corn and made a half-hearted suggestion that he travel to Matamoros and find some students to tutor, but they all knew he wouldn't and both Antonio and Jesusa told him to shut his mouth and get back to work.

"And now you want to leave and go chasing after a train." Jesusa had turned around and now faced Antonio with a finger that glistened with fruit juice. "What kind of greed lives inside you that you would leave us to starve while you have an adventure?"

Antonio glared at Jesusa over the top of their daughter's head. "Men have killed their wives for less insolence."

At this Jesusa only threw the frayed end of the rebozo over her shoulder and shook her head. "Just what everyone would expect."

"Are you so ignorant," Antonio began, "that you can't see I don't have any other choice?" He paused and then he said, "Are you so heartless that you accuse me of greed when you know I'm trying to save us?" He bit his knuckle hard to keep from screaming and, he was surprised to find, to keep from crying, too. "Don't pretend you don't know that."

Jesusa's face was screwed up into something inscrutable, something that looked like despair and resignation and also, tenderness. She looked, too, like she might cry, and Antonio gave the baby to Hugo and he pulled Jesusa to him and his heart hurt for the hard edges of her shoulder bones, the gray circles under her eyes. He kissed her neck and whispered into her skin that he would make it all right, that he would fix everything. She wiped her eyes and said she had to gather eggs, and before Antonio could protest she pushed open the door and was swallowed by the sunlight. The bald quince on the table were already beginning to attract flies.

Antonio took Aura back and gave her a rag doll to hold, and the two men were quiet while she babbled and smacked the doll against her father's chest.

"'Marriage and hanging go by destiny; these matches are made in heaven.'" Hugo looked at Antonio with his eyebrows raised, but Antonio only scratched at a fleabite. Hugo cleared his throat as though working

21

himself up to say something. "I, um, I've been practicing a little out in the brush with a bow and arrow I found at the old house. It's a little thing, probably built for a child, but I've been working on it and I'm actually not bad when I can get myself situated. Anyway, um . . ." Antonio watched Hugo with a sense of foreboding. He knew it would come to this.

"You're not going to Houston. You're going to stay here and help Jesusa."

"I can ride," Hugo said. "And I can hunt, a little. I'll do whatever you tell me."

"I'm going to rob a train. When I need help having tea with the president's wife, then I'll ask you."

"You shouldn't go alone."

"Grind your corn."

Hugo looked hurt, but Antonio pretended not to care, still smarting from the argument with Jesusa. She was disappointed in him, and why shouldn't she be? When they were first married and he moved them into the jacal, he'd told her it was only temporary, that he would stop fighting and stealing and that he'd fix up the big white house and clear the overgrown fields and use a machete to hack away the dark and cluttered history that obscured their new life. And perhaps he had intended to do all that and more, but there was no money to pay for repairs, no workers to clear the fields, no banks to offer him a loan. Antonio never believed in curses or bad legacies—he lived in a poor region in a poor country peopled by ignorant peasants ground down by centuries of exploitation, ruled by a corrupt and avaricious government, bounded on one side by a hostile foreign power with no regard for economic parity or national sovereignty, and unlucky enough to have suffered a prolonged drought. His grandfather could have murdered a dozen Indian tribes and Antonio knew it wouldn't make him or the town any worse off.

And so, after months of returning home scratched and sunburnt and smarting from granjeno thorns, having managed to wrench only a few acres out of the grip of the dense undergrowth that knitted itself tightly across the Sonoro land, he was ready for any chance of escape. When he was asked to join a small raid on a ranch near Zapata, he didn't think twice.

And thus he had scratched out his living for the last twelve years, score to score, though as soon as he came into any money whatsoever, widows and crying children would appear at his side, clutching at his clothes and begging for a little consideration. Always, by the time he'd return home, the little handful of coins he'd place in Jesusa's hands was but a shaving of all he wished to give her. This job, this train, could be his dragon guarding a golden hoard. He'd impale the head, bring home the spoils, and grant Jesusa the peace she deserved.

"I'm going with you," Hugo said again, his face stiffened, with a hard little line settled in between his eyes.

But Antonio was through speaking and he wanted a drink. "Don't be stupid," he said and, softening just a bit, added, "Better you keep your hands clean. Maybe you'll be the one to pull us out of this shit." He handed Aura to Hugo and then headed to the cantina, hoping to straighten his thoughts.

Antonio spent the next week at the cantina, drinking all night and sleeping during the day on a blanket he threw down in the storeroom. One night to straighten his thoughts had turned into two nights to drink off the first, and soon he'd decided to just stay away, preferring the quiet clink of glasses, the murmur of conversation, the neat shelf of bottles, and the patient motions of the cantinero pouring, washing, wiping to the manifold failures both real and expected waiting for him back home. He waged arguments with Jesusa in his mind, the battles intensifying with each drink, and then dozed in the mornings half drunk, imagining the look on her face when he draped a gold chain around her neck and slid gold rings onto each of her overworked fingers.

On the seventh day he made the long walk from Dorado to his jacal, through the little island village. The church tower at the center of town rose four stories high in once-imposing Gothic Revival, a brick and stone edifice capped by a neglected bell tower of red tiles, many of which had fallen and shattered decades before. The other buildings in town unspooled around the locus of the church, with low, close-fitted houses built in the European style and spread outward almost to the edges of the riverbank, their once-gay colors—frog green, persimmon, honey, and sapphire—only visible now in traces, as though the town was forgetting itself, succumbing to an urge to swallow its existence, to allow the name, Dorado, to curl into the sky like smoke and disappear.

Antonio walked through the town, past the last houses and the hill that held the cemetery, and on to the start of the Sonoro lands. When he'd stormed off he was in such a cloud he'd forgotten his machete and now he used his knife and a long branch to bushwhack his way through the dense chaparral, the trees seeming to grow together overnight to create a botanic fortress around the property. At one time, long before he was born, there might have been vast fields of corn and watermelon, wide tracts of grass for cattle, but by the time he was a boy everything had gone feral or fallow. As he'd told Jesusa a thousand times: If the crops wouldn't grow, what point was there in having more of them? No matter. He would build Jesusa a new house. They could even move to the mainland if she wanted. He'd fill up her house with china dishes and clean sheets. So he didn't have anyone to help him? So what? No one then to claim the loot. He stopped and leaned against a tree to vomit. He'd been in worse shape before setting off on a new job. And he was better off alone. In and out, quick and easy. Two horses, four mules. If anyone stopped him on the way in he'd make his face go slack and say in perfectly broken English, "No problems, señor. You want buy my burro?"

When he reached the jacal he was surprised and dismayed to find everything in order. The goats were bent over their trough, the horses were turned out to graze in the sparse field. Antonio saw Jesusa had even repaired a fence post one of the mules had kicked over a month before.

Nicolás was sitting in front of the house skinning a squirrel, two more spotted brown bodies next to him on a tree stump. He looked up at his father without saying anything and continued struggling with the animal's skin.

"Start at the feet," Antonio said. "You started at his back like a rabbit, but with squirrels you start at the feet."

"We thought you'd left already," Nicolás said, resentment clear in his voice, though he turned the squirrel around and stuck in his knife just above the animal's foot.

"Where's your mother?"

The boy pointed with his knife toward the chicken coop, and just then Jesusa appeared in the yard scattering corn for the noisy chickens. She adjusted the red rebozo around her shoulders, and with her arms wide she looked like a gaunt bird, a brown body and red wings. She gave a sharp glance to her husband swaying on his feet before she stooped to go into the coop.

"You have to leave the shotgun with us," the boy said, and when Antonio looked down at his son he saw the first faint brown hairs above the boy's top lip, looking more like dirt than manhood. "I'm the man around here now," and they both silently agreed that Nicolás would do a better job of defending the family than Hugo. Antonio rolled a cigarette and lit it and then, after thinking about it a moment, took it out of his mouth and offered it to the boy. Nicolás pulled short and deep and exhaled up into the blue morning sky like he'd been waiting for that cigarette his whole life.

"I expect I'll be back in a month," Antonio said to Jesusa leaning into the coop to collect eggs.

"I thought you were already gone," she said, giving Antonio her back and narrow rump. "You see we're doing fine without you." Her body was bent in a perfect el as she reached for the farthest eggs, her firm contours hidden inside the generous folds of her skirt. He took a chance and leaned against her and ran his hands down her hips. She pressed into him, ground herself into his body, and he pulled her out of the chicken coop and turned her around and kissed her with such ferocity he hoped it would leave her knees weak, that she might collapse there under the weight of his love. Moments later, when they were in the jacal and she sat straddling him and pulling his hair back so that he watched her full lips and fervid eyes as they made love, she asked him if he was still going to leave.

"You think you're going to take off on me now?" she asked, a wicked little shine in her eyes. "You think you can leave me?" She pulled his hair so hard he was staring straight up at a crack in the ceiling shaped like a seagull. Antonio didn't answer, not wanting to ruin the moment with the truth.

When they were finished and Jesusa was putting back on her blouse,

Antonio grabbed a morral and started filling it with the things he would need, but stopped and ducked as Jesusa hurled a clay mug at his head.

"Son of a bitch!" she screamed. "Coward!"

"What are you doing?" Antonio screamed back, picking up one of the largest pieces of the broken mug and throwing it near enough at Jesusa that she flinched, but not so close as to actually strike her. "I told you I was leaving."

"I want you to get a job! I want you to build us a big enough house and take care of us like you're supposed to. My God, you think you're questing like—like—"

"Like Don Quixote," Antonio suggested dryly, regretting now the nights he'd read the story aloud to his illiterate wife.

"Questing como Don Quixote," she said and pressed her hands against her face in desperation. Then she looked up at him with eyes like two ripe olives. "I don't think you're cursed," she said. "I think you're afraid of being just like everyone else. Just another farmer. I think you can't stand knowing your destiny is right here with us."

But Antonio had turned away, and was back to packing the bag. "I'm going to bring you more gold than you can carry," he said, grabbing tin cups and pans and making a great clatter. "You'll have so much you could throw the little pieces in the water to make wishes."

Tears formed at the corners of Jesusa's eyes. They sparkled in the light that shone through the holes in the thatched roof.

Antonio turned and waved as he led the two horses and four mules slowly out of the yard. Nicolás regarded him sullenly from the front door. Even Aura, cradled in her brother's arms, watched him with what looked like reproach. Hugo had disappeared, likely to church, and Antonio told Jesusa to make sure his younger brother did his share of the work. She was back inside the house before he'd even mounted his horse.

Antonio made it a short distance from the jacal when he heard a large body crashing gracelessly through the brush behind him. He had his pistol out in front of him when Hugo appeared sweaty, bleeding, and out of breath. He had a great pack slung over his back and was cradling a saddle in his arms like a baby.

"You're not going to kill me," he said, though he kept his eyes on the gun as he sidestepped Antonio and plopped the saddle on the spare horse. He looked down at his shirt that was already torn and streaked with blood where he'd been scratched by branches. "Anyway, it looks like nature will save you the trouble."

But Antonio didn't put his gun away. "Get back to the house."

Hugo acted as though he couldn't hear him. Looking anywhere but at the gun, he put one foot on the stirrup and struggled atop the spare horse, who flicked its tail with annoyance.

"Did you hear me?" Antonio asked, his outrage rising at this bald disrespect.

Hugo crossed himself and began a prayer to St. Christopher to protect their journey.

"I said get off that fucking horse!" Antonio screamed so loud that doves broke through the trees above them in fright. But Hugo, though he trembled a little, held the reins lightly in his hands and stared ahead of him, sweat running in two lines down his face. Antonio breathed loudly through his nose. He picked up a riding quirt from where it hung around his saddle horn and thought about beating Hugo down off the horse. Defiance from a younger sibling was intolerable, and everything in Antonio's upbringing commanded that he teach Hugo some manners. How had he gotten it into his head that he could contradict Antonio? How had life not yet sharpened Hugo's soft edges?

And yet part of him was relieved to not have to go to Texas alone, to have someone to talk to on the ride, someone with whom he could share the triumph of opening chests of treasure, someone to see the gold and the jewels reflected crimson and amber on his face and know he'd been right. Hugo had told him he'd do whatever he was told. Perhaps this was Antonio's opportunity to finally teach Hugo how to be a man. Not in the trivial ways like hunting and shooting, but things more fundamental. Like looking out for himself.

He moved his horse close to Hugo's and brought the stiff, braided part of the whip up to Hugo's chin, using it to turn his face. "You'll do everything I tell you," Antonio said. "This is not going to be fun. And this is not an adventure." He thought a second and then added, "If you think you're going questing like goddamn Don Quixote, then get off that horse."

Hugo looked down at the whip and slowly nodded his head.

Antonio held his position a moment longer and then replaced the whip around his saddle horn. Without a word he set them off slowly through the trees, the only sound the steady strike of the machete and the branches falling under its swing.

TWO

Jaime Sonoro's eyes burned from the white-hot glare of the tungsten lights and from the makeup melting down his face, causing the edges of his vision to blur and contort. A vast, boggy patch of cotton spread out from his armpits and clung to the silk lining of his cuera jacket. Beads of sweat slipped down the middle of his back and tickled his spine. No matter where he stood, body odor and the tang of greasepaint followed him. He'd needed to piss for the last five musical numbers, and he'd wanted a beer for the last seven. But those things would have to wait. The crowd was cheering and the chorus girls were crossing their right legs over their left and bowing, their red, ruffled bloomers displayed to Jaime and the other headliners. Then the trumpets sounded, and the girls trotted away as one like a short-skirted centipede.

Jaime jogged to center stage. The accordion squeezed out baroque flourishes like metallic vines growing and unfurling and trailing upward and, blinking into the dark mass of bodies, Jaime Sonoro gave his signature grito, his rooster cry, "¡Quiriqui!" and the music was lost momentarily in the thunder of approving cheers from five thousand fans.

He took a good, diaphragmatic breath, raised his soft palate almost enough to accommodate an egg, and hit a bold but unpretentious F sharp, opening up his most popular song, "Madre Frontera":

29

My mother is the border, though she spat me out halfway.
Now my head is in Tijuana, but my feet are in LA!

He was too seasoned for stage fright and yet as he gestured out at the audience with his open hand, a nervous tremor shivered through his fingers and made them dance in the spotlight. He quickly made a fist so no one would see and he set his face like concrete in a wide grin. By the end of the second chorus, he could stand a little straighter and the hand holding the microphone did not feel so sweaty.

The gringos call me wetback, they don't want me here no more.
I tell them, 'Okay, Jack,' and then I buy the house next door!

There was an interlude and Jaime bent his knees, tipped his hat, and cocked one eyebrow and performed his famous toe-heel dance, striking his heel against the stage and swaying his hips and quickly kicking out his right toe in a bopping but fluid movement evoking a paso doble.

The crowd roared and got to their feet. Jaime could feel the whole building shake as they clapped and stomped, and little showers of plaster rained down on him from above. He had a slight worry the vibrations would shiver the wood beams until the old building buckled and caved in a great mound of gold paint and red velvet. When the song finished he asked everyone to take their seats, and then he turned around and told the musicians they were going to do a few slow numbers next. In the brief seconds of silence between songs the air was peppered with whistles and shouts of "Viva el Gallo! We love you, Rooster!" The venerable actress Sara García once told him, "Only assholes close," but Jaime had always thought otherwise. After the show he wanted everyone humming *his* songs on their drive home.

He'd been on the road and away from his family for four weeks: Detroit, Chicago, Kansas City, Denver, Los Angeles, San Diego, Tucson, every border town in Texas between El Paso and Brownsville, and now at last he was home, the final show a glorious homecoming for him and the other performers. These caravan tours played in American cities with large

Spanish-speaking communities and brought to the people their favorite movie and radio personalities like Luis Aguilar, the hero with a golden voice, or Lola Beltrán, known as Lola la Grande to her admirers, or Pérez Prado, the king of the Mambo. And on this tour, headlining them all, Mexico's guiding light of ranchera comedies, el Gallo, the Rooster: Jaime Sonoro.

"Rooster! Rooster!" the audience shouted when Jaime, this brightest anchor of the firmament, walked back onstage for his encore. All of Mexico's favorite actors had nicknames. Jaime was a movie star for many years before he realized that in other countries this was not the case. In his first big role he'd played a macho, firebrand rancher called the Rooster, opposite Pedro Infante. Where Infante's character had been thoughtful, the Rooster had been brash; when Infante called for patient deliberation, the Rooster provoked conflict, taunting his enemies and firing his pistol wildly in the air. He was a portrait of thrusting, if sometimes misguided, masculinity, and Jaime had enjoyed the entrée into a character so unlike himself, not to mention the chance to act with the incomparable Infante. The morning after opening night the papers screamed their love of the Rooster and, years later, he could not get a haircut without someone shouting, "¡Quiriqui!"

He'd starred in forty films since then, almost all ranchera comedies, a particularly nostalgic form of the Western that mixed music with comedy and tragedy, and seemed to help people pretend that Mexico was not careening at rocket speed out of its agrarian past. Now that Infante was dead, and Jorge Negrete before him, Jaime was the last cowboy left, a legacy he bore with gratitude and pride. The Rooster was a Norteño like him, hailing from the northern ranchlands that abutted Texas. He'd based the character on his scant knowledge of his family's history up north, and plugged the remaining holes with mannerisms cobbled together from folk heroes like Pancho Villa, resulting in a charming, unsophisticated gallant possessing a folksy, black-and-white morality that the public devoured without end. For the millions of peasants who'd walked barefoot out of the countryside and now slept ten to a room in a lice-ridden city slum, Jaime's movies were reassurance that life had not really changed, that somewhere men were still riding horses and defending the honor of women and stringing up bad men from the branches of tall trees. To them the Rooster was proof that the better days lay both behind them and in front.

The cymbals crashed one final time. The other performers gathered around him onstage to take their bows. As the curtain dropped, Jaime's hand was shaken and his back clapped by every cast member and stage-hand. *Always an honor, Don Jaime! They were rolling in the aisles! A real showstopper!*

"A privilege. A privilege," Jaime said with each handshake. And riding high on the successful tour, and knee-weakened at the thought of a long shower and a night with his wife wrapped up in Egyptian cotton, he truly meant it.

Jaime, his elderly father, his wife, Elena, and their three children lived in an elegant Barragán home in Pedregal, an orange-and-white six-bedroom mansion that was long and low like a freighter, an achievement of mid-century modernism, and a temple to a cleanness of form the aesthetic of which blared ever louder for its location in one of the globe's most ornamented cities. In sheltered calm under leafy poplars, hidden by a two-meter-high wall, and flanked on one side by the indigo expanse of a heated lap pool and on the other by a swan pond, Mexico's favorite singing cowboy wrote and read, lunched and napped, swam with his children, and made love to his wife.

And it was into this Elysian dreamworld that a short, frowsy woman with black hair and blacker eyeglasses stepped, first with hesitation, pacing twice in front of the gate, and then with purpose, opening it and marching forth. She let the brass knocker crash against the door twice before she found the doorbell. It gave two low bongs, which echoed through the clean white walls of the house with the ominousness of Raphael sounding his trumpet.

Jaime was in his study reading the trades. María Félix and he had just been named Mexico's highest-grossing stars, and questions and rumors swirled—would they film a picture together? Ignacia, the maid, knocked on the door and told Jaime a woman was waiting for him outside, refusing to be shown in.

"No, señor, I don't think she's from the press."

"I know, señor. I told her you were very tired from the tour, but she won't say what she wants."

"Strange. Almost afraid. She's just standing out there, señor. I can tell her to leave if you want."

Jaime put his magazine down with annoyance.

"To what do I owe the pleasure?" Jaime asked, his tone stiff with forced cordiality. The woman's clothes were appalling: loose, drab, and layered, and topped with a moth-worn sweater of indeterminate age and color. Jaime took her for a deranged fan and he made sure he could slam the door quickly if she decided to make trouble.

"This is yours," the woman said, and she shoved something heavy and rectangular and wrapped up in paper into his hands before he could stop her. And then she turned and jogged down the path to the gate, Jaime blinking and bewildered a second before he followed her, still holding the parcel in his hands.

"Stop!" he shouted, and to his relief she did stop just inside the gate. Jaime was shy of making scenes, and he had no desire to chase down a crazy woman in full view of his neighbors. "Explain yourself," he demanded. "Or else I'll call the police."

The woman's face colored at the word, *police*, and she straightened her glasses and passed one hand through her short-cropped hair. "It's a book," she said. "I'm a rare-book dealer. And this one—it's about your family. I assume. The Sonoros. You're the most famous Sonoro I know, so I called the actors' union and got your address. Okay? It's just a book."

Jaime listened to her with his nose wrinkled, for he realized there was a terrible smell coming from the package in his hands. The book, if that was what really was inside the paper, smelled like rotting meat.

"It smells," he said stupidly, his brain so addled by this exchange. And before he could stop her the woman had slipped through the gate to the street, where a yellow taxi was waiting. He opened and closed his mouth a few times, feeling like a landed fish. The stinking book was like lead in his hands and he stood for a minute marveling at its weight, at how it seemed to want to pull him down.

THREE

Antonio and Hugo were in Houston two weeks waiting on the train, two weeks of rain broken by hours of unbearable humidity and an onslaught of mosquitoes. Antonio had never been anywhere so humid and green, as though the Americans were somehow stealing the water as well. The marshy terrain made the animals hesitant and sluggish, and it worried Antonio that when they had to run, they would not.

They hid out in a wooded area just beyond a cemetery at the city's western border. They slept during the day and ventured out at night, leaving the animals at the camp and creeping on foot past the graves to the rail yard, where they crouched in the soggy grass, tried to resist scratching their dozens of mosquito bites, and watched men endlessly load and unload cars. "When the train gets here we'll know how everything moves," Antonio had told Hugo their first night watching the trains. "In and out quick. Break in, grab what we can, and go. No surprises." True to his promise Hugo hobbled the horses when Antonio told him to hobble the horses, and he gathered water and firewood, and he drew a perfect diagram of the rail yard, all seven tracks, with the number and sequence of every boxcar waiting to be coupled. But he did all this with a heavy air, as though he felt obligated to help rather than eager to abet their crime.

Antonio had a feeling Hugo would try to talk him out of robbing the train, and on their fourteenth night in Houston, he was proven right. Antonio was in a dark mood, and he glared up at the last traces of pink sky through a thick canopy of oak leaves. He chewed the inside of his cheek. The train should come that evening. If it didn't, his calculations had been incorrect, his information bad, his luck gone. They were almost out of food and it was a long trip back, and every day they weren't spotted and detained was another day they'd cheated fate. There was no sense staying longer if the train didn't show up that night.

"Eat," he said before he chucked a rabbit leg at Hugo, who was reading his Bible beside the fire. "That train's coming tonight. We need to get ready."

Hugo caught the leg with one hand, but did not close his Bible, and when he spoke, he spoke to the meat.

"'If any man be in Christ, he is a new creature,'" Hugo said. "'Old things are passed away; behold, all things are become new.' It's Second Corinthians," he said after a pause, "and what it means is that, when Christ died for our sins—"

"I know what it means," Antonio said. "Just say whatever you're going to say."

"It's not too late to go back," Hugo said. "We can tell everyone the train never came, or we can say we stole the gold but it washed away in a storm. We don't have to carry this stain. We can choose."

Antonio nodded and looked into the fire as he ate. "We can choose, eh, padre? Then tell me why I chose to be born a pinche Sonoro with no money, no gold, no nothing except my name?"

Hugo looked down and ran his fingers over and through the grass blades. "If there's no path to righteousness, then what's it all for? If we're marked from birth—this one's destined to be a priest and this one is a murderer—then what's the point of anything? No. God tells us how He wants us to live because every moment is a choice. His instructions are all there."

"You're telling me when men kill one another and children starve that this is how God wants us to live? That Bible's worth more as kindling than anything else."

"I came along so you wouldn't be out here alone, but I've prayed every night we wouldn't find that train. Christ will forgive you if you ask. All you have to do is turn around. I'll be with you. When we get back we can clear the land together. We can move to Nuevo Laredo if you want, or Matamoros. I'll learn how to farm. I'll learn how to break horses. I realize now how my indolence has led to your undoing. But now I'm ready to put away my books and work. Just come back with me. Old things are passed away. Everything can be new."

"Old things don't pass away," Antonio said, watching the flames blacken the rabbit bone he'd just dropped into the fire. "Everything comes back around. Our punishment is that we're always going forward, but always in a circle."

"I want to help you. Can't you see that?"

But Antonio got to his feet and began kicking dirt over the fire. "You've been reading too much. Men think clearest when they're on either end of a gun. There's no question that can't be answered that way."

To this Hugo said nothing.

Antonio looked west into the darkened sky and thought of Jesusa and the children. Of divinity he thought very little beyond the plain truth that knowing love was as close as he wished to come to knowing God. "Get the mules ready," he said.

Seven tracks fed into the massive yard and trains snaked outward in all directions like the bowels of a monster. Great torches burned high up on posts and even late into the night the machinery never slowed. Teams of slick-bodied men hoisted crates into boxcars while sooty boys raced between them with wheelbarrows filled with coal. Foremen bellowed over the hissing steam and clanging engines, directing the workers like oxen. In this roiling cauldron it was easy for two men to go unseen.

There was no moon. Stars shone in the cloudless night like a million shards of glass. Antonio led them to a stand of trees, where they tied the animals just as they had practiced. Then they skulked around the edge of the yard until they reached a ditch near the track leading east. There were many new cars in line since the night before and Antonio strained to see their markings. A whistle screamed as a new engine came in, its light blaring through the yard long and loud, illuminating everything. And before the light passed, Antonio saw it: steaming in the hot night, weather-beaten and streaked with bird shit, was Engine 339. The station agent had been correct. Here was the great beast, finally within his sights.

The train had clearly just arrived and the yard workers hadn't yet had the chance to determine which cars would get decoupled and which added before it continued east. Antonio and Hugo waited while a gang of boys ran noisily past with loads of coal, and then they crept up to the boxcar closest to the ditch and pried open the door. As they lit a lantern and swung it over the interior, Antonio's lips spread wide, for it was exactly as the Idiot had said: crates of honey-colored añejo tequila from Jalisco and pellucid charanda from Uruapan, masks shaped like jackals and devils that glittered with gold and jade and quetzal feathers, a great oaken table inlaid with a mosaic of the Aztec calendar, cypress furniture carved all over with dahlias, and boxes of jewelry containing elaborately strung beads and hammered gold and silver. Antonio picked up a grimacing mask and thought of the overstuffed, pink-faced women who would pass by it hanging in a curiosity shop and titter and shriek, and at that moment he knew that after stealing what he could, he would set fire to the train. He'd never felt any particular allegiance to the patria, but something about standing amid the artisanship of his countrymen, all corners of Mexico represented, made him very much want to stop this delivery of history into undeserving hands. And it had been a long time since he'd had the pleasure of setting a fire.

He put the mask down and told Hugo to keep watch as he went to work opening a crate marked *Hermosillo*. What he unearthed from the sawdust, unwrapped from its cloth sack, and held up to the lantern light caused his heart to flutter, and he thanked God for having sent the Idiot through Dorado. It was indeed a saddle, though the word hardly bore the divine light of what he now held in his hands. The cantle, pommel, and horn were ivory, the horn gleaming white and virginal like a maiden's neck. Great silver conchos flanked the skirt and it was embroidered all over in lush patterns of twisting silver rattlesnakes that leapt in high relief against the saddle's supple brown skin. The vision required to dream something so exquisite and the skill to coax such designs from leather and silver and thread required generations to hone, or the promise of many souls to the devil.

"It's glorious," Hugo whispered, leaning into the boxcar. "It's hard to believe something so exquisite was made by men."

"How many horses you think one of these is worth?" Antonio asked, knowing the answer was in the dozens.

He found three other saddles in the same crate and four other crates besides. He unpacked the saddles and then he and Hugo wrapped them in tanned hides and carried them quietly to the mules and strapped them to their backs. Back and forth from the boxcar to the horses Antonio and Hugo carried a dozen bottles of tequila, all the jewelry they could find, and, on a late impulse, Antonio snatched the grimacing jade mask.

"It ought to be in a museum," Hugo said.

Antonio held the mask in the dim lamplight of the boxcar, feeling in it the weight of a thousand years. Its eyes peered blankly at the two thieves and its teeth stood straight as spears. Poor sons of bitches, he started to say, but thought better of it. "A museum would have to pay, same as anyone else." He shoved the mask in his morral.

"Hey!"

They looked up and saw a boy of about twelve watching them. He was balancing an empty wheelbarrow against his knee and his eyes glowed white against a face blackened with soot.

Hugo sucked in a quick breath, but Antonio had been ready for this. "Put out the light," he said in perfect English, taking care to stretch the *i* in "light" in a practiced Texan drawl. Hugo extinguished the lantern as the boy took off toward the center of the yard, screaming that there were thieves on the eastbound track. Antonio shoved Hugo out of the boxcar and told him to get the animals and head for the main road. Twenty cars on the train and they'd had time to rob only one. It felt like spitting at the ocean. He threw bottles of charanda around the car, enjoying the chaos of shattering glass, and made sure everything was soaked with the sweet rum. With two more bottles under his arms he hopped out of the car before lighting a match and watching the car ignite. The first flames were blue, but soon orange fire overtook everything, and Antonio stuffed a bit of rag into the other two bottles and hurled them at the adjoining two cars. Before fleeing he stood for just a second and watched the flames grow taller than the trees.

He found Hugo on the road, sweating and urging the grumbling mules, and he told him to slow down, made him take several gulps of the tequila, and then started loudly singing an old corrido about a one-eyed prostitute.

"What are you doing?" Hugo whispered as a buggy driver overtook them and cast a disdainful look on the two drunks.

"Just sing," Antonio ordered. He was bitter about not having stolen more, but he enjoyed the chase, the escape. Life without these little frictions was too gray.

A few minutes later, when the mules had had time to catch their breath, two men on horseback came racing up. One shone a lantern in Antonio's face and interrogated the soot-faced boy sitting on the horse behind him. "This them?"

"Naw," the boy answered. "I told you, they weren't Mexican."

Without delay they rode off in search of the fictitious Texan bandits. When they were gone Hugo exhaled a long breath and covered his face with his hands. "Glory to the Father," he said, crossing himself. "Give me some more tequila."

They walked a half hour past the cemetery, following the subtle curve of the bayou and staying inside the trees along the northern bank. The mules sweated in the thick, humid air but kept a steady pace. Antonio spoke to the leader, even stroking his muzzle and wiping the perspiration from under his eyes. "We're going for a swim, padrecito. Enjoy the water now. It'll be another day until we reach the Brazos."

When they were well away from any houses, long past the last felled oak, where the air no longer carried even a hint of smoke from the nearest cook fire, Antonio turned them down the riverbank to a brief, sandy beach.

They began to undress. "You don't want to ride in wet clothes," Antonio had said on the journey into Texas, when they'd reached a river too deep to ford. "You'll chafe your balls so bad you'll beg me to cut them off." Antonio sat on a log to take off his boots.

He'd pulled his knife out of his belt, but hesitated to put it in his saddlebag. He held it in his hand, enjoyed its familiar weight. It was a switchblade, the hilt a combination of gold inlay and ivory or bone. Opening it revealed a curved, murderous weapon of serrated steel that tapered to a smooth, gleaming edge. It was very old, his grandfather's maybe, or someone before him, the inscription in a language he couldn't read so that the characters were lines and wavers, slashes and dots. But it fitted so well the contours of his palm he could have commissioned it himself from a Toledo bladesmith. He decided he didn't want it out of reach. He put his clothes in his saddlebag and then put his boots back on and slipped the knife inside one of them.

"You did good back there, manito," he said, watching a star shoot and disappear behind some wispy clouds. "Maybe you ought to consider a life of crime."

"I'm no Sancho Panza," Hugo said with a weak smile. "This has been enough questing for me." Antonio watched with some pride as Hugo led his horse and two of the mules into the water, his soft pale body disappearing into the river until only the dome of his head bobbed above the current.

The water was warm, but still a relief. Antonio let his head go under and enjoyed the tickle behind his ears and down his neck as he reemerged into the sticky summer night. The horses made great huffs as they surged across and the mules bared their yellow teeth against the mild current. On the other side they stood a moment letting their bodies dry before retrieving their clothes. And there was a brief pause—when the horses and mules had quieted, when the two men stood naked, dripping water onto the sand, when the frogs and crickets held their night songs before beginning another chorus, and the mosquitoes rested before taking flight—it was in that gap that Antonio heard from somewhere in the trees beyond the riverbank a twig snap, that little sound as damning as a gun blast. He knew: They were caught.

Two men stepped out from behind the trees, pistols drawn. Even if they weren't wearing silver badges pinned to their custodian helmets, Antonio would have known them to be police—they held their guns with two hands, one finger indexed along the frame, and took careful, sidelong steps. Such caution for two naked men.

"Cowards," Antonio spat. "You wait until we're naked and defenseless. Why don't you attack men like men?"

One of the officers had flat, cruel eyes. He was older than his partner and wore a thin tie. Antonio thought he could choke him with it if the other man didn't have a gun trained on him. The officer looked Antonio up and down and in one motion brought his knee up and plunged it into Antonio's groin. Blinding instantaneous pain flooded Antonio, spreading through his belly and up to his ears. He fell to the ground because he thought he might vomit. "Get them hands up over your head," the man said as Antonio lay fetal on the ground. "We heard someone robbed a train. Even set it on fire. Posted us up all over the area looking for the men who did it. Said the suspects were white, but I figure two Mexicans out this late can't be up to no good, either."

"Good goddamn." The other officer, who had a nasal voice and small eyes like a weasel, pulled a saddle from its hide wrapping and opened his lighter to see it better. "Where the hell was you greasers planning to sell these? There ain't a Pedro alive has that kinda money."

The one who'd kicked Antonio spoke without inflection. "Probably thinking to boil 'em down and eat 'em."

"Look at this." The weasel-eye brought out a gold necklace made of many linked parts like chain mail that jangled as he drew it out of the saddlebag. "We found a danged pirate treasure."

"Put it back," said the one in the tie, obviously the man's superior. "We'll take it all to the captain."

Antonio noticed the weasel-eye hesitated before putting the necklace back in the saddlebag, and he noted, too, how the man in the tie looked on his subordinate with suspicion, watching until all the treasure was stowed. Antonio sensed that the weasel-eye was a new recruit, that before enjoying the borrowed importance of a police badge he'd been a cattle thief or highwayman, and had only answered an advertisement nailed to a telegraph pole promising twenty dollars a month, a gun, and the opportunity to terrorize people from the right end of the law.

There was a sound of water dribbling on dirt and Antonio looked over to see Hugo was pissing himself. With his hands on top of his head Hugo shook all over from the effort of holding back tears and it was all Antonio could do to not abuse him there. But he would not give the men the satisfaction. Antonio glared at Hugo and gave a short jerk of his head, and Hugo stood slightly straighter and held his breath until his shaking stopped, though when he finally exhaled it began all over again.

Antonio wiped dirt from his mouth and shakily got to his feet, putting his hands on his head as he watched the men through slitted eyes.

"Y'all just can't stay on your own side." The weasel-eye was uncoiling a rope. "Running over here every time you want a free meal."

"Give us our clothes," Antonio said. "There might be women out."

"No doin' Pedro," said the weasel-eye. "This'll be the best thing I see all week." He tied Antonio's hands behind his back, and when he was done he made to thrust his own knee into Antonio's testicles. Antonio was ready this time, ducking and crouching, but it was only a threat, and the sight of Antonio hunched in fear caused the weasel-eye to laugh so hard Antonio knew he could have overpowered him and possibly both men if he'd had just one of his men from Dorado with him, someone quicker to violence than Hugo.

"Sir, I know a farm around here where we could keep some things for a while," began the weasel-eye softly. "Hell, the captain won't know if a couple things go missing. A couple things . . ."

"Shut up," said the man in the tie. "One more word and I'll report you."

"You think your captain won't fill his pockets when you bring us in?" Antonio asked. "Don't be stupid. Listen to your ugly friend."

Antonio stiffened his body, waiting for the blow, but this time the man in the tie punched Hugo in the stomach, crumpling him to the ground. "Keep talking," he said, "all of you, and find out what happens."

"Git," said the weasel-eye to Hugo, jerking him up off the ground and prodding him into a jog. The men led them through the trees to a muddy, rutted path back into Houston, Hugo all the while whispering novenas.

"'I detest my sins because they offend Thee, my Lord, who art all good and deserving of my love.'"

Antonio subtly moved his wrists inside the ropes, rubbing them close together and pressing them against his back. They were a dismal parade—the man in the tie on his horse up front followed by Antonio's horses and mules, then the two naked men tied in tandem, and finally the weasel-eye on a stocky bay, keeping the rear. Antonio saw right away that humiliation was just the first of many torments the men intended for them that night.

"'I resolve, with the help of Thy grace, to sin no more. In the name of Christ, my Lord, have mercy.'"

The ropes were tight, but after a few minutes Antonio was able to maneuver his right hand sideways.

"Cállate," Antonio said, but the sound of his voice only made Hugo start to cry between his prayers, and Antonio wondered if it hadn't been God Himself who'd sent the policemen to the river, just to stick the knife in a little farther.

"'I should love You, my Lord, above all things.'"

They'd been walking an hour and were coming to the outskirts of town when something sharp struck Antonio on the ear. He jumped and turned to see a teenage boy in paint-spattered dungarees standing on the side of the road taking aim with another rock. Antonio ducked and the rock sailed past. There was a whistle and he looked to the other side of the road and saw a pair of drunks sprawled on a sagging porch, leering.

"Do us a dance, sugar!" one of them shouted.

"Why don't you come a little closer?" Antonio shouted back. "I want to know how my balls taste!" This was met with a volley of rocks that seemed to fly at him from all sides.

"Quiet down," said the one in the tie. He spurred his horse into a trot, and as the other animals in line picked up, Antonio was jerked forward, tumbling after the mules at a lope.

The houses clustered and the street grew more crowded. A young woman and man, out for a late stroll, stood on the side of the road and gawked, the woman finally remembering her modesty and covering her eyes. "Animals!" was hurled after them as they passed. By the time the houses turned from clapboard to brick, Antonio had lost count of the rocks, the number of times he'd been called greaser and brown bastard. A gang of ragged children joined the procession, beating tin cans and singing as though it were a parade. Antonio ignored their songs and their taunts until one barefoot boy charged him with a stick. Antonio kicked the child and sent him rolling, but he quickly got back onto his feet and encouraged the other children to assault the prisoners, while spitting invectives so blue the officers eventually halted the procession and threatened to horsewhip the children if they didn't disperse. Antonio watched them scatter, their bare feet leaving wet prints on the neat sidewalks that fronted grand, gabled homes.

Soon they reached downtown Houston, in the dark valleys between sleeping government buildings. The streets here were empty and Antonio was finally confident he could slip first one hand free and then the other. His knife was still in his boot. At the first opportunity he'd cut Hugo free, and then they'd run.

By Antonio's guess they'd almost neared the jail when the weasel-eye rode up front to the man in the tie, making one last stand about turning in the loot.

"It ain't like we'd be the only ones to do it. West showed me a watch he took off one old boy, and I sure have heard the others jawing about how they gave their sweethearts gold lockets and—"

But the man in the tie didn't even turn his head, and spoke straight in front of him. "If your mother heard you carrying on . . ."

Here was a wrinkle Antonio had not expected. The one in the tie was the weasel-eye's father.

"Listen to your papá, little man," Antonio said. "Or he'll give you a spanking."

"Shut your mouth!" the weasel-eye hissed, and he continued to beg. "God sent us this here gold and you just want to throw it away," he whispered.

"Don't talk to me about God," the father said wearily.

"That gold didn't come from God," Antonio said. "Some old Indian dug it up with a rusty shovel." His hands now free, he spoke to assure the men they were still there, and to cover up the sound of his blade sawing through the tough fibers binding Hugo. "That gold's a gift from God like my hook's a gift to the fish." The moment his hands got loose, Hugo looked at Antonio with a tearful face, the same one that Hugo had been giving him since they were young children, and it still infuriated Antonio that he could neither make his brother tougher nor make the world kinder.

"We're meant to have it," the weasel-eye said. "Not taking it is like spitting right in Lord Jesus's face."

"Don't you blaspheme me, you ungrateful little—"

And as the father finally turned his head, about to slap his son across his unwashed face, Antonio stuck the weasel-eye in the side with the grim steel of his knife, ducking behind the flank of the younger man's horse as the stunned father drew his gun. The father shot his son's horse in his confusion, Antonio leaping out of the way just in time. The father's horse then spooked when his companion shrieked and fell, and completed one revolution on his hind legs before throwing his rider onto the street. The ropes binding the horses and the mules tangled. Hugo's horse was tripped first and then Antonio's. The mules and their wares went sidelong. Antonio watched the melee with a sinking heart—there was no time to untangle the mess; they'd have to escape on foot. The man in the tie lay on the ground shaking and checking himself all over, unsure if his horse had rolled over on him. Antonio looked down on him and hoped in the darkness the man mistook him for the devil himself. He stuck in his blade with a slick in-and-out motion, the father expelling a breath and a moan and curling in on himself like an old rind.

"You killed them." Hugo could barely speak, his lips trembling as though from great chill. "Like, like it was nothing. Like wringing a chicken's neck."

"Move your ass," Antonio said, pulling on Hugo's arm. "That gunshot's going to bring someone."

But Hugo wouldn't move, his feet planted impressively for being both tender and bare. The man in the tie was making noises and waving one hand and before Antonio could stop him, he put a police whistle to his lips and blew twice, strong and long.

"Now," Antonio growled at Hugo, and he could already hear faraway whistles answering and hooves beating the packed earth.

"Like pheasants," Hugo stammered. "Like it was—"

"Better them than me," Antonio said, and he shoved Hugo into a slow trot, the man's great bleeding heart, for now, suspended.

The two men, train robbers and now murderers, slipped around the corner of a building. They ran past a block of warehouses and stopped inside a grove of trees. Antonio knew exactly where they were. He'd lead them back to the rail yard. With luck and, he hated to admit, with God's grace, they could jump on a freight train and go. After listening a second and letting Hugo catch his breath, he urged them on, praying Hugo in his bare feet didn't step on a sharp rock or twist his ankle.

They had no gold, no horses, no guns, no saddles, and no clothes. It had all been for nothing. Antonio tried not to dwell on these thoughts as they slunk along the back of a row of houses, trying to be as inconspicuous as two naked criminals could be in the middle of the night. They found some laundry hanging on a fence behind one darkened shanty, and though Hugo was still barefoot, putting on the clothes made Antonio feel that they were not so marked, that they might have a chance.

As they left the protection of the houses and headed for the open ground of the train yard, a short volley of bullets struck the gravel just behind them. Both men started running again. Antonio heard hoofbeats not far behind, but above that a happier sound—the impatient hiss of a locomotive waiting to depart. Antonio said a silent prayer and begged one more favor: *Don't let me die in Texas.*

The smoke-sweet smell of damp fire was still in the air, and there was a current of excitement running through the yard. The workers' movements were faster and more aggressive, like ants after a rock is dropped onto their mound. They hid in a ditch, out of which Antonio peered, searching for riders, but he saw no one, which only made him more certain they were being watched.

He put his finger to his mouth and gestured to Hugo to follow him, and together they scrambled up and out. Shots fired. They pinged the metal tracks and Hugo made a small, strangled gasp, like someone receiving terrible news.

Antonio pulled him limping between two endless lines of flatbeds loaded high with cotton.

"My foot," Hugo whispered. "Something got my foot."

There between the high walls of cotton it was too dark for Antonio to see, but when he bent close he could smell blood.

"Just a graze," he lied. "It's nothing." He bit his lip as an engine far down the yard whistled its departure. He heard men shouting and more horses arriving. Peering around the side of the bed he could see a boy, his hat slightly too big for his head, perched on a horse and arguing with a foreman, who gestured with his long, tin megaphone. Something about the boy was out of place—he was too lanky and clean to be a rail worker. As Antonio watched, a second man arrived on horseback. He had matted red hair under his hat and a filthy red beard, but Antonio could see he was Mexican. The Mexican was older, with glittering eyes, like a man entering a banquet after a week without food. He let the boy do the talking. Then a third man appeared wearing a well-stocked cartridge belt. He was slight and bloodless with a short, neat beard, yet he exuded a quiet confidence. And then the train whistle blew again and the three men turned as one toward the sound and Antonio saw the matching silver stars pinned to their chests and he almost groaned aloud. What did those Ranger bastards call them? The cinco peso.

Shots rang again and Antonio heard police whistles and shouts in every direction. A rider was coming from behind and Antonio and Hugo leapt up into the space between two flatbeds and hugged the cotton, Antonio counting to ten before he let them come out.

"Stop that train!" someone shouted. Antonio led them down one row of cars and then hopped over a coupling and took them down another. He saw clouds of white steam ahead and he urged them on, ignoring Hugo's whimpers about his bleeding foot. Bullets flew around them, but Antonio would not stop. The clouds of steam were moving faster.

"Stop that goddamned train!"

Hugo kept slipping in the loose gravel that surrounded the tracks and finally gave a sharp cry and stumbled. Antonio stopped to help him back to his feet and as he turned he saw the black-hatted head of the Mexican Ranger bobbing up and down, gaining on them. Arm in arm they limped forward. He helped Hugo over one last coupling and finally saw the train, anxious to leave. He jogged them up alongside the last boxcar. Hugo's feet might as well have been made of lead. Antonio reached a hand out to the ladder on the outside of the car, but it whipped away out of reach. Over the *chug, chug* of the engine Antonio heard hoofbeats. The Mexican Ranger was still behind them, his face alight with furious joy. Antonio reached out his hand again, but pulled back when a bullet struck the spot with a clang and a burst of bright red sparks.

"Big jump!" he shouted to Hugo. "You can do it!" He pulled Hugo faster to give him momentum and then shoved him hard toward the ladder at the same instant another bullet struck the train, this one grazing Antonio's arm. Hugo jumped in desperation and without elegance, but his two hands somehow closed on a rung halfway up the ladder and he was dragged some ways before he could kick his feet up onto the foothold. Red and orange fireflies lit up the dark as more bullets hailed. Now freed from Hugo, Antonio could run faster, though his thighs ached and his lungs were twin fires. The boxcar had passed the end of the yard and was accelerating. Antonio took a breath and pushed off, stretching his arms and sailing through the air until he felt his hands close around the iron rung. Hugo reached for him, clawing and scratching at his chest and back in his madness to get Antonio aboard. The last thing Antonio saw as Houston receded into inky depths was the Mexican Ranger, now quite close, too close, slowing his horse and waving one finger at Antonio in the dark, his white eyes and teeth shining through the night and grinning, grinning, grinning.

FOUR

"Get rid of that book," Jaime's father, Juan Antonio, said when Jaime showed it to him. *The Ignominious History of the Sonoro Family from Antiquity to Present Day* by Maria Gaspar Rocha de Quiroga, published in Sevilla, Spain, 1783. The old man glared at it through his Coke-bottle glasses and recoiled. "Some crazy woman comes to the house and shoves a book in your hands and says it's yours? Mierda. It's probably a scam. Our people were farmers. This has nothing to do with us. Throw it in the trash where it belongs."

"No way," Jaime said, pulling it back in almost a defensive gesture, though without letting it touch his clothes. The smell was like rotting fish, and the battered, leather-bound cover—drink-stained and disintegrating and looking somewhat desperate to escape into the quiet indignity of the municipal dump—seemed to look back at him with reproach. "There might be a common ancestor, at least. Aren't you even a little curious?"

"No," Juan Antonio said. "Look at your house, your beautiful family. People obsess about history because they're not happy with the present. Why do you want to disturb your peace?"

Jaime's curiosity was, naturally, piqued. "You know when you tell children not to read smutty comic books, they run straight to them like they hold the secrets of the universe."

Juan Antonio shrugged and got up, grabbing his cigarettes off the table. "Do what you want. I'm saying not to waste your time."

The old man had been living with Jaime for the last year since Jaime's mother had passed, and he was, most of the time, a cherished addition to the family. Juan Antonio walked the children home from school, helped Elena in the garden, and reserved an hour every night after dinner for dominoes with Jaime. He fitted well the shape of their daily life, but Jaime knew, too, of his father's quick temper, his demand for obeisance, and he did his best to maintain an even temperature in their interactions. He let his father go, and he hoped that that would be the end of the argument.

The smell from the book was bad enough that it filled the whole house and Elena asked Jaime to keep it in his office with the door shut. At his desk, he stuck one finger under the front cover and flopped it open, sending out a filthy little cloud of dust. He skimmed over the first few pages and they were all preamble, invocations to various saints and bellicose forewarnings, all written in a painfully florid style that came into vogue when people lived in one pigsty village their whole lives, never had to sit in traffic, and could spend ten years reading a single book. Jaime scanned down the side and estimated there must be a thousand pages. He flipped to the foreword:

The seeds of the Sonoro family may be found in Cain. When Cain couldn't discern why his Father rejected him, he killed his brother and went out of the Lord's presence and fled east of Eden. Cain took a wife, who bore him sons, and the generations spilled across the land like a river overflowing its banks. The sons left Nod, went to Ur, then Troy, then Thrace. Their black hair turned red when they pushed north to Scandza, seizing the kingship only to move south and west: Poland, France, Spain. They ruled for a thousand years, father to son, father to son, their territory shrinking and the bloodline waning slowly until the last Sonoro king was born a pigmentless waif, a specter of the beast-hearted men before him.

Undaunted and in need of gold, the Sonoros fled west again, this time across the Sargasso Sea and into the intemperate furnace of New Spain. And when Moctezuma was struck by three stones, it was a Sonoro

captain who ordered his men to stand aside and watch as the angry mob
brought the king tumbling down off his balcony in a heap of feathers and
blood.

The Sonoros built cities and towns across New Spain and named
them Monterrey, Revilla, Mier, Dorado. Their blond hair browned in the
new sun and their eyes and bellies grew wide when they discovered gold
under the new soil, gold that they took, unquestioning, with the same
pain masquerading as greed masquerading as authority that has traf-
ficked evil from one end of the earth to the other ever since Cain's anger
shattered his brother's skull, and the spilt blood screamed the crime to
Heaven.

It would be a feat to read a thousand pages of that. Jaime had never been very interested in family history. Go back enough generations in Mexico, he thought, and everyone would come to the same sad story. Who wanted to dwell on their great-great-whoever raping his way through an Indian village and initiating a genetic line of traumatized half-breeds? With apologies to Octavio Paz, *this* Mexican had no desire to contemplate such horrors. Though, he now wondered, had he drawn this conclusion naturally, or was he simply responding to a prohibition placed on inquiry by his father, instilling his own roadblock over one already imposed?

But he did pause at the author's mention of the town of Dorado. Jaime knew the Sonoros had, at one time, lived on the island that bordered Texas, though Juan Antonio had grown up across the water in Roma, Texas, married Jaime's mother, a local girl, and moved them back across to Monterrey, Mexico, before Jaime was born. And that was the extent of Jaime's knowledge. Anytime he'd asked about Juan Antonio's family, the answer was always *They were farmers, and they died when I was a baby*, as though this precluded them from having names, identities, pasts. Except that it had worked. Jaime never asked more, never wanted to delve into what was, undoubtedly, a source of great pain. But perhaps he'd never pushed because a desire to know one's roots presupposes a rootedness to begin with. Could a fallen leaf reattach himself to his tree?

.   .   .

Jaime was on Calle Nápoles going door-to-door among the city's rare-book dealers, searching for the woman. He felt ridiculous popping his head into each dust-trap and asking for a short, affronting woman in glasses, but he needed answers. He'd made a little headway into the book. It was both dense and violent, the stories of conquests, mass behead-ings, lechery, and ruin all running together like a movie played at double speed. And the details that lingered long in his mind were sickening. One of his ancestors was a woman who had been born with a tail, and had ap-parently subjected so many men to sexual torture she was burned at the stake. Another poisoned the well water of an entire village and then had it razed, just so he could get them out of his view of a mountain. If half the things in the book were true, he was the son of monsters. But he was a good husband and a good father, a loyal friend and, he hoped, a credit to his country. It wasn't fair, is what it came down to. Why was this his problem? He needed to know why it had been given to him. He needed context.

He was about to give up, get back in his car and leave, slightly worried that someone would tip off the gossip sheets that Jaime Sonoro was hav-ing an affair with an aged bookseller, when he saw one last shop on the street, as forlorn and unremarkable as any of the others, distinguished only by a yellow stained-glass sign that read *Antiquarian*.

He had his handkerchief ready when he walked in, and coughed heartily into it until the woman appeared, gnomelike, from behind a mountain of blue-bound histories.

"We're closed."

"I'm not leaving until I get answers. To start with, why does it smell?"

"Have you read it? A fish rots from the head down. I'll say that."

"How did you come to have it?"

The woman sighed and lit a cigarette. She offered one to Jaime but, touching his throat with a delicate gesture, the singer declined. "The au-thor is a distant ancestor of mine. Don't ask me the lineage because I don't know. Only that, when she died, her children had the book published and this copy stayed in our family."

Jaime waited in silence, compelling her to go on.

"Well, she died right after she wrote it. Supposedly. Maybe her kids thought it was writing the book, or, more specifically, writing a book about the Sonoros that killed her. Who knows? But for whatever insane, eighteenth-century reason—and remember this is at a time when it was common to memorialize someone by binding a book in their skin, so let's be thankful, at least, they didn't do *that*—but despite that the book may have killed their mother, Maria Rocha's children published it and kept this copy for the family. Except, once they had the book, misfortunes began to occur. One son got dragged by his horse. One son fell off a balcony at the opera. You know. It's a whole cursed-object legend. Quel ennui." She blew smoke up to the rafters above her head and Jaime had to laugh at the lengths the woman took to appear as though she didn't believe every word of this story, cuerpo y alma. "My father died six months ago, God rest"— and here she crossed herself—"and I decided enough is enough. We don't need to drag this book through another century. In a couple decades my children will be driving flying cars and getting their dinner cooked by a robot. What do I need to saddle them with some old curse for, huh?" She stabbed out the cigarette in an ink pad and gave Jaime a hard look. "Keep it, throw it away. I don't care. It's just a book."

Aside from forcing him to think about his ancestors, the book forced Jaime to think about his father and the way Juan Antonio had raised him, much the same way that fatherhood had made Jaime examine his own childhood and hold it up against the life he hoped to give his children. And in thinking about his father, Jaime was stung by possibilities lost. Should he have asked his father more questions? Should he not learn what he could now before his father died and all connection to the past was lost? Could his father have been less reticent and more open about who they were and where they'd come from, thus presenting to his son a world already opened, rather than forcing Jaime to grow up making the world anew? (And the irony that Jaime had chosen for himself acting, a profession of eternal fantasy, was not lost on him.) Had he felt adrift, without a sense of self? Or was he now simply indulging in the all-too-bourgeois pastime of Freudian analysis?

He started reading the first pages again, through Cain to Sitalces. He felt an itch at the back of his neck, like one of Elena's hairs trapped inside his collar, and he turned around, feeling someone behind him. But he was alone. He read on, and he had to admit of a little thrill in learning how deep and vast were his royal ties, kingdoms sired by the dozen from his ancestors' ruthless loins. But despite this tiny honor of proximal greatness, he felt a nagging familiarity. Could there be a mysterious biology to it, his blood somehow carrying a memory of this base history? Could crimes be so wicked, and the screams of the innocent so loud that their echoes rang still in the air, audible to anyone who cared to listen?

"Why did we never visit cousins when I was growing up?" Jaime asked Juan Antonio that night after dinner. They faced each other over dominoes. The old man had been about to place a tile and now his hand was arrested. He lay the domino back on its side and looked down at it, rubbing one hand absently over his stubbled chin. "I don't know anything about our family," Jaime continued. "And please don't tell me they were farmers. If this book is correct they were anything but humble peasants, so I'm done with that bull. Do you have any siblings? Who were your parents?"

"Did you ever think that the reason I never said anything about them is because it's too painful?" Juan Antonio asked quietly.

Jaime drew in a little breath and he was ashamed—growing up with neither parent must have felt like living with half a heart. "What was your father's name, at least?" he asked.

"Antonio, okay? I was named for him."

"And what about—"

"You know, your generation wants to talk and talk," Juan Antonio interrupted. "But you never stop to think that some of us stayed safe by buttoning up." He played his tile, wrote down *15* on the score sheet. "Watch out reading that book, boy," he said. "I'd hate to see it turn you mean."

FIVE

After Antonio was able to wrench open the boxcar door and squeeze himself inside, shove enough crates and burlap sacks around that the two men could sit comfortably, when they were panting and resting atop rough-hewn pine crates that shoved splinters through their stolen clothes and into their backsides and sent vibrations shivering up their spines, Antonio was finally able to feel around his body for various gashes and abrasions, and do the same for Hugo.

Hugo was bloodied from his shins down. Once Antonio was able to use a bit of burlap and his own spit to clean Hugo's feet enough to see the extent of his injuries, he saw that one of the bullets had found its mark. He had Hugo stick his foot out the boxcar door so he could try and see it in the feeble dawn. It was not a terrible wound from what he could gauge, and so Antonio bound both of Hugo's feet in burlap and was relieved when he could hobble a bit around the boxcar.

Prying open one of the crates, they had a pleasant surprise: it was filled with tins of cured beef sausages in broth. They were greasy and studded with gristle and were oversalted to the point Antonio believed the meat had probably turned, but he ate six tins anyway, feeling that he'd never eaten, that he might never eat again. They rolled the empty tins out the boxcar door, letting them fall into an ocean of scrubland, hundreds of millions of dry, naked trees. Antonio leaned out, searching the sky for clues about which direction they were headed, but everything was shrouded with a thick layer of clouds that sagged low into the trees and seemed to press into the boxcar, making Antonio feel suffocated. "I think we're going south," he said, "not far from the coast. Judging by the fog." Gray branches of live oaks reached for him out of the fog like skeleton fingers, a strange vision after the oppressive verdancy of Houston. Everywhere, the trees thrust back their heads and looked up at Heaven, waiting, like everyone else, for answers.

"We'd have been better off in jail." Hugo was looking out the door and not at Antonio, and it wasn't clear if he wanted to talk or was only voicing the things that flitted through his mind.

"Don't fool yourself," Antonio said. "They would've hung us from the nearest tree."

Antonio closed his eyes and thought of Jesusa lying in bed, her gown slipped from one shoulder, the children crowded next to her under the thin blanket, dreaming fingers curled into tight fists and dirty toes jutting out over the earthen floor. Or perhaps she was already awake. She'd have set the fire, boiled the coffee, and would stand watching until the sun broke over the jacal, the corn patch, the scrawny goats and ill-tempered pigs. Antonio leaned out the door and looked to where he hoped his wife was, and he imagined she could feel him looking out from the door of the train, even across all that unforgiving distance.

The world flew past, reminding Antonio of a device he'd seen at a tent show, a spinning, circular apparatus inside which a seagull appeared to take flight, the takeoff and landing repeating infinitely. "We should have passed Bay City by now," he said, "or Victoria. Strange that we didn't stop. If we're headed to Corpus Christi they're going to switch tracks at Odem and then we can jump." Gray light was finally starting to permeate the fog and Antonio could just see the dirty red bloom spread out around his forearm where he'd been grazed.

"I told you we should go back. So what happens next, big brother?"

Antonio shook his head. "This is part of it," he said. "No one ever taught you to be a man, so listen good: You need to look out for yourself.

Always yourself. No one else will look out for you. Not me. Certainly not God. So be for yourself. And right now that means running."

"Venga ya," Hugo said with a disgusted look. "You talk such bullshit. No one taught me to be a man? Why, because Papá didn't want to live in that miserable house? Because he left Mamá alone?"

At this Antonio started because he rarely thought of his father, there being precious little of the man to think about. He wasn't a Sonoro, a considerable moral failing in his mother's opinion. He would ride into Dorado on his way to places more compelling, would stay for dinner and a half hour with Antonio's mother behind her locked bedroom door, and then not be seen again for years. Antonio's most salient memory of the man was the back of his burgundy frock coat as his wagon trundled away. But still, he didn't like Hugo's tone.

"Don't speak about things you know nothing about."

"Things *I* know nothing about?" Hugo said darkly. "Yes, you're going to teach me to be a man. Drinking and fiddling with whores and fighting and coming home bloody—if those are the lessons you have to impart, then save them for your own children. If you make it back to them."

"Enough," Antonio said.

But Hugo wasn't finished. "Those were Texas Rangers, you understand? I don't know why you had to burn that train. I saw your face—you were like a little boy who'd just thrown a cat into a chicken coop."

"Go to sleep." Antonio could feel the anger pouring out of his stomach and surging through his blood.

"I thought I could convince you to come back, to live a good life. You know I feel like the older brother sometimes? I feel like I'm the only Sonoro who knows how to be decent."

"You're not," Antonio said, his voice keen as the knife in his boot. "You're not a Sonoro. My mother ran over your mother with her carriage and she felt bad and took you in. You're nothing. I don't even know your real name."

Antonio looked across the boxcar to where Hugo sat in the dark, hatred in his eyes. And his heart cracked open just a little as he realized that, despite every indignity, Antonio had never known his brother to feel hate.

"I'm going to sleep." Hugo wrapped his arms around his legs and put his head down, as though he could will Antonio away, the train, all of it, if only he kept his eyes closed.

Antonio's face flushed hot and he remembered Hugo as a boy: a sweaty mat of curled hair, a toy horse made of tooled leather clutched in his hands, the name No-No tumbling from his red lips. No-No was what Hugo had called him for years before he could pronounce "Antonio." *No-No wait. No-No listen. No-No stop.*

"I'm sorry," Antonio said quietly, but he didn't think Hugo could hear him over the churn of the train.

And as though he'd summoned it, at that moment a whistle sounded. The brakes screamed and the train slowed to a shuddering stop that threw both men sideways. They were in the middle of nowhere; there was no reason for the train to halt. Antonio brought his fist to his mouth and bit down. They should have jumped sooner. The train had been going too quickly, but Antonio now wished they'd have chanced it. He crouched low and looked out. Cool white fog encircled them with more surging in from the east, and he couldn't see up the train or down, though he could hear horses breathing heavily not far away. Rangers? Police? They must have telegraphed from Houston. It was unlikely they were the same Rangers, though he'd heard of Rangers commandeering trains, racing down tracks and requisitioning horses, riding their mounts to death. As he listened to the animals wheeze, he decided that's exactly what had happened. When he heard a man speaking in a high, wavering Southern drawl, he had a feeling it was the Ranger captain he'd seen a few hours earlier.

"Search every one," the captain said. "We'll find 'em."

Antonio put his hand to his lips, though Hugo only stared mutely. Antonio dropped out of the boxcar light as a cat and looked first left then right. The fog was cream thick. It was like standing on top of a mountain. Cicadas droned high in the trees and mourning doves interjected with coos that sounded to Antonio like *You will do, will do, do*. Antonio held his arms up to Hugo and helped him out of the boxcar, setting him down as quietly as he could onto a ground covered in broken twigs and dead, brittle leaves.

Someone on horseback was approaching, but in the fog the sound came from all directions. Antonio had Hugo put his hand on his shoulder, for he was still unsteady on his feet, and the two men staggered into the dense brush. They made slow progress through the trees that wove dry, tangled arms together as though consoling one another. The undergrowth was so knotted in thorny clumps it was difficult to move. Antonio wrapped his arm and fist in a large piece of burlap he'd cut for the occasion, and used them to push branches aside enough to let them pass without getting mesquite thorns in their eyes. They had to choose their steps carefully, land on the outsides of their feet. Alone he could have sprinted away. Alone Antonio Sonoro would have been nothing more than a rumor, a name whispered once and then never again. But with Hugo, his bulk had doubled, his pace halved. The only thing helping him was the brasada. He'd rustled cattle and hidden them in terrain just like this. The trees had a way of swallowing things. A man could be paces from his enemy and never see him. In the early days, when the Spanish first forded the Río Bravo and the tentacles of the king's empire reached every shore, the brush was a labyrinth leading people to their deaths. Hungry men would enter looking for prickly pear tunas or pecans and years later someone would find only their bones. It was still unnavigable for many, but Antonio knew it as if he'd planted the trees himself. There was always a path discernible to the right eye. There was always a way to cheat even what seemed like certain death.

They stopped when they heard more hoofbeats followed by a whistle, and Antonio knew the Rangers had found the open boxcar door.

"Pick it up," he whispered.

"Go to hell," Hugo said. "I ought to call those Rangers right over."

"You wanna die? I'll leave you here and be halfway to the border before you've bled out." Antonio gave Hugo a little shove and they continued.

They would have to hide, Antonio reasoned, conceal themselves in the trees and wait until the Rangers gave up and left. Once the Rangers had moved on, Antonio would leave Hugo somewhere safe and find a horse. It was far from a good plan, but without a gun he was little better defended than a fawn. Antonio stopped. There was a gaunt, pitted oak stump mobbed by gnats that he was sure they'd passed just a few moments before. The morning sun had yet to penetrate the soupy fog, which seemed to be growing thicker, a gathering wind from the east pushing the marine layer inland. Somehow, in the confusion of mist and branches, they'd gone in a circle. He breathed a silent curse. For all he knew, they were now heading back to the train. He looked around him for anything by which he could navigate, but everything was colorless and swirling and Antonio felt panicked. He could practically feel vines closing around his ankles.

And at that thought he looked down and saw that there were vines stretched across the ground. They'd been dormant just moments before but were waking with the coming sun, waxy leaves unfolding, drowsy heads rising and opening their faces to the feeble light. Antonio watched as one after another flower—each the size of a teacup and hued the garish purple of a late summer sunset—awoke and pointed themselves in the same direction like soldiers lining up before their commander. *They're facing east*, Antonio realized. *Even through the fog they know the direction. They're going east and so we'll go west.*

He turned Hugo around by the shoulder and they followed the vines that, now spotted, appeared endless. For one fantastical second Antonio imagined that they originated in his bed, in Jesusa, that he could hold one end and she the other and she could pull him across the distance to her.

Hugo's grasping hands broke branches, betraying their location with every step, but they plunged along another hundred meters. Finally, they came to a felled tree on its side and Antonio shoved Hugo behind it. The fog was beginning to thin, and without this cooling blanket the day was oppressive and warm. The purple flowers, vivid and erect only a moment before, already appeared to wither and wilt, retreating back into their vines until the next morning. Sweat beaded on Antonio's forehead as he covered Hugo in branches and dead leaves and dirt. "Wait," Hugo whispered, "just wait—" But Antonio clamped his hand over Hugo's mouth and made his face savage. He dragged more branches over Hugo and kicked his hands and feet under cover. He was so focused that he didn't hear the horses until they were practically on top of them.

He had just enough time to crouch behind a mesquite. As the last breath of fog vanished, Antonio ventured one glimpse at his pursuers and immediately snapped his head back and bit his lip and cursed his bad luck, cursed his name, cursed Texas and God. The Mexican Ranger was first, his matted hair a greasy brick red in the morning light. The young Ranger was next, a pistol in his thin hand. His hat drooped over his face, but between holding the gun and the reins he had no occasion to correct it. The captain sat atop a shining sorrel with a broad chest. He lifted his pistol, twirled the chamber, tested the trigger, and dropped the gun back in its holster. It was all for show—he had to know Antonio and Hugo were unarmed.

Hugo was silent—Antonio prayed he'd stay that way—and Antonio was able to slow his own heartbeat to a crawl. Far away a rattlesnake fired off a warning.

Don't let me die in Texas. If Hugo could stay silent they might have a chance. There were several meters of brush between them and the Rangers. Antonio could see the heel of Hugo's foot sticking out from under a pile of branches, but otherwise his body was obscured. If the Rangers continued just a little to their right, they'd miss them completely. Antonio pulled the knife from his boot and opened it without a sound. He'd not be taken alone. What were the Rangers doing just sitting there? He wished he could turn around—it was maddening not being able to see his enemies. Besides the horses' steady breathing there was no sign at all that the Rangers were there. The cicadas sang an unbroken note that climbed in pitch, growing louder and more urgent.

"This is the spot, boys," said the captain. "I know y'all are in here somewhere. Men on the dodge always run in a straight line. I know there's two of you, and I know one of you's bleeding. And I know you ain't got any guns. You ain't by a damn sight the smartest criminals I've ever encountered. You left a trail through the brush wider than the Pecos and you made so much noise I'm pretty sure your señoritas could hear you all the way back at the pueblo."

He dismounted and made to speak again, but something in his chest caught and he began to cough long and deep. Antonio had known men like him, consumptives. He smiled. This man wouldn't live long.

61

"I'm Captain Cyrus Fish," he said when he could finally speak again, and he was much louder and spoke with vehemence. "Commander of the Frontier Battalion of the Texas Rangers. Yes, boys, you heard me correctly—the Texas goddamn Rangers. You all've shit on the wrong porch. With me is Lieutenant Casoose, a Mexican not unlike yourselves, and our new recruit, Private Billy Stillwell." Fish spat and twigs snapped as he appeared to now be pacing. "Since last night we've took two trains and ridden six horses damned near to death to track you boys down, and I'll tell you that your story ends right here. I assume y'all are familiar with the ley de fuga? If not, I'll explain it slow.

"By order of the state of Texas under the command of the Honorable Governor Charles A. Culberson, ley de fuga, and I quote, 'allows for the extrajudicial execution of any prisoner or detainee who takes flight upon remand especially, but not limited to, transference from one custodial point to another, thereby nullifying and invalidating habeas corpus, as so determined by an appointed officer of the court, with said sentence to be carried out at the discretion of said officer,' namely, me." He paused and spat again. "Did you catch all that, boys? If you run I can shoot you.

"Now, I will be honest with you and say that I am of two minds in this here situation," Fish continued. "I'd like to administer justice right here and now and leave you all to the ants and the scorpions and the judgment of whatever Catholic hoodoo you all subscribe to. And yet to do so would be to deny the citizens up in Houston the satisfaction of watching you two twist in the wind, to say nothing of the family of the two men you killed.

"And so, because I cannot decide which fate is more befitting your vile and cowardly deeds, I will, in an act of undue mercy, allow you the choice: Do you die now or die later? Consider it your executioner asking if you've got any last words. So I'm gonna count to three. If you come out, I will take your condemned souls back to Houston, where you will be tried and hanged by a joyous and willing crowd. But if you don't," and here he paused for what Antonio took to be dramatic effect—this man could have made a name for himself in the theater, "I will be forced to consider you as fugitives from the law and will execute you as such."

There was a pause. Antonio drew in a quiet breath.

"One."

Antonio looked to where Hugo lay and saw the pile of brush atop him begin to quiver.

"Two."

Branches rustled as Hugo thrashed about, Antonio watching in mute horror.

"Three."

"Ants!" Hugo shot up out of the branches and leaves, shaking and brushing himself all over. "They're everywhere!" he shouted, at that moment so consumed by the ants he was unable to see the three men aiming guns at him.

Antonio stood up and turned to face the Rangers at the moment the one called Casoose fired at Hugo, striking him through the heart and causing him to collapse back into the brush from which he'd emerged.

The scream that came from Antonio was garbled and sounded nothing like words. The sound was so primordial and inchoate it seemed to have existed always, that he'd snatched it out of the ether and, once used, it would return, waiting to give voice to the next unutterable heartbreak.

There was an obscene dark circle opened up in Hugo's chest and a line of blood running down one side of his mouth. Ignoring the three guns trained on him, Antonio fell to his knees and crawled. He pulled Hugo's limp body up out of the brush and cradled him in his arms as though anything could be done. Ants were still swarming Hugo, darting in and out of his open mouth and nostrils. Antonio tried to brush them away, but there were too many, and he had to blink away the black splotches that appeared now in his vision, as though the scene was so devastating his body preferred blindness. The words *My brother, my brother* beat a rhythm in his chest, blood be damned. In this maelstrom, Antonio felt his soul torn in two, and he knew his life, whatever remained of it, would be henceforth split, bifurcated, Hugo's death a large black *X* on the page and all time known only for its proximity to the event—before the death, or after. And Antonio was also aware, as though the very cells that knitted him together pulsed in concert, that this death had opened up a debt that needed fulfillment, that in the countinghouse of his soul he required numeric satisfaction. One brother for three Rangers . . . and however many Texans wished to stand in the way of him receiving his just satisfaction.

"He was decent," he sobbed to no one in particular. "He was good."

Fish had ordered Casoose to stow his weapon, barked at him and for Billy's benefit that in a case such as this where fugitives were unarmed and they were simply tasked with capturing them and delivering them to justice, it was procedure, and far preferable at that, to stick to one's word and not shoot a criminal they'd just promised not one minute earlier to take alive.

"On your feet!" Fish shouted to Antonio. He had his pistol out. Antonio stared down the long barrel but did not move. "On your feet, sir, or I shoot!"

Antonio had a slow feeling, of floating just above himself and watching everyone's prolonged, languid movements as though the scene were acted underwater. He wanted to get up and walk away, feeling that the bullets could catch in the air and never reach him, that the Rangers would stay suspended in the brush and just watch him disappear.

"One last time, sir: On your feet or I shoot!"

Antonio decided to test his theory. He laid Hugo back on the ground and closed his eyelids with his fingertips. He got slowly to his feet and considered the consumptive Ranger holding the gun, his face coloring as he continued to shout. He looked at the young Ranger, whose face was striped where sweat had run trails over his dusty, sunburnt skin. He looked at Casoose, who smiled at him with perfect, white teeth. And very quietly, just to himself, he whispered a promise three times over, a vow he pledged there in the presence of God and Hugo's extinguishing soul: "Dead, dead, dead."

Fish purpled and he spoke all in one breath, his voice growing in resonance like a preacher reaching the thunderous conclusion of a hell-raiser. "The charges of murder of two public officers, theft, arson, trespassing, destruction of private property, public nudity, and unlawfully boarding a train. For these violations against the state of Texas I hereby commit you to death, signed Cyrus Fish, commander of the Frontier Battalion!"

Antonio was about to turn and walk away, slip between the trees like he had as a boy hunting javelinas. His eyes were now adjusted to the terrain. He could see out and around him, everything all at once.

Then came the shot—clipped through the head along the right side of his face. Antonio was surprised to feel the bullet as it entered him. His lips parted and he allowed in the hot metal bee. It opened a door into his flesh, rutted through his tongue, blasted his teeth one by one, sending splinters and fragments ricocheting through his mouth like broken china. It kicked a hole out the other side through his jawbone and kissed his ear and continued its journey because it was in a hurry, hurry, hurry. The ground caught him. It was all around him. He tasted dirt.

Fish holstered his gun and put two fingers on the side of Antonio's neck that was still intact. Antonio could feel the pressure of the man's fingers, searching for a pulse, he could smell the blood on the man's breath as he leaned close, or was that his own blood blooming a halo around his head? He was aware of all this and yet he knew that Fish would find no heartbeat. He watched with a vague sense of fulfillment as Fish withdrew his hand and wiped it on his pants. So was this death? An eternity of watching the living with only a passing interest?

Hugo was there, his toddler face smeared with jam, handing him the little leather horse. *No-No wait. No-No listen. No-No stop.*

He heard Fish tell the others to ride back to the train.

"Ace shot, sir," the boy said. "Ain't we gonna bury them?"

"They're police killers. Let the ants have 'em." This pronounced, Fish mounted his horse.

For a second Antonio thought he was back on the train because there was a rumble that seemed to come from somewhere deep in the earth, though he realized it was only three sets of hooves striking the hard ground and receding. Then nothing. The sky was white-hot and the mourning doves sang, *You will do, will do, do.*

SIX

Jaime accepted that his father would not or could not speak about their family, and so he put his faith doubly in the book to give him answers. Yet the book, too, was coy, spending a dozen pages on some dull anecdote from the eighth century and then hopping to some other equally distant and seemingly random ancestor to narrate an episode from their life. Jaime craved unification, a direct line drawn from the Sonoros in the book to him, and an explanation for why they were as they were, why he was as he was, and whether there was an overlap. And if there was, did he need to fear the day when he would discover it? He felt as though he'd swallowed a bomb and now walked around in anticipation of when the thing might explode. But the book provided neither answers nor solace, or if it did, he had yet to discover them.

"I read today that they owned gold mines," Jaime said to Elena, leaning against the bedroom door. Elena was getting ready for bed, her face slick with Pond's and her hair pinned and wrapped in a silk turban. "Here and in Brazil. The things they did to the workers . . . Well, I don't have to tell you what conditions were like in your average gold mine in the 1600s."

"Come to bed. You've been staying up reading that thing for weeks."

"I'm revolted, but I can't turn away. It feels—I don't know—like I'm meant to know this story."

"If it's torture to read, imagine what it was like to write it."

Jaime looked at her steadily, as that was his thought reading it as well. He was coming around to the theory that the book had actually killed Maria Rocha. Full-body immersion in such a subject would take its toll. It had to.

"Have you thought about it?" Elena asked.

"Thought about what?"

"Writing about it. You keep saying you're going to write a script. Triumphing over evil sounds like a good story."

"Yes, well, when you call it torture you make it sound so appealing."

Elena laid back against the pillow and turned off the bedside lamp. "If you're feeling burdened and overwhelmed it might help to write everything out. San Agustín didn't write his *Confessions* to men. He wrote them to God."

In the afternoons when he wasn't reading, Jaime had taken to buying his children new shoes, bringing them to the big carousel at the park near his house, indulging their whims for ice cream and dolls and balsa wood airplanes, all to prove to himself that malignity was not a genetic disorder. But back at his desk and inside the book, he was never convinced. Roughly five thousand years of history would say otherwise.

And the feeling of being watched followed Jaime in and out of the house, the hair always tickling the back of his neck like something he'd forgotten, something urgent but out of reach. He began imagining men in long trench coats spying on him from behind newspapers whenever he and the children were out. He felt camera eyes on him while he sat alone at his desk reading, could almost hear an electric hum in the background and feel the glare from a small, steady red light indicating he was on air. He'd never been paranoid, but since returning from the tour—no, since he'd spoken to the bookseller—no, since the book had come into the house—he'd been in the habit of turning on lights to peek inside closets, checking always who was behind him, peering through the curtains at his lush lawn, half expecting to see a madman outside wielding a tommy gun.

And so, because his paranoia of what waited for him both within and without was at a peak, Jaime was shocked that he did not see the man in the overlong jacket and wide-legged pants standing nearby as his children whizzed around the carousel on their plaster mounts. It had been a dazzling day, the kind of afternoon Seurat would have captured en plein air. Jaime had proposed that he and Juan Antonio take the older two children to the park while Elena was out with the baby visiting friends. Juan Antonio paid for the children to have a second ride on the carousel and he stood close by watching and waving. Jaime was watching, too, a little farther back, when the sun suddenly went behind a cloud and he looked up to see if rain was imminent. Then a child shrieked followed by several others, and Jaime turned to the carousel to see his oldest, Mito, lying on his stomach on the ground, not moving. When Jaime pushed through the crowd to his child, a man, who wasn't in a trench coat but cut a strange figure nonetheless, was already there picking up the boy and soothing his cries.

"I am Remedio," the man said. "I believe you need some help."

PART TWO
EL
TRAGABALAS

SEVEN

Remedio had lived many places. He never knew their names, but he could remember them by the sky. There was the cool place on the rocky coast where he would sit beside the red-barked trees and watch fog surge in through the gap between two green hills. In this place the air held drops of water that split apart the light in a thousand directions so that the world was forever veiled and soft-spoken and colored the gentle orange of a ripe peach. This place was so beautiful that Remedio had to leave after a short time, the gauzy sky and shrouded hills becoming so familiar they soon stirred him no more than a bowl of weak broth, and Remedio felt the tragedy of letting splendor slide into abstraction.

Then there was the place where the land and sky converged and were one, separated only by a thin strip of ground nailed to the horizon. Here the sunless sky was the unctuous blue of a submerged whale and mirrored in the waterlogged soil that soaked Remedio to the knees. The boundlessness and uniformity of the sky was thrilling to Remedio. He spent every day watching for a cloud, a flaw, a single piece of the picture out of alignment, but it was as if the sky had been unrolled as one piece of fabric, every corner like all the others. In this place Remedio could see that the people dreamed of strawberries, snakeskin, and craggy mountains at sunset—things they'd never seen and couldn't possibly name, but rich in sensuous color and texture. One day a withered, paper-skinned woman came past selling oranges and Remedio left that afternoon, the fruit's bright peel awakening him as if from a spell and reminding him of the days when he used to see the sun.

There was the place where the river split itself. It was a jagged land of burrs and thorns. And yet it was here that the white roses were the most pungent, that the tiger lilies plucked embers from the sun to color their bodies bright as torches. In one day the sky would turn from indigo to gray to azure to white to Mayan gold and crimson, fuchsia and violet, and back to indigo again like a peacock fanning and strutting. Remedio tasted the colors one by one like fruit, letting the juices run down his chin and stain his shirt. But the people in this place were forever looking at the hard ground, digging it, scratching it, poking it, and sometimes stomping their sandled feet on it in exasperation, and Remedio could never understand why they chose to put their faith in the brown dirt when the sky offered such richer bounty. He'd lie in the spot where the river reconverged and became one and listen to the dragonflies beat their stained-glass wings over the water and watch the sky, envying the birds and the trees and wishing he could get just a little bit closer.

Remedio had lived many places and he'd lived a long time with men, and he found their endless dispositions fascinating. Whereas Remedio was the only one like him, men littered the earth in trickles and hordes and yet no two were ever the same. Though they might have been born in the same village or even to the same mother, their struggles and desires and wishes and fears were so personal as to make it impossible for Remedio to say for certain what men were and weren't. And he'd tried. But as soon as he'd form a hypothesis, making up his mind that men were inherently good or bad or that men could change or not, he'd encounter proof to the contrary and have to start all over again. A single unifying concept of humanity seemed at once so achievable and yet so reductive as to render it immediately false. And so after a while he gave up this preoccupation and instead looked for parallels between them and him. He played a game with himself: Remedio is like a woodcutter because he clears the clutter and makes way for new growth. Remedio is like a surgeon because he only takes away what's rotten and leaves behind the good flesh. Remedio is like a mother because he inflicts discipline on those who need it. He avoided comparisons between himself and dogcatchers, judges, fishermen, and anyone in law enforcement for he knew how often earthly punishments were tied to instances of luck and unluck, and he did not wish to entertain the possibility that such a flawed system could extend beyond the hands of men.

He traveled as well, for his work took him many places—cities, villages, lonely homesteads absent even of buzzards. He liked the cities. He would wander the broad avenues lurking in bookstores, listening to a beggar play the accordion, stepping aside as little girls shrieked through the streets in starched pinafores. One day he saw a postman in a green uniform like a soldier, struggling down the street with a heavy mailbag on his back. Remedio had forgotten all about postmen. A long time before, when messages were glyphed onto papyrus, Remedio remembered sitting under a cypress tree and watching the sky until a gray speck became a bird that flew straight for his master's waiting hand. He followed this postman as he walked up one side of the road and then the other, stopping at every building.

What swift fingers the man had sifting his deliveries and slotting them *tot, tot, tot* into mailboxes. Remedio checked the man's work after he'd finished and found no mistakes. The doctor's medical catalogs were not confused with the lawyer's notarized letters. The scented love notes for the handsome bachelor on the third floor had not found their way even by accident to the lonely amputee in the basement. Once the man had emptied his bag, Remedio followed him back to the central post office, a grand building with a gilded ceiling like a church, and he was startled at the volume of letters he saw there carried on conveyor belts operated by hand cranks. The letters flowed through the veins of the mighty beast, and how many permutations of need were contained within! *Please send money, please come visit, please stay away, please say yes*—as many words as stars and almost all asking for love in some form or another, and a reminder that they were not alone. That humankind had devised something so ordered was a miracle to Remedio, that out of the swirling chaos of their hungry souls men had managed to build a system for delivering sympathy, joy, remorse, anger, felicitations, admonishments, and cheap sentimentality. Remedio felt a kinship with the postman. It was a comfort to him that men strove to an ideal of such precision, that because he had paid the postage and written the recipient's address, the sender had every expectation his letter would reach its destination. Every letter an address, every message an audience. If they believe that is the way, Remedio thought, then it should not be difficult for them to comprehend their destinies. Remedio is like a postman because, like a letter, every person has a terminus.

Remedio never knew who he was to collect until he was close enough to see their face. There was a markedness to them, a kind of pallor that Remedio could see, like an absence of lumin. And on their faces were always written the nature of their crimes. Murder, incest, theft, cruelty—the variations were endless. Men were most inventive when they were devising ways to be wicked.

He had only once refused the collection of a soul. The baby from where the river split. On the baby's face had only been written *In arrears*. He'd never before had reason to doubt that a soul was going to the place where it belonged, had never had cause to question the judgments that came unbidden and unseen. But he could not take the baby. He'd watched the unlucky child open and close his fist and flail his arm until his mother took the tiny fingers and closed them inside her own. The child's pallor was difficult to see bathed in the light of his mother's eyes, but it was there and unmistakable. And Remedio saw, too, that his theory had been utterly wrong, that the situation in which he found himself resembled nothing of an improperly addressed letter. So that day he'd stalked away from the hacienda empty-handed and angry, and vowed to take no action on the baby until he'd come to some resolution of his own.

Sometimes Remedio was gone for years. But he always returned to the place where the river split, where he watched the baby grow into a man who defiled himself with violence and drink. Remedio was often tempted to take him. Perhaps he'd been wrong. Who was he to ask questions? To make assignations? But just as Remedio would find himself straightening his tie and clearing his throat and readying himself to make his approach, the man would carry a neighbor's child to the doctor, or he'd comfort his wife as she wept for their poverty, or he'd take some of the gold he'd won at knifepoint and give it to a friend whose stillborn crops baked lifeless under the unforgiving soil. The man fascinated Remedio intensely. It was as though he were aware of the precariousness of his own existence, that he wished to perform some balancing of accounts within himself, committing murder and then saving a family from starvation on the same day, net equal. And for the first time, Remedio had the opportunity to watch and see, would the pallor disappear? Could the course reverse?

Now Remedio watched as this same man struggled on the ground, the pallor still there, stronger in fact, his many crimes lettered about his face in print as tiny as fleas, while the man he called his brother dissolved like the last star in the morning sun. Remedio said aloud, "I know what you want. I'm not wise, but I know enough. I could take him now. I should take him now, but I won't. I'm not convinced. Strike me down if you like, but I tell you I'm not convinced."

THE SONORO FAMILY

BY MARIA GASPAR ROCHA DE QUIROGA
Published 1783
Sevilla, España

The Sonoros had gone up the stairs in wooden shoes and down again in silk slippers, and repeated the performance so many times that no one remembered which stage of the cycle they lived in anymore. Fortunes made; fortunes lost. Of course it was inevitable that certain of the family would turn to larceny. Theft is only thus called if the victim holds power enough to indict. And the Sonoros were practiced thieves.

In the province of Texas, between Villa de San Agustin de Laredo in the north and los tejidos to the south, lies a great river sometimes called el Río Bravo, for its difficult and mighty course. But do not be swayed by its lofty name. The riverfront there is so dense and wild and impenetrable by civilized men that only those brave or godless enough may make their stead. Fanged beasts called onzas prey on Christian flesh, and flora of every infernal species blooms spiny and spiteful in diabolical abundance. The southern region of Texas is a dread place, impossible to govern, and owing to the aridity of the climate and the Río Bravo's peculiar penchant for disappearing altogether in the interminable hot months, impossible to contain. Bandits and brigands may cross in and out of Nuevo Santander in New Spain as they wish to terrorize the gentlefolk of the colonies.

And yet it is not the river's fault that men abuse the privilege of her crossing. As we blame not the brook for swallowing Ophelia, so shall we blame not the Río Bravo for opening her arms to men and affording them infinite vices. Evil has not its genesis in the Sonoros, but it finds in them a willing and procreative host.

Recall, however, these words, imparted to Moses himself: "The Lord! The Lord! A God compassionate and gracious, slow to anger, abounding in kindness and faithfulness, extending kindness to the thousandth generation, forgiving iniquity, transgression, and sin; yet He does not remit all punishment, but visits the iniquity of parents upon children and children's children, upon the third and fourth generations."

EIGHT

Antonio woke up because someone was screaming—it was a harsh, rasping shriek, full of phlegm, not entirely human. He wouldn't realize until later the screaming came from him. The sound woke him from his charcoal dreams. A lantern fashioned from an old tomato can swung from a rafter and cast weak orange light up and down the walls, making the room where he lay appear to rock like a boat. In this hot, dark place Antonio opened his eyes for the first time in three weeks and his body was suddenly galvanized, alight with electric pain so loud and swift he closed his eyes again and saw it explode blue and yellow and white across his brain.

It felt as though an animal had clawed deep into his neck, was still clawing at that moment through muscle and sinew, searching. He could feel every severed vein and every shred of torn skin decaying under the breath of the filthy air. His face felt seared by a hundred embers, the ends of so many cigarettes ground into his skin only to be pulled away and returned again and again. Inside his mouth his tongue had swollen to fill the entire space. The sides pressed into the empty sockets where once had been his teeth—now reduced to a bitter, stony grit spread between his tongue and the roof of his mouth. The bullet must have traveled all the way down his throat and into his gut, for he felt he'd swallowed handfuls of broken glass. Even the paltry bit of spit that oozed down off his tongue and into his esophagus scorched him. His arms and legs were heavy and engorged. Whatever poison was inside strained against his skin, skin that felt taut and translucent like an overripe plum. And he was violently hot. His clothes were soaked and strangling. His heart beat so fast he thought it would burst.

He had to be in Hell, sentenced to burn for his cruelty to Hugo and for not having saved him, for even taking him to Texas in the first place. Straining his eyes he looked for flames or a spit, but he couldn't turn his head and could see only the tomato can lantern. He picked up his hand and had to look a while to recognize it—the skin was purple and the fingers, swollen to twice their size, had a curling, boneless appearance like grubs. He brought his hand up to his face to touch his mouth, to assess what remained of the lower half of his face, and the brief moment of contact between his fingers and his jaw was so painful the room blackened and he thought he must have fainted. When he finally raised his hand again and looked at it, the fingers were smeared with blood.

He dropped his hand back against the bed and cried. He was so thirsty. He needed to be cut open. He'd done it to horses after a snakebite—split the skin and drain the pus and maybe, if the infection had not spread, the horse escaped with only a scar.

He heard animal noises outside, braying and bleating, the animals' frightened chatter spreading and intensifying. One animal let out a sound like a woman screaming, or a harpy seizing her prey. Then Hugo was in the room looking down at him with watery, half-lidded eyes. Antonio begged him for forgiveness and renewed his vow of revenge. *I'll make it right!* he screamed inside. *They'll pay their debts!* Hugo only looked at his feet and said nothing. Small, spasmodic movements shook Antonio's ribs, tears wet his eyes, and a gurgling noise came from his throat. He heard movement nearby but he couldn't see who else was in the room. He tried to call out but no sound came to his lips, if he still had lips. A hard wind blew into the room and his fever turned to chills that blistered his skin with goose bumps and racked him with shivers that caused him to silently beg for death. *I want a grave next to the house*, he thought, *so that sometimes I can*

climb out and watch Nicolás and Aura play in the melon patch. I'll make it
right, my God. I'll make it right.

Antonio closed his eyes and the last thing he saw before he fell asleep
again was the hole in Hugo's chest as he lay dead in the brush. The hole
grew until it overtook Hugo, the trees, the Rangers. Antonio stood at the
edge of the wound, a concentric, caverning hole of purples, reds, and
pinks, until he finally stepped inside and fell down into the path the bullet traced, down all the way to the center of his brother's dry, lifeless heart.

The next time he woke up the room was dark again. The animals had
quieted and the chill was gone from the air. Antonio woke with some mix
of relief and disappointment. To live meant he could avenge Hugo; to die
meant he would finally find out in which direction the scale tipped.

His fever was down, and his clothes were now brittle around him. He
turned his head just slightly, and even that small movement flooded him
with pain. He was not in Hell. He was in a small jacal with mud walls and
a tall, thatched roof. As his eyes adjusted he could make out the things
in the room: rough wooden furniture, unlit candles, two sleeping mats
rolled up in a corner. He was lying on a grass bed that was raised off the
floor and his body was covered by a rough wool blanket pulled up to his
chin. He brought his hand to his face again. The fingers were no longer
swollen but were still covered in rust-colored blood, now dried and flaky.
He brought them trembling to his face, which was wrapped in bandages
so tight he couldn't open his mouth. Despite the bandages he winced
as pain billowed out from the touch. He was dismayed to see his fingers
again painted red.

He took a series of shallow breaths through his nose, counting up and
down to four several times. His hands and arms were numb and slow to
obey but he was able to bring them carefully up to his chest and pull the
blanket off, letting it drop to the floor. One, two, three, four, four, three,
two, one. He pictured each number as he took short, choppy breaths,
trying to focus away from the pain sparking small fires across his body.
He rolled onto his side and had to lie like that for several minutes. He
couldn't scream, and so his silent tears fell sideways down his face and
wet the bandages under his cheek. When he was ready he pushed himself

up on the bed, blinking stars out of his eyes. He had no idea how long he'd been in this place but his legs looked thin inside his pants. No telling how long he would still need to recover.

There was a small mirror hung on the wall across the room and he had a desperate urge to go there and see for himself what remained. He put one bare foot tenderly on the dirt floor and then the other, and his legs shook and threatened to collapse from the strain. His spine throbbed, resisting having its vertebrae stacked one atop the other. Antonio held tight to the bed with both hands before he was sure he could take a step, all while continuing to count. Then, unsteady as a new calf, he slowly brought himself across the room on bandy legs, feeling victorious and a little stronger with every step.

Cracks like veins traced the mud walls. It was dusk—an orange-purple light came in through a window gridded with iron bars. The mirror was flocked with dried sage, and its medicinal smell reminded Antonio of his mother. He could see her panting through the white house with smoking bundles of the stuff, convinced the Indians under the ground were forever giving her children mal de ojo. Before he looked in the mirror he prepared himself. *I'm alive*, he thought. *Remember that.*

His eyes were the same: green and deep, except for a ring of conquistador gold that shone around the pupils. And his hair, what little of it he could see, was the same: wavy and thick and wild like a thornbush. But the rest of his face was unknown, obscured from the middle of his nose down, behind dirty bandages the color of which ranged from chocolate brown to guajillo maroon and the alarming crimson of fresh blood. The bandages were wrapped so tightly he worried they might be holding his jaw in place. He felt around to the back of his head, running his fingers over the rough weave, trying to find the place where the bullet might have left his skull, but he couldn't feel anything. Whatever was under the bandages was monstrous, that much was clear, and he had to see it, how much of his grotesque core had been wrenched out of the darkness and brought violently to the surface, naked for all.

He found his knife lying on a table and he used it to cut through the bandages behind his head. He thought he might faint from the pain—the gauze had fused to his skin and pulling it off felt like being flayed alive—but he breathed and counted and the bandages finally lay in a pulpy heap on the floor.

He confronted himself again in the mirror, his eyes tracing the contours of his own face like returning to a home destroyed by fire. His strong jaw and full lips were gone, replaced by a wide, yawning cavern that now encompassed the lower half of the right side of his face, with blue and purple edges as frayed and tattered as the bandages, and a center so deep and black it might have gone on all the way to his soul. His nose was askew and partially eaten by infection. The left half of his mouth was untouched, but the right half had disappeared altogether, the lips blasted away leaving two lipless halves that did not meet, hanging open in a permanent grimace like the jade mask he'd grabbed from the train. He was a beast and a monster, a hideous apparition. How could he go back to Jesusa, brotherless, penniless, and deformed? How would he ever again hold his children? They would shun him and they should. He was a walking nightmare.

He'd had dozens of women in his life and they'd all come willingly, hungrily. To be handsome is to live above mortals, to be forever forgiven, never held to full account because such is the eye's craving for symmetry. Now confronted with the shame and the shock of his body stripped of all fine pretense, he could only shake his head at the villain in the mirror and watch in horror as the villain shook his abominable head, too. He pulled back his arm, made a fist. The shattering of the glass slowed his breath, quelled the rage and fear for the space of two heartbeats, before he was again as jagged and fragmented as the shards now littering the dirt floor.

He became aware of a glow gradually filling the room. He turned around and saw an old woman holding a candle and a boy of about twelve watching him from the doorway. He straightened and breathed hard through his nose, showing no repentance for the broken mirror.

"We have food," the woman said, and she beckoned him into an adjoining room. She was very small, shorter than the boy by a head. In her white braids and embroidered blouse she looked like a doll made of old leather. The room into which she led Antonio was small, with pots crowded into corners and straw mats laid on the floor. A low breeze blew in through a door covered by a long piece of frayed fabric. He lowered himself onto one of the mats, wincing and trying not to cry out. His bones creaked and popped from disuse, but he eventually arranged himself with his legs crossed.

"You should not have removed your bandages," she said. "The last time you took them off you almost lost your nose."

Antonio tried to answer but the sounds got caught on his tongue, which still felt quite swollen, and wouldn't pass through his half lips. Instead of his voice he heard strange gurgling sounds and he startled, thinking they couldn't possibly have come from him. He tried again, sure he was just hoarse, but only wet garbles came out.

"Yes, you tore off your bandages more than once. You were fighting the devil in your sleep. Your tongue will heal, but your teeth are gone."

In the flickering candlelight Antonio could see she had lost one eye to a cataract and was on the way to losing the other, but she moved around the room with confidence, instructing the boy to make a porridge of cornmeal and milk while she pulled bundles of herbs from various containers and added them to a molcajete she'd placed on the ground. "My nephew found you," the old woman said. "He was looking for a runaway goat and followed a vulture circling something in the chaparral. You and another man were there. The other man," she said with a little shake of her head, "was already gone."

Antonio closed his eyes, wishing he could ask if they'd buried Hugo. As if reading his thoughts, she said, "My nephew got some men from Refugio and they buried him in the cemetery there. I lit a candle for him," and she indicated a small red votive lit inside a shrine to the Virgin of Guadalupe. "Whoever suffers in the body is done with sin," she said, quoting St. Peter as she watched the small flame burn steady and upright. "And one has to suffer to deserve."

She held a large bunch of weeds with yellow flowers and bluish leaves and she pulled the heads off the flowers and dropped them into the molcajete, whispering under her breath. When the flowers were all in the basin she took the tejolote and began grinding them down with firm, patient strokes and it was not hard to imagine the old woman's ancestors sitting in the same spot a thousand years before. "This will help with the swelling," she said without looking up.

She told Antonio to lie on the floor. The boy offered to hold Antonio down, but the old woman shook her head. Antonio's eyes filled with tears as the old woman applied the yellow, burning paste to his wounds, but he did not cry out, only keeping his eyes trained on the single, small fire and the round, impassive face of the Holy Virgin calmly watching his suffering as she watched everything from inside her cage of light. The old woman worked with deft hands. The burning mixture finally mellowed and cooled and began to numb the bottom half of Antonio's face. Then the old woman replaced the bandages, binding his face tightly, but leaving his mouth open, slipping her thin, childlike fingers into the dressing and tugging at precise points. Close up, she smelled sweet like cinnamon and rosewater.

"I couldn't find the bullet." She fixed him with the eye that still held a lively shadow of brown. "You are El Tragabalas," she said with a small smile. "The bullet swallower."

The boy held a bowl in front of Antonio. The porridge smelled mild and sweet. He took it and nodded his gratitude and put it to his mouth, for a lusty hunger had overtaken him. He opened his lips and let some of the warm liquid into his mouth and immediately doubled over and let it dribble out onto the dirt. The porridge, so innocuous in its clay bowl, burned his raw mouth and throat as though it were made of pure chilies. Hunger stabbed him in the ribs with urgency and so he tried again, but he was able to let only a few drops pass through to his stomach.

The old woman motioned for her nephew to help him, and so the boy crouched on the ground next to Antonio and took the bowl from his hands and very slowly coaxed everything down.

"You were a tricky one," the old woman said. "You lost a lot of blood before my nephew found you. The wound in your jaw was so infected I could smell you a half mile from the house. The maggots are the only thing that saved you. I spent a whole day just pulling them from your jaw. The Holy Mother must have been with you." She paused and considered him. "Was the other man your brother?"

Antonio looked at her but didn't answer. He was grateful for her kindness, but he didn't owe her anything of himself. Now that he was awake and able to walk he needed to find a horse and get after the Rangers.

"I see," she said. She gestured to the boy, who now held a brass cup in his hands. "Since you got here my goats haven't been right. They cry all night and don't want to eat." The boy dropped several small pieces of charcoal into the cup followed by copal resin before handing it to the old woman with the solemnity of an altar boy. "Now that you're awake I'm going to see what kind of haunt you've got on you. I think the hole in your face and the bullet in your stomach are the least of your worries."

She lit the resin and the room soon filled with thick, sweet smoke. She told Antonio to lie down and she produced a brown egg, which she dipped in a bowl of salted water. Antonio tried to get up, wanting no part in peasant superstitions, but this time she did enlist the boy's help and he pinned Antonio to the floor with surprising strength. She held the egg in her right hand and, after crossing Antonio with it, proceeded to rub it over his body with short, vigorous strokes. Her figure grew hazy in the smoke and the dim candlelight.

Again Antonio was reminded of his mother—a proud, fearful woman who'd married badly and spent her life trying in vain to protect her dwindling inheritance with spells and herbs rather than hard work and prudence. Every time Antonio or Hugo would cough his mother sent for the curandera, a bruja who laughed loudly and smelled like salted fish. His mother believed the bruja had cured Antonio and Hugo of yellow fever when they were children. But Antonio had seen through the woman's tricks, the way her answers were always vague enough as to never be false, how the Sonoro family's salvation was always one payment out of reach.

Now, in the darkened jacal, the old woman rubbed the egg over Antonio's chest, supposedly pulling bad humors from his body like a magnet and trapping them inside its hard shell. She brushed it lightly over his bandages, his neck, down his arms, and over the palms of his hands. Antonio was dizzy from the smoke and the heat radiating off the clay walls like an oven. The old woman finished the ritual by running the egg on Antonio's feet. It tickled him, but his mind was again on the bruja.

Antonio remembered the fever, remembered screaming in the night, imagining a coyote at the foot of his bed. The bruja answered his screams with spoonfuls of tequila—her round toad eyes still taunted him in his nightmares. The bruja had banished his mother to the other end of the house, assuring her that she and the Holy Mother were ample caregivers. The days he and Hugo spent in bed were long and torturous—they took turns over a single chamber pot, which quickly overflowed and spilled onto the floor.

"There's blood," the old woman now said with alarm, and showed Antonio the egg, which she'd cracked into a bowl. He lifted his head and glanced briefly at the yolk—in the middle sat a small bloody teardrop, the end of which stretched long and tapered. The old woman watched him for a reaction, but he turned his head and said nothing. *Peasant nonsense*, he thought. *Seeing something in nothing.*

The bruja's cures had nothing to do with them surviving the fever, but his mother had wept at the woman's feet and given her every piece of silver in the house. Superstitions were a trap waiting to swallow the searching and the sick.

The old woman began brushing Antonio with a bundle of green leaves while reciting Ave Maria, the boy somewhere in the dark, echoing her prayers. The smoke made shapes in the air: a gun, a train, a child's frightened eyes. The old woman's chants grew louder and the boy's grew as well until they were practically shouting. Antonio rolled over on his side and shut his eyes. A gun, a train, Hugo whimpering in the dark. "'Holy Mary, Mother of God, pray for us sinners now and at the hour of our death.'"

"Enough!" Antonio knocked the dish containing the egg out of the woman's hands and it shattered, spilling yolk and albumen across the floor. The sound of his own voice surprised him. It was rough and garbled, only a touch of his former self in it, but it suited him. It matched what he felt inside. He'd swallowed the Ranger's bullet and now carried that bitter memento inside him, his own thwarted death living on in his body, casting him into the gray limbo between this world and the next. He looked at the egg, the bloody teardrop now burst open and spread across the yolk in a constellation of red dots, foretelling a thousand wounds to come. If the bullet was still inside him, had he actually survived? He'd swallowed a darkness that could grow like the hole in Hugo's chest, devouring everything. Perhaps one day the bullet would decide to continue its journey and slip upstream into his heart, his throat, his brain. Was it possible to survive such a wound?

If the old woman was upset that Antonio had knocked the egg onto the floor she did not show it. She crossed Antonio and crossed herself.

"You have a shadow," she said. "He will catch you."

NINE

Remedio had stepped off the path the minute he'd refused collection of Antonio's soul. It was painful for him to stray like that. Excruciating in a way he imagined was almost physical. He'd been given a task, and by not completing it, he felt like a part of him had been torn off, left behind while the rest of him continued on. He'd lost something of himself that day, and the ache was constant in him now. He worried what would happen if he continued commanding his own course. What would be left of him after too much compromise, too much exposure to humans, too much visibility? It was a question he decided to put off answering for a little longer.

It was in the city where he found the actor. Remedio watched the actor and his father, the actor's guileless children. What untroubled people these were, whose greatest sin that Remedio could discern was insularity. Outside the ramparts of their happy home children starved and cried and were beaten and died alone in the dark never having received their birthright of love, and the actor and his wife meanwhile danced the hokey-pokey with theirs and made great splashes in the blue swimming pool. Remedio knew far better than to ask why, and yet this and a hundred other questions clouded him like gnats as he drifted through their house at night, picking up beautiful things and putting them back down.

Did observation change the nature of the observed? Remedio wasn't sure. He'd watched the actor, the actor's father, the actor's children, and he could see they remained in stasis, their lives unrolling like garden paths, unsurprising and pleasant. But if there was a debt to be repaid, if the Sonoros were still found in arrears, Remedio would be tasked with taking one or possibly all of them. Besides being unjust, Remedio reasoned, this would put him in a position to again refuse collection of a soul. And he did not wish to do that.

He saw the actor struggling to understand his history, to find his own light self in the murk of his ancestors, and to come closer to his unyielding father. Remedio thought he could help the actor, just a little bit, nudge him in the venal direction in which all Sonoros headed one day or another. Remedio would help the actor and thereby prove that the path was just. Then Remedio could continue his work in rectitude, and without the pain of another deviation.

The city was loud and busysome. On a street corner Remedio appeared behind a tree and stood without blinking, momentarily shocked by it all. Office girls sat outside Sanborns smoking in kitten heels. A man barked, "¡Los perritos! ¡Los perritos!" while four mutts in pink tutus spun about on their hind legs to a tune played on a clarinet. An announcer with a satin baritone hawked Nescafé from a car radio, while barefoot boys darted between stop-start traffic selling chicle and cigarettes. A sweet potato vendor wiped his forehead with a rag before rolling his pushcart forward, leaving in his wake a honey smell and the mournful sound of his steam whistle.

When Remedio approached the actor and his family in the park, he saw the boy child giddily clinging to a white plaster horse and bobbing up and down in time to an old rag. The actor wasn't watching the children. The actor's father was, but a bad hip made him slow. Remedio linked eyes with the boy—he had a stout, freckled face and black eyes like a bird—and Remedio watched as the child stood up on the stirrups and climbed onto the horse's back just as it reached its zenith. His right foot foundered atop the rounded head of the saddle horn and his face broke open in terror as he tumbled from the carousel onto the ground, hitting the cement with his knees and then his hands and sprawling wide.

Remedio reached the child first. He lifted him from the ground and the boy's cries almost immediately subsided. The actor and his father came when Remedio was already carrying the child to a park bench. "Careful," the old man said to Remedio. "Don't crowd him," he barked at the children and parents who gathered in close to watch. And Remedio saw how quickly the old man could transform his inward shame for the boy falling outward into anger. At the park bench Remedio poured water from a flask onto the boy's legs and dried and dressed his scrapes and scratches, finishing with rainbow-colored lollipops for the boy, his sister, and all the other children who'd gathered to watch the operation.

"That was remarkable," Jaime said at the same moment his father asked a pointed, "And who the hell are you?"

Jaime looked with shock at his father, any unease he might have had about Remedio now vanished in the relief he felt at seeing Mito patched up and with no broken bones.

"Are you a doctor?" Juan Antonio asked, arms folded. "What are you doing walking around with candy and gauze pads?"

Remedio looked steadily at the old man, considering the question. Remedio is like a doctor because he tends to the diseased? He was not sure what he would say, though he was unable to lie.

"Well of course he's a doctor," Jaime said. "I'd like to ask why you weren't watching the children."

"The hell I wasn't watching them," Juan Antonio said. "That fool boy climbed up on the horse like he didn't have the sense God gave a rock."

"You can't say that about my son," Jaime said, feeling his cheeks color. He dropped his voice because he did not want to make a scene in front of the doctor and the other parents at the park. "But you walked them over there; you were supposed to be watching them. We can discuss it at home."

"Your son should know better than to climb up on a moving carousel."

"He seems to be feeling much better," Remedio finally said. The boy was now swinging his legs from the park bench and enjoying the spotlight as the other children congratulated him on his toughness.

"He's normally very cautious," Jaime said to Remedio, "but who knows where children get these ideas. His mother and I will have a talk with him."

"A child's soul is a bird in flight," Remedio said.

"Exactly," Jaime said. "Would you care to join me for a drink? My house isn't very far. It's the least I can do."

"Thank you kindly," Remedio said, and he could feel the heat coming off Juan Antonio's eyes like two burning coals.

At home, with a healthy glass of Cutty Sark in hand, Jaime could get a keener look at the stranger. He had careworn brown eyes and firm, some-what large features that could have been sculpted by an Italian master. His skin was lined, but it was difficult to place his age, and Jaime thought he had rather a good face for film. His clothes, too, were difficult to cat-egorize. His jacket was too long, his pants too wide, and his hat was of a shape Jaime thought may have belonged to another century. But what were clothes against a seemingly magical ability to mend his child?

"To the kindness of strangers," Jaime said, and as Remedio had de-clined a drink, he raised his own in the air and then took a long sip. "I want to apologize for my father's behavior at the park. I don't know what's got into him. Perhaps he's starting to feel his age."

"It is difficult to watch oneself approach the end."

"I'll drink to that," Jaime said with a little laugh. "Time will claim us all, won't it? You know what Borges proposed," and he tipped a little more whiskey into his glass. "That all time has already passed. That all this is only a memory. What do you think of that?"

"I think any man who believes he understands the true nature of time is in for a surprise."

"Very profound," Jaime said. "What kind of doctor did you say you were?"

"I have studied human nature for a long, long time," Remedio said.

"A Jungian," Jaime said and nodded wisely. That accounted for the man's strange clothes, he thought. "Well, I hope you find little to study here. All happy families are alike—am I right?"

Remedio considered this. "I don't agree. Happiness can have many faces." And he was awed at how the words came to him, how he was able to open his mouth with little foreknowledge of what he would say next. Stepping off the path seemed to be making him more like men. He wasn't sure whether he greeted this change with gladness or dread.

"My wife is going to love you," Jaime said. "Please stay for dinner."

And after dinner, when it was quite late and Jaime and Elena were expansive and wine-drunk and both insisting that cabs were scarce, they begged Remedio to spend the night. And as they'd invited him in and it was late and they were so very certain that they wished him to stay longer, what could he say?

TEN

Antonio spent another two weeks in bed before he could move around with-out difficulty, and it was two weeks after that before his bandages could be removed. He stayed in the jacal with Cielita, the old woman, and Manu, the orphaned child of a neighbor who she referred to as her nephew to make the boy feel he was not so alone, a circumstance that Antonio felt with a sharp pain in his chest. The pair lived quietly in the brasada with a small herd of goats and ventured occasionally into the nearby town of Refugio to cure croup, set broken bones, and sell herbs and potions for everything from lazy eyes to broken hearts. Once he could get up, Antonio helped around the farm by replacing wheel felloes, repairing the fence around the goat enclosure, patching the cracked mud walls of the jacal, and teaching Manu to braid lariats. When he was strong enough he carried water for the old woman's daily bath, for she insisted, for reasons he could not divine, on being fastidiously clean. And when he had done this for a week without his arms shaking from the strain and without feeling faint from the heat, he told Cielita he wanted to visit Hugo's grave. And so the next morning while it was still dark—for even with his face bandaged and a bandana tied around that, he didn't want to be seen—he and Manu set out for town.

The air was clotted with monarch butterflies on their migration south, and by the time Antonio and Manu reached town and the sun had risen, the insects sagged by the thousands in the trees, a living autumn of orange and brown. Some people believed the monarchs were the souls of the dead, and that they traveled every year to Michoacán for Día de los Muertos. Trying not to step on or brush up against any of the butterflies as they walked, Antonio wondered, if Hugo were one among this horde, would he know him?

They walked past the iron gates of Mt. Calvary Cemetery and Manu only had to shake his head for Antonio to understand—whites only. Down the street and around the corner was a small wooden sign that read *Santa Cruz*.

Antonio had fashioned a wooden cross and used his knife to carve Hugo's name and dates as neatly as he could, though in the coming dawn he was ashamed at how primitive it looked, how childish, not at all suited to the life it represented, a life spent treading the divine path, always seeking out that which would ennoble, a life undeserving of the rot of the Sonoro name. But neither could he leave the grave unmarked, and so when Manu pointed it out—marked now with a large rock tied up with a yellow ribbon—Antonio knelt and dug his cross into the ground before wiping angry, regretful tears from his eyes.

I never should have let you come. I never should have told you. I should have died instead. I wish—I never should have—

How many times could he repeat this refrain? It had been running as an unbroken tune in his mind for weeks. Would he repeat it forever? Or could he entertain the idea that he'd been spared for a reason, that God wanted him to kill the Rangers, that he'd lived precisely to enact violent justice? He couldn't wash the malevolent eyes of the Mexican Ranger out of his memory, nor the self-righteous voice of the captain, nor the quavering but just as deadly hand of the boy Ranger. For they played unbroken in his mind, too, and he knew only one way to put those memories to rest.

He knew better than to expect anything as foolish as a sign from Heaven, but there in the graveyard, on hallowed ground, perched atop the inflection point between two decisions, he couldn't help indulging in a little superstition. *Give me a sign, brother. Show me that I'm right. That this is what you want.*

He knelt in silence, waiting. Behind him he could hear Manu chewing mesquite beans. Grackles chattered noisily in a nearby tree and a chorus of cicadas answered. Wagons and mule trains were beginning to roll into town, their creaking wheels and the distant shouts of teamsters carried into the cemetery. A strong breeze blew in from the east and, answering this call, the tree nearest Antonio seemed to alight as thousands of butterflies took wing, the effect like a school of golden fish rushing up and away to Mexico.

Antonio stood and crossed himself, satisfied.

When he returned from the cemetery, Antonio announced that he would soon be on his way.

But Cielita would not hear of it.

"You're weak as milk teeth," she said. "When you can carry me on your back for a mile through the brush, then you'll be ready. Leaving before then is a death sentence."

Antonio cursed her and called her a stupid old bruja, but he knew she was right. He still had to use one hand to steady the other as he scooped up beans with a tortilla and brought them to his mouth. Pursuing the Rangers would mean months on a horse and days without food and water. Even with the strength of two men it would be almost impossible. Almost. His advantage, and it was a great one at that, was that he, Antonio Sonoro, was, in the eyes of the state of Texas, dead. So he braided his lariats and strained goat hair from the cheese Cielita preserved under the house in clay pots, and waited for the day he could leave.

At night, when Manu lay snoring on his petate, Cielita would beckon Antonio outside, where she smoked marijuana from a short, wooden pipe, and she would ask him to describe the stars.

"The scorpion," she said from her low wooden chair one night, "does he look angry?"

Antonio crouched on the ground and considered the constellation, the fishhook tail curving north and the insect's red heart pulsing bright in the wan glow of a crescent moon. "No, abuelita. He's just hungry and wants some tamales."

The old woman laughed, shaking her whole body. Antonio's throat was still too raw to allow smoking, and so the old woman brewed him a tea from the crushed flowers of the plant. He leaned against the outer wall of the jacal and enjoyed being pulled into a deep calm that brought him down and sideways like an ocean current.

Cielita was so quiet and still that after a while Antonio thought he should carry her inside to sleep, when she said, "It's the strangest thing. I was born in New Spain, which then became Mexico, then the Republic of Texas, and wound up in the United States, and meanwhile my house has always stood in the same place. The Texans call me Mexican and I've never even crossed the Rio Grande. What is it like on the other side?"

Antonio placed stones in the path of a line of black ants and he watched with mild interest as they scrambled over their new obstacles. "It's the same as here," he said. "Always some pendejo trying to take what's yours."

"Your gun works just as well over there."

"Yes, and the gallows, too."

The wind stirred the dead leaves that still clung to the trees and the air around Cielita was thick as ever with cinnamon.

"I've never known anyone who took so many baths," Antonio said, massaging his shoulder, which was sore from carrying buckets of water to the house from the creek. "It's not healthy."

Cielita looked at him a moment before speaking, one corner of her mouth raised. "I was sixteen when the Mexican army under General Urrea took Refugio," she finally said. "This was just after the Texans lost the Alamo. No one thought the Mexican army could lose, but still, we were cautious. When it was over we knew we'd be living under someone's thumb. I saw Urrea ride through with his men—he was so handsome in his plumed hat." She took a draw off the pipe and exhaled up toward the sky. "And he had the longest sword I'd ever seen."

Antonio almost fell backward laughing.

"During the battle I brought water to the men," she continued. "They called me pasita, little raisin. To be so near men from the capital, men in white breeches and gold buttons—they were like nothing I'd ever seen." The clouds in her eyes mimicked the field of stars above. "One boy used to whistle at me whenever I came into camp. I resisted him as long as I could, but one day I was careless and he caught me when my hands were full and took me back to his tent. He was only a couple of years older than me and I remember being so shocked that without his fine clothes he was just as dark as I was." She paused, and when she spoke again her voice had darkened. "He was a rude boy. I did not know then how many shades of cruelty men carry in their paint box. When he let me put my clothes back on he told me I smelled worse than his horse. 'Like a shit-wallowing sow,' he said." She shook her head slowly and it was clear the words rang in her ears still, sixty years later. "He told me he'd whip me if I told anyone what we'd done. I said of course, and I gathered my things and I left. But not before I snatched his hat."

"You stole a hat?" Antonio playfully wagged his finger. "You're a bad one."

"I saw it sitting there next to the door of the tent. It was black leather with a big brass eagle on the front and a ball of bright red feathers coming out of the top. I'd never held anything so beautiful in my hands. It was like something a king would wear. I only wanted to take it for a little while, to make him search the tent for it for a few days, just to get back at him for what he'd done. I took it home and tried it on and it felt like a crown. I thought, why should this boy, as brown as me, have something like that? What made him so special? The weight of it on my head and those red, red feathers . . ." Her voice trailed off in the memory. "Well, how was I supposed to know Urrea would shoot him for something so stupid as a missing hat?"

Antonio said nothing and went back to piling more rocks in the way of the ants.

"After that the army left and then the next month we learned the Texans had won. We thought maybe there would be no reprisals." She yawned and stretched out her legs, causing a small chorus of cracks and pops to arise from her bones. "But that was wishful thinking. That's when we started calling our new neighbors los diablos tejanos." She looked at Antonio with her good eye and he had the feeling her vision had gotten better with the marijuana. "The harm we don't intend hurts the worst, and the door into Hell is always open."

"It sounds like the bastard had it coming."

"Not for me to decide."

Antonio made a sucking sound with the corner of his mouth. *Who knows?*

"I never forgot what he said though, and I've taken a bath every day since I saw his body, bareheaded, lying in a ditch. Maybe that's my penance. I've never felt clean since."

"Do you still have the hat?"

She shook her head. "I buried it in the ditch that night. For all I know it's still there."

She faced Antonio, searching him behind her cataracts.

"You're getting restless," Cielita said. "You think you're ready to leave."

Antonio inhaled through his nose and knocked down the pile of rocks, startling the line of ants so that they scattered wildly, just to remind them that the world is chaotic even when it seems full of design.

"You never stay still," she said. "You're always crouching, ready to run. You're going to go after the ones who killed your brother, aren't you? A fool's errand. Go back to your children. Give them the luxury of a living father."

"I can't go back until my heart is at peace. Maybe that's my penance."

"Who were they? Bandits, too?"

"Rangers," he said. "Los Rinches." Cielita gasped and crossed herself, but he continued. "When I was younger we'd see them sometimes on the other side of the river. We'd sling rocks at them if we had good cover. The cattle rustlers would throw us a couple centavos to keep them distracted. 'Rinche, pinche, cara de chinche,' we'd yell. We didn't know they were allowed to cross the river." He lifted up his shirt and showed her a pink scar along his side shaped like a comet.

"I thought that one looked old," she said.

"I was seven the first time they shot me. I was nine when I saw them rape a woman doing her washing near their camp. And when I was fifteen I was at a cousin's wedding in Matamoros when they burst into the reception. They shot up the room. They killed the groom's aunt and hit two others before the cowards lit back out to the ferry. They got the land, fine, but it's not enough. They want submission. They want to feel good about it when they rip things out of our hands. But they won't get me again. And they won't get my children, either. I have to go after them. I have to make it right." He stood and kicked dirt over the ants, stomped them with the heel of his boot before they could make their way into the jacal.

"Your brother doesn't want your blood to spill with his," Cielita said. "Go back home. God has given you a reprieve."

"I have to make it right," Antonio repeated. "I have to."

Bats screeched and streamed across the windless sky. The night brought no relief from the heat. Antonio took off his shirt and fanned himself with it. The goats bleated and pawed the dirt. They'd stopped shrieking through the night, but they were still anxious whenever they heard him moving around the yard.

"I'm going to bed," Cielita said.

"Hold on." Antonio swayed over the old woman. The marijuana had made him unsteady, but he was certain he could support her weight.

"What are you doing?" Antonio got his arms under her even though she kicked her feet. "You're tipsy, you jackass," she said. "You're going to trip on something and break your head and then we're both cooked."

But Antonio ignored her. He swung her around to his back, one hand under her right thigh, the other holding her hands, which clutched at his skin and pulled his chest hair. By now he knew the brush around the jacal even in the dark. At first Cielita struck him on the shoulders and screamed for him to put her down, but soon she was whooping and shouting like a drunken vaquero, kicking her tiny heels into his sides and telling him to gallop, horsey. Antonio stumbled through the brush with the old woman on his back, picking up speed and dodging branches and cactuses. He felt strong and agile. The woman was a bundle of kindling, no more a burden than the wind. They ran to the creek, stopping when Antonio could hear the trickle as the thin vein of water threaded over rocks and between knots of grass.

"I can't talk you into staying?" Cielita asked as he carried her back home. "Manu's learned so much having a man around." She'd stopped her cheers and now lay with her head against Antonio's bare back. They were almost to the jacal. Antonio could smell the goats, fetid and sweaty.

"I'll never be able to repay you," he said.

"We all play our part. Do you pay the deer for his trouble when you shoot him?"

"Even still. If there's anything . . ."

He put her down at the curtain that served as the door to the jacal and she straightened her dress and smoothed her hair before going inside. "Kindness is its own reward," she said, "but cruelty is a self-inflicted wound."

"Good night, buelita."

Antonio did not follow her inside. He took his knife out of his boot and began sharpening it. If he made his knife ready, perhaps he'd see the Rangers in his dreams. He sharpened it until a piece of grass dropped on its blade split in two.

When he finally lay on the floor, he entertained himself before sleep by imagining running the knife into the stomach of the Mexican Ranger Casoose, and the white one named Fish (to the boy Ranger, Antonio would grant the kindness of shooting). Their lips would hang open, vainly gulping air like carp. His fingers on the knife handle would be able to feel every tooth of the blade as it sliced through muscle and tendons like ripe squash. Their faces when they saw the knife withdrawing from inside them would disfigure in shock, each ceasing to be a face at all but only an extension of the carnage. He would erase them. He would turn them into vessels of hurt. It was a better vision than picturing again and again the moment Hugo's soul left his body.

On the floor of the jacal with his shirt rolled up under his head, Antonio pictured all of this and dropped warmly into sleep.

·   ·   ·

When his bandages were removed for good, Antonio went to Cielita's copper coffeepot, for he'd broken her mirror, and looked at his face stretched across its curved surface. A deep red river, shiny, jagged, and raw, now ran from the tip of his right ear to the edge of his mouth, where it formed a depression, the center of which was too far down inside his skin to be seen, and from which fresh blood still oozed. The flesh over his nose and lips had healed, closing over the open wounds, though his mouth now sat crooked with only one half able to fully close. The side of his nose appeared gnawed, a large piece lost to rot. He ran his finger along the seam that was now the focal point of his entire face, where the old woman had done her best to sew the two halves of his cheek together after the bullet ripped them apart. He winced from the contact. Even the air stung, and he knew that riding a horse across the dusty ground would make his wounds much worse. He covered the right side of his face with his hand and looked at his strong brows and firm left jaw, his green eyes—the eyes of a Visigoth, his mother had proudly told him—and for an instant it was the same face he'd always seen, handsome and unspoiled. But as he brought his hand down to reveal the gash, which seemed to open wide and slowly swallow the bottom half of his face like a sinkhole, he knew the wound ran far deeper than the path the bullet had traced.

Cielita asked one favor of Antonio before he went in search of the Rangers. She had an arthritic sister living in Corpus Christi, a two day ride to the south, and she wanted Antonio to deliver a package of medicine to her, herbs to ease her pain and reduce the swelling in her joints. "She has a blue house under a giant palm tree next to the water," she said. "You won't miss it."

He wanted to leave before dawn while the day was cool. Manu brought out their only horse, a sleepy red dun with a stripe down her back. "She doesn't go fast," Manu said, grooming her and feeding her eggs, "but she's reliable." Cielita packed him beans, tortillas, coffee, and a thick package of dried goat meat rolled in paper. To this she added the copper coffeepot, a wool blanket, a gray felt hat like the gringos wore, a spoon, a cooking pot, rope, matches, and a leather canteen.

Antonio tied a bandana around his head. He would give the world only half a face, show only what would not terrify, and this, he told himself, was how everyone else lived anyway. The darkest horrors of his soul had been dragged up to the surface, but were they so different from the iniquities that lived in all men? Now anyone who saw his face would know he was a monster and there was some relief in that. Still, he could not bring himself to suffer stares and derisive cries. He would wear the bandana.

Cielita watched him tie the cloth around his face and when he was done she held out a pair of boots. They were tall and well-suited for moving through brush.

"Como los Rinches," she said when he tried them on. "You look like a Ranger."

Antonio winked and squatted low, stretching to break them in.

Antonio added the package of medicine to his saddlebag, hugged Manu goodbye, and thanked Cielita.

"I'll send money for the horse as soon as I can," he said.

Cielita waved this idea away. "I wish I could give you my gun," she said, "but I know you'll find one when you need it."

In response Antonio pulled the carved steel hilt of his knife just out of his belt. "You're right," he said, his eyes alight above the bandana.

Antonio mounted the horse and the leather reins were soft in his hands, the animal warm and powerful beneath him. Cielita was right—he didn't like to sit still. Movement was power. Running was living.

"One more thing," Cielita said, and she pulled something small from a pocket in her skirt. She took Antonio's hands with both of hers—they were birdlike under her onion skin—and intoned a blessing before crossing him and then licking her thumb and pressing it to his forehead. When he looked down he saw she'd placed a prayer card in his hands, the Virgin of Guadalupe printed in color on heavy paper. "The Holy Mother loves us all," she said, staring hard into Antonio, and he had the unnerving feeling the old woman could, if she wanted, see more behind her cataracts than she let on. "No one is too wicked for grace."

He thanked her again, nodded to the boy, clicked his tongue, and gave the horse a gentle squeeze with his thighs. He pointed the horse south and tried not to think about his chances of finding the Rangers in all the vast latitudes of Texas, and instead focused on the sound the knife would make as it entered their skin, and the blank, lightless quality of their eyes when he brought them to the ground.

As he rode away, a large red bird watched him from atop a huisache. The bird tilted its head, blinked twice, and kept its gaze on the figures of horse and man as they were folded into the brush.

ELEVEN

One night turned into several as Remedio told Jaime and Elena that he had traveled far to reach Mexico City and he did not yet have accommodations—both statements, in a strict sense, true. They gladly opened their home, and the children were likewise eager to have a new adult to dance and sing for and who also kept them amply supplied with candy. Remedio, who'd never spent this much time visible and among humans, was aware that in even this short amount of time he was undergoing transitions: from a loosened tongue, which now readily supplied answers in any proximity to truth, to a loosened conscience, which provided him the latitude to administer iodine and Band-Aids to soothe the children's scrapes, but also to sharpen the emotional perceptions of everyone in the house, increasing the amplitude, so to speak, of every interaction so that the maid cried when Elena complained that they were out of eggs, and the children were driven to hysterics over use of the television remote control. Remedio, who had never before changed, was becoming more like them by the hour. And while the old ache of straying was still there, he could feel it less and less the closer to men he allowed himself to drift, something in their brash embrace of both free will and contradiction bleeding onto him, seeping into his core, and insulating him.

Juan Antonio was the only one who objected to the new houseguest, and he made his feelings well known in the mornings when he complained that breakfast was late because Ignacia was squeezing fresh orange juice for Remedio, in the afternoons when he claimed Remedio had gotten the newspaper all out of order and lost the fútbol scores, and in the evenings when he said he wouldn't play three-person dominoes with Jaime and Remedio, that a game split thus was as stimulating as a tea party for schoolgirls. When, on the third day, the children insisted that Remedio pick them up from school instead of Juan Antonio, the old man finally reached his limit. He stalked into Jaime's office and slammed the door and stood with his arms folded. Jaime waited a full minute for his father to say something before he realized part of his punishment was having to speak first.

"What is it, Pop?"

"Get him out of the house. You don't know anything about him. No references. No friends. For all you know he could be an axe murderer."

"You've been watching too much *Perry Mason*."

"What's his last name? Where's he come from? You've got to keep your family safe, you know. You can't invite in every jackass off the street."

"You're one to talk about people with no family history."

"That book's poisoned your mind. Your head's so stuck in the past you can't see what's right in front of you. I told you to throw that thing away. It's a curse."

"Do you think people are created in a vacuum? That we appear out of thin air holding onto nothing from before? Refusing to be part of a family is not the same as not having one."

"Don't go turning over stones, boy," Juan Antonio said with an authoritarian look that made Jaime want to scream. "Are you happier because you know more about the past? Hm?"

"Happiness has nothing to do with—"

"Aha! So why bother?

Go back to making your little cowboy shoot-'em-ups."

Jaime sat very still; he didn't even blink. He stared at a spot on the rug where two flowers, one red, one blue, kissed and twined and gave birth to a halo of golden rosettes. Most of the time he could pretend that his father was proud of him—he could pretend; he was an actor, wasn't he?—but every so often the old man would betray himself and out would slip his true feelings. At these times Jaime simply had to hold himself together and survive it, because Juan Antonio was either too oblivious to understand the harm his words caused, or, Jaime worried, too callous to care.

"I need to get back to work," Jaime said, and he opened the book and bent his head low over it and wouldn't let the first tear drop onto the greening page until his father had left the room.

Sometimes Remedio itched to take Jaime, his father, his son, to close the debt and be done with it. He found himself standing at odd hours outside Jaime's study, his bedroom. He'd stand there a long time, his hand hovering just above the door handle, waiting for a signal to turn it.

He had also sown sufficient chaos in the Sonoro household so that the morning's milk curdled by late afternoon and the radios turned on of their own accord to news programs blaring the day's disasters. He'd so effectively disharmonized their life, that even he did not foresee the scorpion.

It was brown and amber, the color of dying leaves, and was first discovered by Ignacia inside one of her slippers when she got out of bed. She shrieked, her petite toes suspended centimeters from the thing's gnashing claws. She dropped her slipper and the scorpion scuttled away under her doorsill and into the house, where Jaime and his family had awoken to the maid's scream with the shared certainty that their sanctuary had been violated. Jaime rushed downstairs with a wooden club he kept in case of burglars, and he found Ignacia standing on a chair in the kitchen speaking rapidly to him in her native language from Chiapas, strange clicks and too-round vowels that had traveled up and down green mountains for centuries, one word repeated inside the noise that Jaime could discern.

"Tzek," she said, "tzek, tzek."

"Sec?" Jaime asked.

"Tzek," she said again. "Scorpion. A man-killer. She was in my shoe and now she's somewhere in the house."

"Jesus Christ," Jaime said, and ran the hand that wasn't holding the club down his face.

Juan Antonio and Remedio appeared and Elena called down the stairs to ask what was the matter.

"There's a scorpion loose," Jaime shouted. "Stay upstairs and get the kids into one room."

"A lot of fuss over a little insect," Juan Antonio said. "I guess breakfast will be late."

Ignacia gave the old man a hard look, but didn't move from the chair.

"I don't suppose ant poison would work," Jaime said, looking with suspicion at the gleaming white floors, half expecting the thing to dart out from under a cabinet.

"You have to trap her, señor. Trap her, and then you hit her with a brick, como pah! Pah!" And she mimed slamming a brick against her hand.

"How the hell did it get into the house?" Jaime asked.

"Through a crack in the wall," Remedio said, speaking for the first time that morning. "Or up a tree and under a windowsill. Down through the attic. They're incredibly agile and they can fit through almost any space."

"Your children are always leaving doors open," Juan Antonio said. "Doors wide open. Lights on. They think electricity is free."

"Leave the kids out of this," Jaime said. "We don't know how it came in."

"You probably let it in going in and out of the garden, you old fool," Ignacia said, clearly still smarting from Juan Antonio's complaint about breakfast.

"The insolence!" Juan Antonio's face was growing red, and Jaime flinched a little, waiting for his old man to really blow his stack. "Are you going to let this filthy indio speak to me like that?"

"You can't call me that, old man!" Ignacia screamed. "Just see if I clean your ass when you get too old and start pissing yourself."

Into this melee came Elena and the children, all of whom had just heard their prim maid scream the words *ass* and *piss*. The baby's chin quivered and Elena looked horror-struck.

"That's totally uncalled for," Elena started to say before Jaime cut her off and ordered her and the children back upstairs.

"They have to eat," Elena said, putting the baby on her hip and helping the other two children onto chairs. "You can't expect them to sit upstairs and starve."

As Jaime and Elena continued to argue and Juan Antonio quietly abused Ignacia, calling her a viper and a savage under his breath as he searched the cabinets for instant coffee, Remedio felt a sharp sensation in his side. Clutching himself, he slipped out of the kitchen and into the living room, where he leaned against a wall without a sound.

He'd easily shattered the family's gilded peace, and in so doing had brought them all closer to their true natures. He could see the pattern laid out neatly before the Sonoros—an ouroboros of cruelty, pride, and privilege endlessly feeding on itself and giving birth to generation after generation of willing sinners. He should take them all, that very moment. What, then, was the problem? He unbuttoned his shirt and looked down to see red welts on his right side, the scorpion crawling now down his pant leg and circling up and over his boot. He pressed a finger to one of the welts and was surprised to feel something sharp beginning at his skin and going deep inside, what would be his spine perhaps, or his liver or neck. He buttoned his shirt and leaned down and picked up the scorpion by its tail. It was long and lean, and it thrashed in Remedio's hand. He considered it, remembering a dry place long before where burnt-back men had carved scorpion likenesses into stone pillars in the desert. He'd never understood exactly why they worshipped the false-idol scorpions, but he believed it might have had something to do with bringing close what one hated and feared, making alliance with that which is cruel and seemingly random in order to placate it, in the hopes that one would not be the next victim. And this made a lot of sense to Remedio.

He let the scorpion down onto the palm of his hand and admired its hard exterior, its rich honey color. He slowly closed his hand over its quivering body, ignoring the stings that came again and again.

Jaime came into the living room as Remedio was still holding the thing in his hand. As Remedio looked up and saw Jaime he dropped the scorpion's crumpled body to the floor, a sudden thought sending a quick shiver of recognition through him. Jaime asked him what he was doing and Remedio held up his hand, red and welt-swollen. "I took care of it for you," he said.

As Jaime watched, the scorpion stirred and stood on its eight legs, flicked its tail once, twice, and then thrashed its claws before it sprinted away, disappearing under a sofa and out of sight.

Jaime looked at the floor in something of a stupor, unable to comprehend what he had just witnessed, while Remedio stared dazed at his hand. So this was pain. He finally looked down to where the scorpion had just been and the shiver of recognition blossomed into a full-body sensation that he would later decide was fear. He needed to leave. And yet he stood rooted to the floor, momentarily allowing gravity to hold him firm against what was a clear signal to go.

And Jaime, meanwhile, looking from the floor to Remedio, one to the other, his mouth unable to form the words to ask why, by God, was Remedio unfazed by seeing the scorpion spring back to life?

TWELVE

Antonio stayed off the sendaro, preferring the cover of the brush. In the eyes of the law, Antonio Sonoro was dead, but still he did not wish to see anyone. Even this early in the morning women with tinajas balanced on their shoulders would be returning from the creeks with water, and farmers would be leading cows or goats up the path to town. And everyone knew the road to Corpus Christi was lawless.

He pulled his hat low and brought his blue bandana up over his nose, allowing only his eyes to be visible in the narrow gap. The sun broke slowly, turning the world from blue to pink to yellow before clouds overtook it and washed everything Antonio could see gray, the color of smoke rising from an extinguished fire. The horse plodded amiably through the brush, picking her feet up and over fallen mesquites and wending through a tight labyrinth of naked oaks, thick clots of brown grass, hidden fox burrows, and red ant mounds. He'd also taken a large file from Cielita, and this he used to file down barbed wire when he and the horse encountered it. There was a saying in South Texas after every square acre had been split between the new American owners, portioned, and fenced: Cuando vino el alambre, vino el hambre—when the wire came, so did the hunger.

They went thirty kilometers the first day. At nightfall he followed the fence surrounding a cattle pasture until he came to a stock pond and he

ELIZABETH GONZALEZ JAMES

let the horse take long, greedy swallows of the warm water. There was a sorghum field nearby and after she'd had her fill of water he turned her out to graze. Then, going back to the pond, he broke off a nopal pad, squeezed out the slime inside, mixed it with some water in his cooking pot, and then strained the mixture through his bandana into a cup. He'd seen worms as long as his leg pulled from screaming men and others that squirmed under the whites of the eye. Hell, he thought, would look a lot like Texas. He used some more of the clean water to wash the dirt and sweat from his wound, wiping away the line of blood that had run and dried from the corner of his lip to his chin. When he looked up from the water the scorpion was low in the sky and he believed Cielita was sitting in her little chair, smoking her pipe and thinking about him.

The horse was in high spirits the next morning as they set out before dawn again, Antonio still keeping them off the road. They were nearing the coast—the air tasted of salt, and seagulls and grackles fought over the same meager scraps—and Antonio knew the road would be choked with wagons carrying shipments to and from port. The wind was stronger this close to the coast, too. Dry leaves shook like rattlesnakes, making it difficult to hear approaching riders. And though they were well concealed in the brush, Antonio saw signs of people all around him: broken branches, bent, trampled grass, hoofprints preserved in the dry soil that mapped the wanderings of a dozen bandidos.

All day Antonio was also aware of large numbers of turkey vultures with heads like raw meat flying south. When the wind momentarily waned he could always hear large wings overhead. The birds were assembling somewhere in frightful numbers and it made him uneasy that he and they were going in the same direction. As afternoon approached Antonio also began to smell something foul. The smell grew and grew the closer he drew to the Nueces River, and as the number of birds in the sky doubled and tripled, he knew something abominable lay ahead.

He and the horse reached the Nueces in the late afternoon when sunlight caught brief shimmers of water between its banks—a trickle in some places, a still pond in others, but mostly nothing at all.

Ten thousand dead cattle lined the banks, their withered, emaciated bodies like strange skeletal rocks and alien stalagmites. Ribs broke through bloodless skin and the whites of thousands of skulls showed through where the tops of their heads had been baked away. They were heaped at the water's edge, and continued as far as Antonio could see. They lay with their necks stretched toward the empty riverbed, lured by the hope contained within a faint smell of water, only to drop dead of disappointment. The sky seethed with buzzards, the smell strong enough to lure them from all over. A fog of flies hung over the river with a loud drone that Antonio only then realized he'd been hearing for the last hour. Antonio was so overwhelmed by the smell he had to jam the bandana into his mouth and breathe through that, and even still he could taste rotting flesh, death, and desperation.

One bull calf stood among the dead and lowed, attempting to summon his mother. Weakened by thirst and his long journey to the water, he'd gotten stuck up to his knees in the river's quicksand mud, and he pulled at his legs in vain as he waited to slowly starve to death, life-giving water only inches from his lips. Antonio got down off the horse and approached it. Without looking the animal in its eyes he drew his knife and slit its throat, a meager bubbling of blood coming to the surface and spilling down the calf's pale chest. Its legs buckled and its head dropped straight down, stuck too deep to even fall over. Antonio heard wings close overhead and he got back on his horse and rode the rest of the way across the river, wishing to see no more.

Antonio was tired and he knew the horse wanted a rest. There was a watering hole nearby, shaded inside a mesquite grove where the river bent and the landscape dipped low and, even in the driest weather, would still hold water in the deep. Mesquite seeds rattled in their pods as the relentless wind drove through the chaparral and Antonio was uneasy. Water would attract men, and it was getting dark. He paused before entering the grove, listening for anything carried on the wind, but he heard nothing and brought the horse inside and was pleased to find the pool low but full enough. He let the horse drink and he washed his face and let the cool water run down into his shirt and tickle his chest.

The horse drank for a long time. She finally brought her head up as the sun sank and the light outside the grove was imperial purple. Antonio had one foot in the stirrup, about to mount her again, when the wind stopped for several counts and he heard two men approaching on horseback, nearly upon them.

One man was singing drunkenly off-key: "'If all the girls were bells in a tower, and I was a clapper, I'd bang one each hour!'" The other man gave a full-throated, raspy laugh. Antonio smelled cigarettes and tequila. He was hemmed in with the river at his back, but he wasn't afraid. His knife called to him and his hand twitched in excitement. He tied the horse and took off his bandana and put it in his pocket. At that moment he wanted to look like a monster. He opened his knife and held it gently in his hand. He slowed his heart and turned away from the men, who by now had quieted. Their horses stopped and he knew he'd been spotted.

"Hombre," said the singing one. "You lost?"

Antonio remained facing the river. He was still and calm, a jaguar in tall grass. Behind him a gun cocked.

"That's a pretty knife," the man said. "Let me see it."

Now that they were close he could hear their horses breathing—rapid, wheezy breaths and snorts. They'd been ridden hard and would not go much farther.

"Hombre. I don't like talking to myself."

A shot flew past Antonio's ear and splintered a tree on the other side of the river. The dun reared and squealed, but Antonio didn't flinch. He counted backward from ten and alerted each muscle in his body to be ready.

The men climbed down off their horses and Antonio was pleased. Courageous from tequila, they wanted to rough him up before killing him, to prove their strength before one another because every man knew death was preferable to appearing weak.

"Hey, joto," said the wheezy man, "come see what I gave your mother last night."

Antonio turned around slowly and took one step forward into the waning light, bearing his naked, gruesome face like Judith delivering the head of the Assyrian. And he contorted it further still, stretching his lips wide in a smile that he summoned from the darkest part of his soul that craved violence, that wished to scramble to the top of a mountain of bodies, bloodied but victorious.

"Jesus Christ," said the singing one, and he crossed himself. "Es un monstruo."

"No," Antonio said. "Soy el Tragabalas." And he took advantage of their hesitation and plunged his knife deep into the stomach of the singing man, splitting him open and spilling everything inside him onto the dirt. The man staggered a half step, not yet dead but no longer in control, and Antonio caught him and held him in front of him as a shield.

The other man fired his gun but missed, instead striking the stabbed man in the arm. Antonio maneuvered the body, which was now limp and nearly slipping from his grasp, and shoved it against the man with the gun, knocking him to the ground and pinning him down. Then Antonio climbed on top of the two men, the dead one holding the live one in place, and brought the knife into the other man's side, just under his ribs.

"My brother," rasped the man. He struggled against the weight of the two men and the steel in his stomach. And for only a second, as he watched the man writhe, Antonio felt remorse, that men couldn't pass each other without drawing a weapon, that they were no better than animals fighting to the death over water and a few dusty rocks. Then he was tired of the man's breathing, which sounded like a rusty hinge, and he pulled the knife quickly from his side, causing him to scream and choke before he finally quieted and his arms and legs ceased their convulsions.

The horse took a long time to calm. Antonio fed her prickly pears and stroked her muzzle until she would allow him to lead her away from the river. He'd need a new horse. This one was useless to him if she was frightened by gunshots and gore, but he'd have to wait until he reached Corpus Christi. The dead men's horses still wheezed and thick streams of snot dripped from their nostrils to the ground. They wouldn't move again until morning. Antonio rolled the men apart and searched their bodies and their saddlebags. Between them they had five guns—three pistols and two rifles, one of which was a gleaming Remington-Keene—as well as a handful of bullets, a thick roll of bills, and a large bottle of tequila. Antonio drank a healthy plug before he pointed the dun south and spurred her into a lope. She was tired and cranky but he chided her until she picked up her pace. He could reach Corpus Christi in an hour as long as he kept the horse moving.

The moon was low and bright now as he came out of the mesquite grove and met the road. He passed two Mexican teenagers in high-peaked sombreros cutting hides from the dead cows and adding them to a tall pile on a cart. The boys ignored Antonio, rightly figuring him to be the source of the two gunshots, and paused only to sharpen their knives against stones they kept in their pockets. The land was so flat and feature-less Antonio could count the lamps burning outside the stagecoach inn in Nuecestown back west. Farmers had cleared the brush all around. In a wet year the fields on either side of the road would have been lush with cabbages, corn, and onions, but now there was only an unbroken expanse of brown dirt, fallow land bounded by a fallow river. The pitted road was mostly empty save a few barrileros, their battered wagons full of precious well water.

He took the road because there was no cover to be had and the two dead men posed him little threat. Anyone who found them before dawn was a bandit like himself, in which case they'd rifle their pockets, maybe swap boots, and be on their way. Besides, he thought, Antonio Sonoro is dead and dead men can't be arrested. This thought cheered him along with the money in his pocket. He'd been to Corpus Christi many times before, always arriving with his pockets full of money earned selling sto-len cattle and leaving with his pockets empty, the city's poker dealers and whores all a little richer. Tonight Antonio planned to dine on shrimp. He'd drink beer chilled on ice. *Everyone should enjoy their own death this much*, he thought. *Pity I've only died now.*

The breeze was hot and salty and the stink of dead cow began slowly to be replaced with the stink of dead fish. As he neared town, traffic on the road increased, though he noted with some unease that it was all going out. He saw many hastily packed carts bearing whole families pulled by knock-kneed horses. An old man sat atop a collapsed buckboard at the side of the road eating a watermelon. Antonio slowed and tipped his hat. In answer the man slowly brought his right forefinger up to his right eye and pulled down the lower lid, exposing the pink flesh underneath. Antonio straightened on his horse and nodded. It was a warning known to all travelers in rough country: *Watch out.*

The road crested a slight hill before it dipped low to meet the bay, and from this vantage Antonio could see black smoke rising from the town. Horses galloped past—three, four, five—ridden by Mexican men with panicked faces. After another kilometer the carts began again, the road suddenly thick with refugees. Antonio let four wagons pass before he stopped a man leading a donkey carrying a boy with a withered arm.

"What's the matter?" Antonio demanded. "Where are these people going?"

The man wiped his face with his sleeve. "There was a festival today in Little Mexico. Everyone was there. A Yankee was killed—I don't know how. Some dispute over cards, I heard. Everyone said it was the Lozano brothers got him. The Yankee was the son of a judge and now there's a posse searching homes and burning everything." The man ran his sleeve over his face again, which was newly sheened with sweat. "They're shooting any Mexican they see, so you'd best turn around."

Flies lit about the donkey's eyes and ears, causing it to shake its head and grunt in exasperation. The boy on the donkey's back watched Antonio and the slow, sorry procession of carts with half-lidded interest, as though losing their home was only the family's most recent betrayal. Antonio unfolded several bills from the roll he'd found on the dead men and passed them to the man leading the donkey, careful to make sure the gift went unnoticed by anyone else on the road. "It was two men you say killed the Yankee?" he asked. "Did they catch them?"

The man took the money and bowed his head in appreciation. "No," he said. "They took off toward the river. Heading to San Antonio probably."

Antonio could almost feel the knife hum in its leather sheath. "Yes," he said, "heading to San Antonio probably."

The man pulled on the donkey's halter and they joined the others plodding away from Corpus Christi like branches washed upstream in a flood.

Antonio thought he ought to turn around, damn Cielita's arthritic sister. But he'd promised the old woman.

As he neared town, Antonio heard screams and smelled the sharp, yeasty smell of burning straw and clay. One sign over a little tumbledown shack read *Boots polished or oiled. Done by white labor.* He winced at the sight of grown men who shrieked and cowered at even distant gun blasts, who left their own rifles and pitchforks leaning against the adobe walls of their shanties to flee on foot, running only for the chance to run again later. The drought had hit the city hard, and everyone, regardless of color, had seen their cisterns dwindle and in some cases dry. He'd read in the newspaper that officials were telling people to put potash in the water to kill the wiggle tails so they could drink it. Scarcity had pushed everyone to the edges of their sanity, and Antonio knew that indiscriminate violence would continue until the sky opened once again.

Corpus Christi was a port town of about five thousand that lay along the southern bank of the Nueces and followed the river to where it emptied into Corpus Christi Bay. Little Mexico, a term coined by the whites and grudgingly adopted by the Mexicans, sat on the backside of a bluff that overlooked the water. It was a collection of a hundred or so adobe and wood-frame houses, many of which were now ablaze, as well as a church and a small wooden cantina. Antonio strained through the fumy dark to see the large palm tree with the blue house underneath where Cielita's sister lived. He was a ghost in the chaos, unseen amid wailing women, frightened horses, children hidden under blankets. He steered the horse into a narrow alleyway that ran along the back side of some unburned homes. Heat rolled through the alley in waves. The strip of exposed skin between his hat and his bandana began to prickle and sting and after only moments near the raging huts his throat was raw and raked with smoke that had begun to take on the sulfur scent of burning hair. On the other side of the homes he could hear a man shouting in English, "Don't put out the flames! You souse 'em and I'll shoot you where you stand!" Guns fired. A flowerpot filled with dead roses shattered near his horse's feet and Antonio ducked his head and pressed her on.

They followed the alley behind the houses, across a broad caliche road, and had turned into another narrow slip between rows of homes when Antonio caught sight of a tall palm tree just beyond the last house. The strong Gulf breeze sent papery bits of burning palm fronds coasting like fireflies to alight on everything flammable. As Antonio passed behind a house with bright gingham curtains hung in the windows, a gust struck the bay side of the home and flames suddenly billowed from the roof, where moments before there had been only smoke. The horse reared at the flash of heat and fire and spun Antonio around several times before he finally kicked her hard in her flank so that she dropped her forelegs and continued moving. They emerged and were now riding against the wind and Antonio gulped the briny Gulf air as he would have gulped water.

Cielita's sister's house sat untouched by the flames at the edge of a hill where the land sloped down to the railroad tracks and the water beyond. Antonio tied the horse to the palm and didn't bother to announce himself or knock—the door was open and the old woman lay dead on the floor, a rifle in her hand and cartridges scattered about. She must have died loading her gun, the woman no doubt as feisty and fierce as her sister. Antonio knelt and closed her eyes, and said a silent prayer.

He took off his bandana, and was busy washing soot and sweat from his face in a trough that fronted the house, when a voice startled him.

"I knew it was you." Antonio turned and his breath caught. The young Ranger was standing before him, a black silhouette against the still-burning homes, his pistol drawn in his pale, child's hand. "I saw you sneaking through the alley," the boy said, "and I figured you aimed to put the fires out. It was your green eyes tipped me off. You're the only greaser I ever seen with green eyes. Just now when you took off your bandana and I seen that scar I said, 'Dang, that's a ghost.'"

Antonio let out a low sigh. The Frontier Battalion was tasked with policing the violent southernmost triangle of South Texas from Laredo in the west to Corpus Christi in the east, and south to Brownsville, within which vast radius Cyrus Fish and his men held jurisdiction over every

Mexican body that walked or crawled. Of course they would be in this melee up to their filthy necks.

"That's right, puto," Antonio said. "I'm a ghost. So put your gun away."

"Captain Fish checked your pulse. I seen him blow half your head off." The boy's voice was high and fearful. Antonio knew the boy was afraid not only because he was a killer and that the boy was just a boy and looked to have come from a place where people hesitated to shoot one another, but because he'd now seen him resurrected like Lazarus. Coupled with the giddiness he no doubt felt at finding this apparitional fugitive, Antonio was confident the boy was far too excited to present any real threat other than misfiring his gun. The *Ranger*, Antonio corrected himself. Billy Stillwell. He wasn't a boy, he was a Ranger. And yet when he looked at the boy behind the gun it was no longer the skinny Ranger he saw but his own son, Nicolás, only eleven but eager to drink and shoot, and just as eager to run to his mother with a quivering chin when the world was too mean. This boy had probably only recently been allowed by his own father to drive a team, but a few years removed from carving obscene words on the door of a school outhouse. His too-big hat seemed like a costume and Antonio felt in that moment that they were both playacting, that someone offstage had given them lines and shoved them before the lights and that nothing more than happenstance had cast him as the ruthless bandido and Billy Stillwell as the guileless Ranger wishing to bring him to justice.

"How much smoke have you inhaled?" Antonio asked, stalling without knowing why. "You're seeing things. You'd better run along before you hurt someone."

"Get on the ground and put your hands on your head."

What was wrong with him? He'd dreamed about watching the boy twitch and writhe on the ground, had prayed to God to send the Rangers to him, and now one was here and he hesitated. He put up his hands and took a step toward the boy, and the boy in his inexperience and fear allowed this, only telling Antonio again to get on the ground.

"I died once. You think I can't do it again?"

"On the ground!"

"Quiet, now." Antonio took another step forward. It was a funny thing about frightened men and guns—the closer the target, the harder it was to hit. Decent men—and most men were decent even if they were holding a gun—did not care to see the whites of the eyes of the man they were attempting to shoot. Antonio quietly slid one foot forward again, but kept his hands up on either side of his head. *Don't do this*, he thought. *Save yourself. I don't want to do this.*

As if reading his mind, the boy fired his gun, grazing Antonio's shoulder above his heart with the red-hot pain of a whiplash and causing him to cry out. The boy twirled the gun around his finger until it was pointing back at Antonio and then glared at him with all the ferocity he could muster. "Next time I go an inch lower. Get on the ground." Antonio blinked and saw the boy had aged twenty years in the span of the gunshot. Now he had a man's eyes, reckless and broken.

"Go back home to your mother," Antonio pleaded. "I'm a ghost. Let me haunt in peace."

The boy squinted at him from behind his revolver, only making sense of the world by seeing it through sights, and Antonio believed he and the boy were of one mind in that instant, their crossed fates binding them body and soul. Antonio knew what the boy would do. The boy would shoot, and Antonio would kill him. Something about it was unavoidable, as though he'd concocted the scheme to rob the train only so that he and the young Ranger would arrive at that moment, all of history pushing them toward that particular collision like tectonic plates crashing together to create mountains. The boy would shoot, and Antonio would kill him.

"One last chance, you son of a bitch. And this time I'll make sure you're dead."

Antonio turned around, his last attempt at cheating the situation. Perhaps the boy harbored some vanity about shooting a man in the back. He'd taken several steps in the direction of the horse when, as if by instinct, as if responding to a vibration carried on the wind, Antonio pulled the gun from his belt, turned around, and fired it at the same moment the boy fired his own gun at the escaping outlaw.

The two men realized as one that the boy's gun had jammed. He cradled it in his hands like a broken toy as blood spread across his chest.

Antonio strode over to the boy and took the gun and threw it far past the blue house. As the boy dropped to his knees and then face-first to the ground, Antonio doubled over and vomited. Two dozen he'd killed and yet this felt different. Even the boy's blood seemed redder, thicker. Antonio straightened and couldn't look at the boy on the ground because it might be his own Nicolás there. *I wasn't here*, he told himself. *When I ride away it'll all be gone.*

No, stop that. He was glad he'd killed the boy, to have repaid one-third of the debt. And if the young Ranger was there, the others were nearby. Tonight he could collect in full everything that was owed. He tied his bandana around his head again and mounted the horse, and he did not see that light flickered still in the boy's eyes. The big palm tree shivered in the wind.

Antonio would not ride through the fires again. He rode down the hill that sloped beneath Little Mexico and led downtown. He would skirt behind the houses closest to the water's edge and meet the main road there, hopeful the Rangers were distracted by the exodus out of town. He slowed the horse as they neared the neat, gridded streets, each side flanked by wooden homes and commercial buildings with second-story arcades. He was uneasy as he saw he was the only rider on the street—even the wooden sidewalks in front of the saloons were clear. He pulled the other pistol from the saddlebag and slung it into his belt, put the remaining bullets in his shirt pocket, and turned the horse off the boulevard and into a smaller residential street lined with bright, white homes. Antonio was aware of being watched, knowing that even at that late hour, behind every lace curtain of every lead-paned window sat a man or a woman or a child hoping, praying that this terrible man would be gunned down before their eyes.

Antonio had the pistol at the ready when he heard a gun blast and felt a bullet fly past his ear.

"Hya," he called to the horse, shortening up the reins and driving her north toward the docks. There was a train line that ran that way and he urged the horse on, finding himself back in a familiar and happy role of outrunning his enemies. More gunshots sounded as the horse thundered through the deserted town, but each was wide, hitting shop windows and splintering wooden railings. A bullet struck a water barrel and another nicked his hat. "A little lower," he called over his shoulder and let out a grito, a full-blooded "Ah-ya-yah!" that echoed off the wooden facades and down the dusty streets.

He'd covered only a few blocks when the horse slowed and then stopped, panting, drenched in greasy sweat, refusing to go on. "Move it," he shouted, and kicked her with both legs. "Move it, you lazy bitch," but her head was hung and her breaths were shallow and quick. The train tracks were only a couple blocks away at the docks. Antonio's feet hit the dirt a second before a volley of bullets struck the ground around him. Far down the street two clouds of dust raced toward him and Antonio lit out for the tracks, hating to leave all his provisions behind.

The horse whinnied behind him and Antonio looked back to see the dun had been hit and brought to her knees. Her shrill, pain-filled cries were carried on the wind and wrapped around Antonio still running, before disappearing at last over the water.

Antonio met the railroad tracks behind an ice factory, though he saw no trains. He looked left and right and a few hundred meters down to the docks where the tracks ended on a pier, and saw only an old iron steamer bobbing in the waves. A line of abandoned carts, half loaded with crates, stretched out from the bay. Plenty of places to hide, but Antonio didn't want the water at his back.

There was a lumberyard nearby with planks piled three meters high. Antonio ran there and hid in the narrow gap between two stacks of crosshatched boards, counted his bullets and readied his pistols, and watched the road. He regretted that he hadn't more bullets than the ones in his pocket, but his hands were steady. And what were a couple of riders? If they were part of the mob that had been burning Little Mexico, they would be easily dispatched. And if they were the final two Rangers . . .

The sky was black and seagulls soared low over the docks looking for fish heads. He waited a beat and then heard the riders coming closer, the horses throwing up dust before them. He held the barrel of the pistol out of a small gap between the oak boards and slitted his eyes and had to swallow several times as the two riders became five, then ten, then twenty, then thirty. Still, this was likely only the mob, not the Rangers. Dentists and coopers and rubes—they would be poor shots, though they were many.

"Hey, idiot," Antonio heard in crisp Spanish from somewhere in the stacks behind him. "You're in my shot. Move over unless you want your head blown off."

THE IGNOMINIOUS HISTORY OF

THE SONORO FAMILY

from Antiquity to the present day

BY MARIA GASPAR ROCHA DE QUIROGA
Published 1783
Sevilla, España

Antonio Baltazar Sonoro of Valencia had a friend once, a lesser noble named Tohias Tadeo with whom he shared his passions for stag hunting, pig farming, and commissioning self-aggrandizing works of art for local churches. To Tohias, Antonio Baltazar gave all of the best of himself (which, admittedly, was not much), pouring, through hours of midnight conversations and dozens of bottles of sweet Tokaji, all his successes and desires and glad and bad fortunes, his opinions on the members of court, his ambivalence about his wife and children, and his stunning ignorance of Catholic dogma despite being a benefactor of the Church beyond measure.

Antonio Baltazar was always too happy to share these confidences and Tohias swallowed them with an insatiable hunger, living vicariously through Sonoro and always asking for more. Many years into their friendship Antonio Baltazar confessed, with a red face sweating sticky wine, that he had been for some months entangled with the young niece of the marqués and that the pair of fools were in love. This was, at last, the gem that Tohias sought.

Tohias told the marqués of the affair. The niece was sent to Girona to join the Capuchin order, Tohias was named un vizconde, and the witless Antonio Baltazar was thenceforth shunned from all dignified society. His wife seized the opportunity to return to her ancestral home in Geneva with the children, and lived out the rest of her happy life weaving tapestries of cuckoo birds, while her husband suffered the loss of his beloved pigs to ague, and had all his likenesses in all his favorite churches painted over with the face of St. Sebastian.

And though this dishonorable end stung Antonio Baltazar, he realized that as much as Tohias had violated a sacred trust, so he had been in the wrong, using his friend to bolster his own image of himself the way an actor may wear false shoes to make himself taller. The veils that surround a single moment are infinite.

This story has been used for hundreds of years as a cautionary lesson for all Sonoros: Forge no friendships. Look inward for all you seek. A Sonoro's only friend is himself.

THIRTEEN

CORPUS CHRISTI, TEXAS—1895

Antonio turned around and saw the barrel of a rifle protruding from around the side of the lumber behind him. The stacks in the lumberyard were three meters high, and spaced wide enough apart that a man could crouch between them. Antonio had hidden behind the first row of five, and as he looked around he counted another five columns. Most important, he could see between the boards and still remain hidden from the posse. Antonio glared at the rifle, bristling at being called an idiot, but as there was no time to straighten out the man's etiquette, he moved just out of the way.

"How many of you are there?" Antonio asked, readying his gun.

"Six."

"Not bad," Antonio said. "I don't have many bullets."

The man cursed. "They're lucky I don't have my pistol. It wouldn't be a fair fight for them if I had my pistol."

Antonio rolled his neck and ignored the man's boasts. The approaching horses made a sound like kettledrums. The man behind Antonio gave a loud, high whistle that Antonio knew to be the one used by overseers to signal quitting time in the cotton fields. "Get ready," he called to the other men hiding in the stacks. "On my count."

124

Antonio let out his breath and aimed his pistol at a bearded man in dungarees and a straw hat.

"Three."

The wind blew in off the Gulf and mixed with the dust kicked up by the posse. In the dark, dusty, smoke-riddled air, it was difficult for Antonio to keep eyes on his man. He felt in his shirt pocket, hoping magic might have replenished his ammunition, but only the same small handful remained. He squinted his eyes and quieted every muscle, even his heartbeat. Every bullet had to count.

"Two."

Five riders split from the group and headed up a small hill, presumably to surround them to the rear and trap them inside the lumberyard. They were going to be hemmed in: the posse on one side, the five riders on another, and Corpus Christi Bay stretching wide behind them.

For a second Antonio closed his eyes and saw Jesusa, saw his family sitting down to dinner, and his heart ached to hear Nicolás's singsong chatter when he was little, to hold Aura in his arms and feel her perfect skin against his cheek. He remembered the prayer card in his jacket pocket that Cielita had given him and he crossed himself.

"One."

As the first riders reached the lumberyard Antonio and the others opened fire. Antonio struck the man in the straw hat in the left shoulder and dropped him as he clapped both hands over the wound. The one who'd called Antonio an idiot brought down six in quick order, while a seventh spooked and rode back toward town. If there were five others in the stacks they couldn't shoot worth a goddamn, though the man behind Antonio more than made up the lack. Antonio brought down one more before the remaining posse dismounted and arrayed themselves around wagons and wooden crates and returned fire with zeal, unloading their repeating rifles into the stacks at a volume that caused Antonio to duck and curl against the wood, praying no bullet found a fortuitous path between the boards and into his spine.

"Hey, idiot," said the voice. "Why don't you and me take the five at the rear?"

"Go to hell," Antonio said, his body compact against the wood with his arms on top of his head. "And if you call me 'idiot' again I'll slit your throat."

Auburn hair and one brown eye appeared around the side of the stack and then darted back behind the wood. The bullet spray continued and Antonio clenched his teeth.

"Move back on my signal," the man said.

"Look, pendejo," Antonio said, "you might boss your little pizcadores out in the fields, but I'm no cotton picker, so you shove your whistles up your ass. We need to stay in here and keep moving. They'll think we're fifteen instead of seven. Then we can pick them off until there's no one left."

"The brush line begins just behind us across a field," the man said quietly. "If we take out the five in the back and grab their horses, we'll be hat-deep in the chaparral before anyone up here knows we've gone."

Well, there it was. The benevolent stranger was granting Antonio the opportunity to escape the fray and leave the others behind. And wouldn't it be just his bad luck if the man got a head start and left Antonio to cover them both? Something in the man's accent was also amiss. It was the way he said *chaparral*—too close to how the Americans would have said it, with a *sh* at the beginning of the word instead of a *ch*. It was a minor error, but it cast doubt over all his other words.

"Turn your chin just slightly to the left," the man said, and when Antonio made no move to obey, he added a pointed "Please." The rifle fired two rounds, the bullets whizzing so close to Antonio's face he felt their heat as they went past, and Antonio heard two groans and two men he hadn't seen fell to his right, only a few meters away. "The men hiding in here are sharecroppers," the voice said. "They couldn't shoot a rabbit in a snare. You want to stay and die with them, be my guest."

Antonio considered his options. "We'll move back when I say," he finally said, and he waited for a lull in the shooting. "On the left." At last the hail of bullets slowed. Antonio took off his hat, brought up his head, and looked through the boards. Two men squatting low were advancing to the stacks and the posse held their gunfire to give them a few seconds to cross. The rifle behind him fired and one man was hit in the chest, while the other rolled behind a wagon wheel.

"Now." Antonio scuttled along the ground on his haunches, hugging the side of the stack behind him, and managed to crawl behind it before bullets struck the area where he'd just been. He paused to catch his breath. He couldn't fire without holding his gun around the side of the stack, which, now he'd been spotted, was too risky, so he ducked again and waited. He was now in the space where the man with the rifle had been, and a small pile of casings lay amid a litter of wood chips where the boards around him had splintered. Antonio looked down the row and saw one man in the next stack over and another two beyond him.

"You can't see the riders in the rear," said the voice, still one row behind him. "Move one more back at least."

"The others should be moving around, too," Antonio said.

"They're safe where they are. No one moves."

A very round man, whose shirt buttons strained over his belly, had crept into Antonio's sight and he was able to angle his pistol without untucking his body and fire, striking the man in the neck.

"You're not Mexican," Antonio said.

"And thank heaven for that."

"Why are you shooting your own people?"

The rifle fired two more rounds and Antonio heard two more bodies drop. "My own people?" the man asked, sounding incredulous. "My good man, Texans are pigs who've been taught to stand upright and ride a horse. I'm English."

Antonio took another look at the men down the line of wooden boards. The one closest to Antonio nodded to him as he hastily reloaded a rusted navy revolver. He had a thick mustache and kind eyes and Antonio could tell by the way he held the gun—with his left index finger straight down the barrel—that he was a lousy shot. He had only six bullets left. How much time would that buy him? Antonio sighed and said, "We'll move again on my signal." He paused and counted slowly under his breath, all the while cursing himself, the Englishman, Mexico, the entire population of Texas. "Now."

Antonio scrambled quickly around the stack behind him. Three walls of lumber now separated him from the shooters in front and two from the rear. Antonio looked down this row and saw a man lying on his back, his boots askew and his body still. Next to him sat another man who'd thrown his gun on the ground and sat with his hands clasped in prayer, apparently offering his final confession. The Englishman had moved back one row as well, and Antonio peered through the gaps between the boards and saw that he was not much older than Antonio and was smartly dressed in a gray sack suit and a bright red tie. He had reloaded his rifle and stuck it between two boards at the edge of the stack and crouched with it on his shoulder, muttering. The gunfire had ceased altogether and Antonio wished to peer around the side, to know where the riders had scattered, and plot his escape. But he knew at least five sets of eyes were trained on the back side of the stacks, waiting for the slightest movement. He hunched down with his gun ready and flicked his eyes left and right, prepared to stop anyone from entering their wooden fortress.

"So, whitey," Antonio whispered, "how many are they? Five? More?"

"None," the man said flatly before he pulled the gun away from the boards, turned around, and slumped against the stack facing Antonio. "They're not there." He said it so weakly it sounded as though he'd seen himself on the other end of his sights.

Antonio swore. "They're in the trees." He cursed himself again for having followed the bad advice of a gringo. He was always better off on his own.

"We could run for it," the man said, but his voice betrayed him and it was clear he did not believe his own words.

"We wouldn't make it three steps." Antonio shook his head. "We'll move back up," he said. "Pick them off one by one." Though he, too, was given away by his own voice. He had six bullets. Even if each one found his man there would be reinforcements.

"I'm running low," the man said, producing four cartridges from his pocket. "I've not proven myself a worthy ally, I'm afraid."

Antonio took a deep breath and tried to prevent his mind from tumbling downward. "You move one up on my count," he said. "We'll go together after that, zigzagging and firing from different spots. If we can confuse them we'll buy a little more time."

"My name is Peter Ainsley," the man said in English, his voice heavy with resignation. "I'm pleased to make your acquaintance."

"Antonio Sonoro," Antonio said, his pulse quickening. "Now move on three. One." Everything seemed quiet, even the wind. "Two." Antonio sat without breathing, feeling for vibrations in the ground through his boots. "Three."

Peter dashed around the side of the stack and moved up, while Antonio scuttled sideways and picked up the dead man's gun and the one the praying man had thrown on the ground. He signaled the Englishman and tossed the better of the two pistols to him. Just as Peter caught the gun Antonio saw movement over the Englishman's shoulder and he fired, striking a man in the head.

"I count fifteen," Antonio said. "Ten in the front and five in the back." A shot rang through the stacks to his left and a man screamed. Antonio saw that the praying man was now slumped over, and in the same instant the Englishman's rifle fired and struck the shooter who was so far away Antonio could only see him as a slightly darker presence in the darkness all around them.

"Fourteen," Peter said.

"I'll go left. You work your way to the front."

"I can't see your face," Peter said before he moved up one row. "A man who won't show his face is a man not to be trusted."

"Then don't." Antonio peered out toward the front of the stacks and saw a bearded man in a white felt hat. Antonio fired at him and missed.

Peter fired two shots and then moved up again. "Go smooth on the trigger," he called behind him. "Pretend you're dragging your finger through mashed beans."

Antonio screwed up his face at the analogy but peered out front again and saw the man in the white hat. He drew his finger slow and smooth over the trigger and watched with satisfaction as the man fell.

"Sorry for my performance back there," Peter called. Antonio moved up two more so that he and Peter were both in the first row facing opposite sides. "For a second I thought we were boiled, but fortune may favor us yet."

"Don't get cocky," Antonio said. "If I see a break I'm gone, and then you're on your own, whitey."

"Some gratitude. I saved your life."

"And I saved yours. Consider yourself lucky. No one's ever called me 'idiot' and lived."

Peter dropped another man who collapsed into himself like a pile of rags. "Oh that," he said. "Joshing, that's all. You Mexicans take yourselves far too seriously."

Antonio crawled to the next stack on the left. He caught a bullet in his boot heel and the wood was blown clean off. Peter followed a second later, and a bullet grazed his leg, a misfortune he lamented mostly for its having damaged his suit. He dropped next to Antonio and the two men were side by side for the first time. "Stop following me," Antonio said, loading the last of his bullets into the pistol.

"I think we make a good team," Peter said. "I haven't had this much fun since I left Manzanillo."

"There's no team." Antonio strained to see out to the sides. He felt like an insect trapped under a cup, or Moctezuma made prisoner in his own palace.

"It's your pride saying that. I'm a dead shot and an asset to any duo. What I lack is local knowledge and stealth and, judging by your appearance, I'd guess you're amply supplied with both."

"You talk too much."

"Then we're agreed," Peter said. "We finish off this rabble and go west. I'm going to hazard another guess that you're headed to Mexico."

Antonio got to his knees and struck a man he saw climbing a tree to gain a view into the stacks. "If you follow me out of Corpus Christi I'll shoot you."

"Details," Peter said and waved his hand. "It so happens I'm also headed to Mexico. I've had quite enough Texan hospitality."

"I'm not going to Mexico. I've got business here."

"Geography dictates we head west, my friend. Unless you're in possession of a boat."

At that moment Antonio knew how he could escape and he blamed the boy Ranger and the jabbering Englishman for muddling his head. "There's a reef road," he said, mostly to himself. "Mountains of oyster shells under the water. The Indians used it. You can cross the whole bay that way. The bastards won't know what to do. It looks like you're walking on water."

"You're sure?"

Antonio nodded. "There's a rock that marks the beginning of the road. It looks like a dog."

"Splendid," and Peter gave a short, hopeful laugh. "Fucking splendid."

Suddenly a shrill police whistle cleaved the night and initiated a chorus of howling dogs. All shooting ceased, and as Antonio and Peter peered through the boards, they saw rifle and shotgun barrels pointed in the air behind crates and wagons as though a general was riding in to inspect them. Antonio knew who it was that caused all the men to crouch at attention, the only person for whom they would pause.

"Who's this now?" Peter asked, and Antonio only shook his head.

"I want him alive!" Fish screamed as he rode closer. "I want him alive, you hear? Discharge your weapon and I will discharge you!" He rode his horse as close to the lumberyard as he dared and Casoose was there as well, looking down from his frothing paint with amusement at the tattered posse and the numerous dead.

"Antonio Sonoro!" Fish screamed, and his voice was abraded and coarse as though he'd been coughing or screaming or crying or all three. Antonio was only sad he hadn't been there to see the Ranger's face when he discovered the dead boy. "That's right, you son of a bitch, I know your name! And I know you're in there! He was sixteen. Hardly more'n a kid. If he'd had kin I never woulda took him because I knew I'd never forgive myself if anything ever happened." Fish paused to let out a scream that was close to the sound Antonio had made when Hugo was shot. Antonio bit his lip, regretting having lost the presumption of his death. But now he knew where the bastards were. Now he could lead them anywhere he wanted. They would follow him to the other side of the earth.

"You're surrounded," Fish shouted over the wind. "There is no escape. I'll wait all night, all day. I'll wait weeks if I have to, until you're so hungry you eat your boot leather. And when that runs out I'll wait until you're so hungry you drag yourself out of those stacks with your fingers worried down to the bone, when the angel of death's sitting on your shoulder. When you crawl out of those stacks desperate and begging for mercy, I'm gonna take your hand and pull you up onto your feet. And then I'll look you in your snake eyes and I'll kill you."

"What the hell did you do to him?" Peter cocked one eye and looked at Antonio with a mixture of amusement and fear.

"And anyone else in there," Fish shouted, "come out with your hands up and you'll get a fair trial. Don't throw in with this coward, this child killer. He's got no more sympathy than a scorpion and he'll do you no better."

"'Sympathy of a scorpion'?" Peter mumbled. "Someone's been teaching the Texas Rangers to read." He pulled his face away from the boards and sat down. "I guess we wait."

Several minutes passed. Antonio heard a murmur that turned into hoots rippling through the posse. Then light flickered in between the boards like lizard tongues, and when Antonio looked again through the crosshatches he saw that six men now held torches. It took no time to see what was about to happen. He stood up and looked around him for a way out but, absent wings, nothing seemed likely. In a minute the entire perimeter of the lumberyard was on fire.

"Barbarians!" Peter shouted as he scrambled to his feet. "Common Huns! They ought to know that building next door is an ice factory. My father owns one of those damned things in Rangoon, and they've got a nasty habit of exploding. If it catches fire we're all properly fucked."

Heat broke in waves and battered down the passages between the stacks. Peter and Antonio moved to the center of the yard, where they found the man with the kind eyes and the other two farmers who'd been hiding from the posse. Their faces were slick and panicked and they looked up at the night sky as though to wish on a falling star, to beg clemency from the drifting clouds.

And then even in all that chaos and crisis, Antonio was furious that these men should burn for the crime of being nearby when a white man was killed. And he was furious with himself, that a few moments before he'd attempted to disappear into the chaparral and leave them behind to die.

"Give us all your ammunition," Antonio ordered the three men. Turning to Peter, he said, "We're going to cover them so they can run. You can, too, if you think you can make it," he added, but the Englishman knew as well as he did it was a slim proposition even with two of them shooting.

Peter pinched his lips together in a grimace, but he nodded once. They all got as close as they dared to the back of the lumberyard that abutted the field and the brush beyond. Peter and Antonio shoved one stack of boards over on its side and climbed it to gain some vantage. Then Peter fired one shot out through the flames. Antonio's skin felt like it was scorching through his clothes. When Peter's shot was returned, he and Antonio fired in the direction of the shooters as the three men took deep breaths and barreled between the burning stacks of wood toward freedom. Antonio fired again and again, everything he had, all the while praying for a miracle, for these men to be saved, that if God had any mercy to grant, He give it to these men, to their wives and children, to all those that came after, a line that might extend forever, infinite, opening like those purple flowers uncurling before the sunlight, if only they were given the chance to live.

The last thing he saw before the flames got too close was three bodies slipping into the trees.

The fire was now advancing to the center. Black smoke covered them like ink. ". . . put our heads down and run!" Antonio shouted, for the fire was making a sound like crashing waves of broken twigs. ". . . one of the boards like a shield!"

Peter was crouched on the ground, coughing into a tight space he'd created between his knees. Antonio screamed at him to get up and even yanked on his arm to try and drag him to standing, but it seemed the Englishman had made up his mind to die. When Antonio looked up he could see nothing but orange and yellow, the light so intense it was just as bright with his eyes closed. He felt his skin blistering. When he tried to lick his lips he could taste his own roasting flesh. He heard a muted sound that he vaguely registered as an explosion, the sound inside the fire now as loud as a train. And then for a second he saw there was a break in the wall of light, a black space he could see and maybe even reach if he was quick enough. He took a step and remembered the Englishman on the ground. He owed him nothing, goddammit. But to leave him . . . He kicked the man hard in the side, startling him enough that he got to his hands and knees. By grabbing his shirt collar and the scruff of his coat, Antonio dragged Peter toward the blackness, which, as they stumbled closer, he could see was a break in the flames where two stacks had collapsed away from one another. Peter seemed to have gained a little breath and Antonio no longer had to pull him. Peter crawled and Antonio staggered, and through the smoke and the firefly bits of burning wood that pirouetted through the air, Antonio could see the water, the last streaks of moonlight painted across the bay and stretching to the horizon. He tripped forward, lusting for water as he'd never wanted anything. His feet were on dirt and then grass and then sand and finally, finally, he was in the bay: his boots, then his knees, then his whole body. He fell face-first and let the warm waves take him as though he'd returned to the womb.

When he sat up the water lapped his stomach. Peter was beside him watching the burning lumberyard, his hat resting on one knee and his red tie, impossibly, not the least bit askew. As his eyes adjusted, Antonio saw that not one but two fires raged. The lumberyard was a bonfire, the stacks of wood providing fuel for twenty-five large fires that merged into one colossal inferno. The second fire was on the lot adjacent to the lumberyard, at what he took to be the ice factory. Flames had already devoured one wall; black, bilious smoke poured out of the roof and bruised the sky. Three loud pops sounded within the building, followed by an explosion that lifted the roof clear off and sent it flying into the street. Antonio watched in disbelief, too dazed to even duck.

"That would be the methyl chloride," Peter said, getting to his feet.

"The Rangers," Antonio muttered, for he felt like his head was still in the water, everything murky and obscured and sounds reaching him at only half volume.

"Blown halfway to Canada, I hope," Peter said. "The boiler would have exploded first and taken out that wall. If they weren't burnt to a crisp or struck on the head they'd be spooked at the very least. Now," he said, hitting his hat on his knee and putting it back on his head, "about this reef road. I'm very keen to walk on water. In England we're taught that privilege is reserved solely for Jesus Christ, and I'd very much like to prove my vicar wrong. Shall we?"

Peter was looking at Antonio, whose bandana was soaking wet and now hung around his neck, and took in his face with quiet solemnity. "Have you ever heard of the Man in the Iron Mask?" he asked after a moment.

Antonio only blinked to clear his eyes of soot and seawater.

Peter continued. "There's power in a mask. Behind there a man could be anyone. If you have secrets, friend, rest assured I'll never speak them."

Still in a half stupor Antonio followed the Englishman out of the water and north along the beach. It was still dark; the sun was sluggish. A thousand ducks sat in the shallows, their staccato calls merging until it was a constant drone like bees. They reached the rock shaped like a dog and, with a little tapping about in the muck, found the reef. Thousands of years of sand and oyster shells had washed up and accumulated to create the passage, two long arms reaching out from opposite sides of the shore and just touching in the center. It zigged and zagged, and several times the men went off the track and bogged in the sucking mud, but they made their escape out of Corpus Christi just as the first fingers of dawn grabbed hold of the horizon. They sloshed through the water in those last moments of darkness, kicking up phosphorescence behind their boots, the blue-green clouds at their heels mirroring the blue-green clouds in the sky as the Milky Way faded from view and was overtaken with orange, persimmon, magenta. Antonio stopped and said aloud, "Isn't it beautiful?"

FOURTEEN

After the scorpion incident the entire household felt bruised and leery, like kicked dogs all settled in various corners. Ignacia had been given the rest of the day off, Juan Antonio went for a walk, Elena drove the children to her mother's house, Remedio claimed he was overheated and needed to lie down, and Jaime shut himself in his office to read and to unconvince himself that he had seen a scorpion reanimate itself. His head was bent low over the book, with only fifty or so pages to go. He almost dozed off in this position, realizing with a start he'd been reading the same paragraph over and over, and upon waking he saw two things at once: Nearing the end of the book, Maria Rocha had started using the first-person *I*, inserting herself into the narration as though she were no longer retelling history but beginning an autobiography, questioning her motives and justifying her choice of subject.

> *The reader may wonder why a person would undertake an exploration of such a deviant subject as this most dark and odious history. And to the reader I say, Indeed! In compiling this history I have swum in the stuff, smelt its foul stench in my hair, shrunk from its virulent advance in my nightmares. Why sequester myself inside this fetid inquiry, why subject my mind, my heart, and my godly soul to the taint of history's*

most villainous breed? It began as an intellectual pursuit, attempting to construct a definitive account of the bloodline from antiquity onward, but has since transformed into something beyond historical record, something I had no idea I was writing until I had written it. Plainly: It is a documentation of the genesis of evil in our world. Like the estimable botanist Carolus Linnaeus, I have identified a specimen, named it, sketched it, and am now publicizing my findings that others may recognize evil, too, and once named, tear it root and stem from the soil, choke it out, render it lifeless, impotent, and unrealized. I wish to do the work of the inquisitor, and pray that swift and terrible execution will follow my weary hand once the ink has dried on these scant pages.

The other thing Jaime was aware of was Rocha's insistent use of the word *oscuridad*, or darkness. He counted seventeen uses of it on one page. Flipping back through a few chapters he noted it was there as well, the word sticking out because she had used it in rather an unusual way, giving it a shape and a personality, movement, and sometimes even intent.

The darkness hovered over Sidria Antonianetta Sonoro, prone on her quilt and her limbs already beginning to stiffen, before it drifted to Plutarco Antonio, the eldest boy, and sat upon his bed canopy watching the child sleep.

This wasn't a metaphor, Jaime realized. Maria Rocha wasn't describing darkness in the traditional sense, but something more like a shadow, something man-shaped and conscious. How had he not noticed this before? He flipped to pages at random—Yes! There it was, and there again. The shadow man flitted through the narrative for thousands of years, cleaved to the Sonoros seemingly in perpetuity. And touching the back of his hand to his neck, for he felt the watching presence on him again, Jaime turned to look behind him and saw the shape of two feet beneath the doorsill. A second later someone knocked. And when Jaime opened the door he was unsurprised to find Remedio.

"Do you need to see a doctor about your hand?" Jaime asked him, concealing any nervousness in his voice inside a veil of concern. "Those stings looked pretty bad."

"Oh, no," Remedio said easily, and he showed Jaime both hands, completely free of wounds. "I think your maid was mistaken about it being a man-killer."

"Was she?" Jaime sat back down at his desk and felt like he was waking up from a dream, as though a shell was cracking open around him and he could see and hear things anew. He watched Remedio, a complete stranger who'd been living in his house for days, and he saw, for the barest second, malice in Remedio's eyes, a bright white flame that was gone as soon as Jaime was aware of having seen it, if he had seen it. For the first time—and why, he asked himself, was this only occurring to him now—it truly struck him: Who had he invited into his home?

And as quick as the malice had appeared, Remedio's face returned to its usual expression of solitude and yearning. In this Jaime recognized something of himself, and he thought perhaps it was this that had prevented him from seeing the truth before. But no, he needed to stay focused, not slip into fantasy. He stiffened his spine and thought of his children, and he tried not to picture this man hovering above their beds at night.

"You're almost finished," Remedio said, indicating the open book. He strolled close and flipped a couple of pages, his eyes scanning the text and appearing to read it upside down. "I'm curious—what have you taken away from it?"

Something about Remedio touching the book stoked a territorial urge in Jaime and he pulled it a little closer to himself. *Mine*, he thought, though he understood this reaction had been prompted by nothing. He took in a breath and had to think for a second. "I think I'm coming to see just how little I've understood."

"Of yourself?"

"Of everything. Myself, this country, the goddamned Spanish. I knew, but I didn't *know*. I didn't know the scope of it. They stole a hundred and eighty tons of gold from the New World, they obliterated an entire mountain in Bolivia that was basically made of silver, and the Indians I killed, millions of Indians—"

"*I* killed?"

Jaime looked up in surprise. "Excuse me?"

"You said the Indians *I* killed. Do you mean the Indians the Sonoros killed?"

Jaime looked at him, his face blank.

"You know, the Bible says children will pay for the crimes of their parents."

"Lucky then my father's been going to confession every week for decades. What's your game, huh?" Jaime asked, his voice growing an edge. "You want money? Is that why you weaseled your way into the house? And why this sudden interest in the book? You think I'm hiding some gold mine?"

Remedio laughed quietly, the first time he'd ever been able to employ that little affect. The actor was becoming more like the others all on his own.

Jaime was angry now, for some reason his father's words springing up in his brain like a painted monster in a fun house. *Go back to making your little cowboy shoot-'em-ups.* "Is that it?" he asked, getting louder. "Have you been hanging around hoping to siphon off whatever you could?" He wouldn't say aloud exactly how long he feared Remedio had been *hanging around*, but the picture was becoming clearer, that this man, whatever he was, had likely been stealing from his family for ages. Oh how they'd had to scrape when Jaime was a little boy, washing clothes in the creek and trading eggs for shoes so he could go to school, when his ancestors sat atop mountains of gold. And there the thief stood in his own house and Jaime had invited him in.

"You need to leave," Jaime said. He saw recognition in Remedio's face, what Jaime took as an admission of guilt, and he was satisfied that he'd solved at least one mystery.

"I won't trouble you another moment," Remedio said and turned to go.

"Don't come near me or my family again," Jaime said, having no idea if such a command was his to make, but feeling he needed to say it aloud nonetheless.

Remedio turned around and gave Jaime a look of restrained triumph. "The past is not so far away as you might think. Nor the future, for that matter. No man lives free from history," he said, and then he was gone.

THE IGNOMINIOUS HISTORY OF

THE SONORO FAMILY

from Antiquity to the present day

BY MARIA GASPAR ROCHA DE QUIROGA
Published 1783
Sevilla, España

In so documenting, I run headlong against the utmost question: How must a goodly and conscientious woman live a righteous and contented life whilst carrying the loathsome truth that elsewhere her brothers and sisters suffer under the iniquitous bonds of evil, that evil surrounds her, that evil waits with lupine hunger behind a tree to carry off her children and gnaw at her harrowed bones? That ultimate judgment waits is, ofttimes, not solace enough.

But I digress, and I must offer an apology, for no historian's or biographer's lens should be turned toward herself. Yet I fear the fixation has changed me, plunged me to my crown in greed, violence, and hatred, wherefore perhaps my work has suffered, my inquiry soured, my very humors altered for the worse. By turning my gaze toward that which is vile, that which is vile has now turnt its gaze upon me.

And yet I cannot look away. I fear—oh my God, I fear!—that in looking at them I recognize myself. It is easy to curse the Sonoros, to spit on their name, wish the stain of their existence could be dashed against the river rocks and washed clean with lye. And yet they have made me, made us, who we are. How may one regret their own existence?

FIFTEEN

Antonio and Peter had been walking for eight hours and had barely gone thirty kilometers. Antonio took them on a meandering, circuitous route north, knowing the Rangers would expect him to go in any direction but that one. He would lead them in a circle, stop, reverse their path across the circle, walk into the tall grass, and then move in the opposite direction, all to confuse the Rangers and obscure their path. Between them they had Antonio's nearly empty pistol and a small derringer that Peter kept in case of emergency, the rifle having been left behind in the fire. They had no horses and no prospects. It was early afternoon and Antonio knew by that time the fires in Corpus Christi would have been long extinguished, the bodies tallied, witnesses bullied and their secrets disgorged. And he knew that when the Rangers did not find the charred remains of a disfigured bandit, another posse would be summoned, armed, and provoked into a spitting rage with appeals to their most foundational notions of justice, retribution, and racial superiority. What Antonio didn't know was whether Fish would call on his men to simply find that murderous Mexican and tear him limb from limb, or if he would widen the appeal to include all Mexicans, to hold Antonio up as an example of a failed people, contemptible savages who needed benevolent Protestant discipline to straighten their naturally crooked dispositions. Antonio had heard a dozen men make these speeches—they even came all the way into Mexico on occasion, preaching that didn't those poor brown bastards wish to live a good life, to live decently like their neighbors across the water? And when these promises of salvation went ignored the men always threw down their Bibles and picked up their rifles, for that was what they'd wanted to do all along, and shouted that such an indolent race didn't deserve the soil under their feet. And then the unspoken rejoinder: Why should a little thing like a river stop the mighty spread of Texas? It was this belief that Antonio could see coloring every Texan's eyes when he spoke to them—he could read it in the way they looked him up and down, in the fear that arched their brows just slightly and the machismo they summoned to try and disguise it. To kill a Mexican was to lay claim to something that should be theirs, that could be theirs if only they were so bold as to take it. The posse would grow, for who wouldn't trade a pickax for a shotgun, and the Rangers would spread the story on the telegraph lines and the post roads and up and down the train tracks until the entire state would be looking for a Mexican with half a face. And so Antonio kept them circling. He wanted to catch Fish and Casoose where they didn't expect him, but first he needed some distance. When the fight came, *he* would dictate its terms.

The other reason Antonio moved them through such a dizzying path was the hope that he could lose Peter, that the Englishman would get tired and sit down somewhere and Antonio would just keep moving. The Englishman was loud, he never stopped talking, and his mere presence in his dandy linen suit and strawberry-red tie was offensive to Antonio, sticking out in the chaparral like a long-limbed parrot. He felt trailed by a child, though even that comparison was unfair, as most children would have at least known to walk on the outer soles of their feet and slip sideways between branches. The Englishman was not large, but he created enough destruction as he moved that, after an hour of walking, Antonio stopped him and told him that he needed to be stealthier or Antonio would kill him before he had a chance to give up their position. After that the Englishman lowered his voice and was a little better about how he moved through the trees, though he still kept up a ceaseless dialogue about the differences between Mexico and the United States, Mexico and England, border politics, how to avoid diseases at whorehouses, the merits of faro versus poker, the Irish, cotton farming, and English football. Antonio said nothing, focusing only on their direction.

"I asked you, good man, did you ever read any poetry?"

Antonio turned and glared at the Englishman over the top of his bandana.

"I rather enjoyed it myself. Of course, they worship Tennyson at Oxford, but I was always more partial to Byron. This morning when I was sitting in the water watching those fires I couldn't help thinking about his poem 'Darkness.' It's quite a brutal vision—lots of burning and hellfire and all that. And there's one line that's been stuck in my head all morning and I think it's rather funny considering the circumstances: 'The crowd was famish'd by degrees; but two of an enormous city did survive, and they were enemies.'" The Englishman paused and seemed to be waiting for Antonio to respond, but Antonio was busy looking for a trail that would bring them to water. "Well, that's us," Peter continued, "the two who survived. And I daresay from the fact you've been trying to dodge me all morning, you consider me your enemy. You didn't think I would notice, eh? Well, I'm happy to say the feeling is not reciprocated. This is the most fun I've had since I left England, and a damned sight more entertaining than running a cotton farm." He sighed and wiped himself with a bandana. "I assume the boll weevils hit you as well, those bastards. We were clearing ten thousand pesos a month until 'ninety-three. I'd been sending all the money back to my father—it was his farm in the first place, and how would a person even *spend* ten thousand pesos in Nuevo Laredo? And so when the cotton was lost I paid all the workers and didn't have enough left to book even a third-class passage back to Europe. Oh, I wired. I sent telegrams every day for a month asking my father for money and I never heard a word. I know they're not dead because I saw in a newspaper my younger sister's been married and there was a photograph of the lot of them having champagne with the Earl of Lytton. But I suppose they're done with me and, truth be told, I think they were done with me years ago. *I* was the one they sent off to run their sweaty foreign ventures. I can't say

144

I've been a remarkable son, but I don't think I've done so badly, either. But anyhow, here I am, cut off, Saint Jerome in the bloody wilderness. It's not all bad, though. I think now I'd find returning to England difficult. The thought of sitting through one of my mother's interminable dinner parties seems laughable once you've killed a man. I'm starting to get back on my feet, too. I was in Corpus Christi negotiating a little importing venture when those baboons came through with their torches. They burned my favorite cantina, the bastards. I had no choice but to fight back. I've some notions, too, of turning my life into a book: *A Gentleman in the Brasada*. What do you think? Or, *An Englishman Enters Mexico*. Or, *Adventures Along the Rio Grande: Episodes from a Mexican Cotton Farm*. Or my favorite, *Peter Ainsley: The Gentleman Assassin*.

"When I ran into that lumberyard last night I thought, 'Peter, you're a damned fool.' Now I'm so very glad I did."

Antonio was silent during this speech as with all the others, though he had been listening. Beyond the obvious things that vexed him about the Englishman there was another, deeper something about the man that Antonio found insulting, and until he listened to him speculate on aggrandizing titles for his unwritten memoirs, he hadn't understood what it was. There was a reason the Englishman was loud and clumsy and possessed a generally bright and unflappable nature: he was merely pretending to be a bandit, spending a holiday slipping into someone else's life, trying on their clothes and firing their gun, all the while intending to flit back to a life of carriage rides and china teacups, and simply shake off all the fear and danger like brushing dirt from his boots. Antonio was being used. Yes the man had saved his life, and yes he'd saved the man's life in return, but despite how chummy he was, Antonio felt the Englishman viewed him as a specimen, a rare animal he could follow and record. In San Antonio there was a photographer's studio Antonio knew where visitors could have their picture taken with what was advertised as a real, live Cherokee Indian. Well, never mind that the Cherokee never lived within a day's journey of San Antonio, but the real Indian was a Mexican from Guerrero wearing a headdress stitched together by the photographer's wife. But when the Yankees came to Texas they expected to see Indians,

145

and even a Mexican with a feather duster on his head would suffice. And Antonio realized he was this Englishman's Indian, and sooner or later he would be expected to whoop and fire his pistola in the air and guzzle tequila with one arm wrapped around a comely señorita because the Englishman had read books about bandidos and didn't he know exactly how they were?

"Stop walking," Antonio said, and he turned around and faced Peter, and he didn't like how the Englishman looked at him calmly, with a smile hiding just behind his lips as though Antonio wasn't capable of strangling him if the mood took him. "I'll take you as far as Mathis and that's it. This isn't a fun adventure and I'm not your fucking guide. Maybe when the Rangers catch up with you they'll let you play for your freedom in a game of dice or fire arrows at chickens, but there won't be any deals like that for me. I need to find them before they find me, and I need to deal with them by myself. You rich people read too many books. You all think everything's going to work out fine in the end, and maybe that's because for you it always does."

"Are you finished?"

To answer, Antonio hawked out a wad of yellow phlegm that landed just near the Englishman's tooled boots.

"You're very presumptuous. I never asked you to be my guide and I doubt you'd be of use in that capacity anyhow. I'm no tourist, mind you. I lived in Mexico for six years and I'm quite certain I've seen more of your native land than you have. It took you twenty minutes of speaking to me to figure out I wasn't Mexican and that's got to count for something. I'm aware of the stakes you're under. They're different to mine, yes, but you forget I'm now the dreadful bandit's accomplice. Their bullets won't discriminate. You forget, too, that I'm a dead shot and a damn sight better than you. You leave me at your own peril. I'm an able outdoorsman, I have no quarrel with banditry as a profession, and I think I make for an amiable and devoted companion. And I know the location of every cathouse south of the Colorado." He adjusted his tie and folded his arms. "I've had my say. I leave the decision up to you."

Antonio pulled a mesquite pod off a tree and chewed one of its beans slowly with his remaining teeth, letting the sweet pulp sit along the side of his mouth. The Englishman was right—he was a dead shot. He would let him stay for now, but he promised himself he would cut him loose or kill him at the first hint of trouble. "I'm in charge," he said and spat the fibrous insides of the bean onto the ground. "I say where we go and you listen to me. If you don't like it you can go hide out with your whores. And I'm not here for your entertainment. If you even think of asking me to fire my gun in the air I'll slit your throat."

"Noted," Peter said.

"Keep your eyes open for smoke," Antonio said, starting to move again. "We need to steal you some clothes that don't make you look like a banker."

"A banker?" Peter stopped and screwed up his face, and Antonio was pleased he had finally found a way to insult the Englishman. "There's not a banker alive that could afford this suit." Peter let a few seconds pass in silence before he said, "Did you say, 'Fire arrows at chickens'? By God, man, is that how you think whites settle their disputes?"

They continued heading north, and before sunset they reached Mathis, where they were able to steal Peter some clothes that were hung to dry on a wire, as well as a hatful of chicken eggs that they cooked in the shell over coals. Peter balked at his new workingman's attire, which he claimed was scratchy and ill fitting, and he was not at all cheered when Antonio pointed out that at least the clothes were clean. He would not assent to bury his suit and tie—"I can't throw away my suit! They wouldn't let me in the same room with a decent whore in clothes like this"—and so he carried them in his arms like a sleeping child. They spent that night in a dry creek bed. As Antonio fell asleep he could hear in the distance the lonely psalm of a shepherd, singing the brush to sleep.

Near a ranch outside Oakville they found some cows straggling in an arroyo. Antonio and Peter drove the animals before them in the direction of the ranch, where they hid out until dark. In the shadows they stole away with two well-muscled paints. While this made their journey faster, the farther west they went, the more dire was the drought. Out there water did not flow, not even in the imagination. Antonio and Peter were surrounded by gray chaparral that blanketed the featureless landscape, rising out of the chalky soil like witches' fingers.

They rode for three days, still doubling back and circling, obscuring their tracks, and surviving the high temperatures on intermittent meals of sweet prickly pear tunas. When they'd find a patch of nopales, they'd stop and gorge themselves, the juices spilling down their chins, and then they'd scrape thorns off the youngest cactus pads and eat them raw, for Antonio was too wary of lighting a fire.

"If I owned Hell and Texas," Peter said, fanning himself against the heat and squinting in the unrelenting sunlight, "I'd rent Texas and live in Hell. We're still south of the Nueces, aren't we? This paradise is what the Texans won in the war? If you ask me, the Texans ought to fight Mexico again and force them to take it back."

"I've heard of men out here holding up trains," Antonio said, "just to steal the water from their boilers."

"Yes," Peter said, eyeing Antonio, "remind me someday to thank you for rescuing us. We might've done better to burn to death in Corpus Christi."

Antonio kept them moving, hoping they would come across someone whom they could ask the Rangers' whereabouts as well as the size of the posse. But they saw no one save a large red bird that Antonio would occasionally catch watching them from a tree branch. They continued aimlessly northwest, for Antonio didn't want to admit to Peter or himself: he had neither a plan nor a clue.

After ten days Antonio knew they would not last much longer. Animals had picked clean every coma tree. Even the cactuses had started to dry up. Antonio figured they were maybe another day's ride from Espantosa Lake near Carrizo Springs—the only spot Antonio felt sure would have water. If they found more cactus he could go another three days maybe; Peter probably only one. The heat was making Antonio delirious. Rocks became enormous blackberries, while tree stumps were mythical toads with gills and horns. He had moments of terror, believing what the Englishman had quoted from his poem was true, that they were the last two survivors of an apocalypse. They were so alone, so alone, two men on a raft a thousand kilometers from shore. Creatures swam in and out of Antonio's vision on bird's wings. He would find himself speaking to them, asking where he could find water, and again and again they gave the same answer: *Too wicked for grace*.

The Englishman was uncharacteristically silent, his tongue having finally succumbed to extreme dehydration. His face was pink and raw like a newborn mouse, the sun finding ways to burn him despite his bandana and hat.

"I heard los Rinches can ride one hundred and thirty kilometers in a day," Antonio said at night as they rested against their saddles. He would still not permit them to light a fire, despite the fact that Peter had spent the day clutching his stomach and moaning that he had the runs from so much uncooked cactus. The Englishman now lay splayed on the ground with his shirt open, tufts of golden hair stirring along his chest in a weak breeze. He hadn't moved in an hour and Antonio might have given him up for dead except he could see his eyes open and moving right and left across the night sky as though tracking some celestial game of table tennis.

"I've been looking for goat tracks," Antonio said. He felt compelled to speak. With the Englishman's words dried up with the rest of him, Antonio realized in the silence how he'd depended on the chatter to distract him from his own condemning thoughts—how he'd run from one certain death to another, how his chances of finding the Rangers were as good as finding a teardrop in the ocean. He hadn't seen a footprint in days, and he feared the silence and darkness and dead trees would swallow him and the Englishman up. "I'd like to know what kind of reward they've put up. No Mexican since Cortina has cracked ten thousand—you think I've managed?"

His tone was light because what else could he do? To sit there and enumerate all the ways he might die in the next day, two, three—there was no point in that, and besides, he was a fatalist at heart, a worldview he'd picked up from Jesusa. "If you're born to hang, you'll never drown," she was fond of saying. When they first met she used to tease him about being a "rich boy," no matter that he had scarcely more in his pockets than she did. "For you, the world is anything you want it to be," she said one night as they sat near where the river split with their feet dipped in the warm water. "For me—I know where I end up."

"And where's that?" he asked in a playful tone.

She looked at him as though he were very stupid and she spread her arms out to indicate Dorado. "I can go anywhere I want as long as it's right here. They'll bury me in my mother's front yard next to the washbasin and they'll put a little plaque next to it that says 'She died as she lived—doing everyone's laundry.'"

Antonio laughed. "If you can see the future I hope you'll tell me if I'm still handsome when I'm an old man."

"It's not seeing the future. It's seeing what is. But it's better that way," she said with a little smile. "When things are good, it's a gift. And when they're not, it was always going to happen. Either way, you never need to worry." This was one of her many strengths, Antonio thought, and one that set her apart from the rosary-clutching ninnies who believed they could straighten their teeth and fatten their cows by praying enough for it. Jesusa was fine without him, perhaps better. When he returned she would not throw herself at his feet out of gratitude. He'd have to prove himself, win her back by making her life easier for once, instead of harder.

"We're not too far from Valdez," Antonio said, turning to Peter, who hadn't moved or spoken in over an hour. "We should come upon a house soon."

Peter garbled something and Antonio had to demand he repeat himself. The Englishman's lips were bleeding and he seemed unable to open his mouth. Antonio took a cactus pad from his pocket and split it open to reveal the slimy, viscous inside. He indicated that Peter should rub it over his lips.

"Valdez," Peter said a moment later when he could open his mouth. "We go."

Antonio shook his head. "Valdez is full of outlaws. Trains don't even stop there unless there's a deputy on the platform. If anyone thought he could make money or cut a deal or just to stick his foot in someone's ass—"

"Valdez." Peter was sitting up higher now, seemingly animated by the thought of escaping the brush. Valdez was a violent place—hot, dry, forlorn, and filled with a transient population of thieves and murderers. Three sheriffs had died in shoot-outs in one year. An entire town filled with men whose moral center rested on guns and gold was the last place they should go.

Peter managed to tear off a piece of cactus pad and chew it slowly before spitting it on the ground in a great green glob. He pushed himself so that he was sitting all the way up, and Antonio could see the great effort with which he spoke. "I know the madam. Good friend. Has food. Please." His eyes were still moving back and forth in the dark in a motion that appeared involuntary and his cheeks had begun to hollow so that his normally jaunty expression was slack.

Peter tried to focus on Antonio as best he could. "You saved my life," he whispered. "Please. Do it again now."

Antonio got up, startled because it wasn't Peter he saw on the ground, but Hugo, his brother, asking him to save his life. He took two steps back and blinked and now it was Peter's face again, but hollowed and skeletal. Their faces flickered, one to the other and back again like two sides of a card turning and turning.

Suddenly an orange glow appeared in the distance, a fireball that erupted and burned no more than ten kilometers away. Antonio's heart sped up. He climbed a tree to get a better view, and by the time he reached a high branch another glow appeared not far from the first. In minutes there was a wall of flame stretching across the horizon. It wasn't a wildfire, for the flames stayed in place. It was the Rangers, lighting fires at intervals and creating a perimeter to flush out the two men, to drive them into the open like animals.

Antonio cursed under his breath, believing he'd put more distance between them and him. Whether the heat had made him slow, or the lack of food and water, or Peter's inability to conceal his movements—it didn't matter now. He hefted Peter onto his horse and tied the two animals in tandem. In minutes they were moving again at a slight jog. They were indeed not far from Valdez and soon Antonio could see the lights from the whorehouse like a beacon summoning lost ships. The orange glow stayed steadily behind, maybe even moving forward like an advancing army. Behind every tree he expected to see a gun pointing at his head.

When they'd almost reached town Antonio had to turn the horses loose, for their brand would be immediately recognized. He pointed them north away from the Rangers and struck them hard with a branch, causing them to bolt. He tied his bandana around his face and put Peter over his shoulder and then staggered the last stretch up to the back door of the whorehouse, a grand wood-frame building with a second-floor balcony that faced the street and a red light swinging over the front door in a gentle breeze. Two teenage girls were sitting on a back staircase smoking and watching Antonio with unfriendly eyes until he dropped the Englishman at their feet.

"Get the señora," he barked and they picked up their skirts and stole up the stairs without a word. From the vantage of the staircase Antonio could see the orange line, longer now, pinning him against the building. It might have circled the whole world. In a moment a woman in a tightly corseted black dress appeared glowering down at Antonio from the top of the stairs. "No Mexicans," she said. "We don't serve Mexicans except on Christmas," and she flapped one thin hand to indicate he should go away.

"He says he knows you," Antonio said, picking Peter's head up off the ground and twisting his torso to face the madam. "His name is Peter Ainsley."

The woman was already milk pale, but she seemed to lose even this as she heard Peter's name. She hesitated, bringing one hand up to the velvet buttons fastened around her throat. Then she signaled to someone Antonio could not see inside and two large men appeared. They picked Peter up and brought him up the stairs as the madam peered out into the darkness. When they passed her with Peter she gasped and put a handkerchief to her mouth. "My room," she said as they carried him through the door. She watched Peter disappear into the house before she straightened herself, put the handkerchief back in her pocket, and looked at Antonio still at the bottom of the stairs.

He was beginning to sway; he could name at least twenty different foods whose smells skimmed over the air to him, whispering seduction in his ear.

"Well," the madam said, "I reckon you want to eat."

Antonio had to hold tight to the rail to reach the top and once there the woman put out one hand to stop him. "I told you we don't serve Mexicans, and I have some guests here that would take great exception to seeing you on the premises. If you know Peter, that'll get you a meal. But after you've eaten you need to get on out of here. This ain't a charity."

Antonio nodded and followed the madam into a sparse but brightly lit kitchen. He looked up and blinked at the light shining down on him from the ceiling. It was not the usual orange-yellow glow of an oil lamp, but a bluish-white incandescence that gave a strange, sickly pallor to everything. The madam saw him blinking and looking up at the light and down at his hands. "Electricity," she said. "We're the only place in Valdez that's got it." She pointed to a table and he sat down while she picked up a broom and used the handle to poke awake a redheaded girl of about fourteen, asleep on a rag-strewn cot in the corner.

"Get up, Josephine," the woman ordered, and when the girl was slow to stir she struck her once across the calves, eliciting a scream. The girl sat up rubbing her legs and glaring at Antonio, intuiting the cause of her interrupted sleep. "Fix him a plate," the madam said, "and then see that he's on his way."

"Water, please," Antonio said, and his voice seemed covered in nettles.

The girl dribbled a few spoonfuls of water from a pitcher into a tin cup and dropped it in front of Antonio with bald disgust. He finished it in one swallow and asked for another, and when she rolled her eyes and made no move to accommodate him he yanked the pitcher out of her hands and brought it to his lips under the bandana, not caring about what he spilled, only that he wished to dive down into the pitcher and drink forever.

Through the kitchen walls he could hear what sounded like the waning end of a party: laughter, clinking bottles, bad piano playing. The girl was watching him with her eyebrows raised. "Most men would take off their bandana," she said.

"I eat with it on. Makes the food taste better."

"Is that a fact?" Antonio could see the greenish remnants of a bruise around her left eye. She watched him with defiance, in no apparent hurry to prepare his food. "I heard coyotes won't eat a Mexican," she said, "on account he's too spicy. Is that true?"

"Sí," Antonio said. "If Jonah had been a Mexican, that whale would have spit him right back onto the boat."

The girl giggled. "That's good," she said, turning toward the stove. "You're funny." Soon she set a plate of eggs and biscuits before Antonio, a thick cut of greasy bacon, and a pot of coffee that was so fresh off the stove it was still bubbling. When he'd eaten everything, he used an end of stale soda bread to sop up the bacon drippings, and when that was gone he leaned back in his chair and contemplated asking the girl for another helping.

The kitchen door banged open then and the madam poked her head in. "You're still here," she said, looking with annoyance at Antonio. "Peter's asking for you. He says if I turn you out he'll break my neck." She looked around the kitchen as if searching for answers somewhere among the tins and burlap bags. "It's a fine thing for him to drop in here and start telling me my business." She glared at Antonio, who was silent. He was trapped. No telling how close the Rangers were now. Running out into the brush might mean running straight into trouble, though hiding in a well-known brothel was hardly a better alternative.

"There's a room in the cellar," the madam said. "You go down there now and don't come out until I get you. And if you even cough down there I'm not responsible for what happens to you. And you"—she turned to the girl, who shrank even when the madam wasn't holding the broom— "if you breathe one word of this to anyone I'll turn you out to the dogs." She let this threat linger a beat before she turned back to Antonio. "Well, get up," she said. "I'd like to get a little sleep myself, for Lord's sake." She opened a door in the kitchen wall that was barely perceptible in the wood paneling. It opened onto a dark staircase leading down into a moldy cellar, where Antonio could hear cockroaches scuttling across the floor. The madam had a candle—for apparently the electricity did not run down to the basement—which she did not offer to Antonio, and it painted her face a ghoulish green and gray. She opened a door to a tiny cell that contained a bed and a chamber pot and nothing else. She brought the candle up to

Antonio's face and looked at him carefully. "Take that rag off your face," she commanded. Antonio hesitated and she repeated the order. "I've got to protect my inventory," she said.

He untied the bandana from around his face and she brought the candle so close to him he could feel it burning the still-tender skin around his jaw.

"El Tragabalas," she whispered. "I saw your picture at the post office. There's a reward for you."

Antonio looked at her steadily. "I can leave before anyone sees me."

"It's too late for that," she hissed. "I've let my death in."

SIXTEEN

Sometime later, Antonio was awakened by the kitchen girl kicking open the door carrying another plate of eggs and biscuits, coffee, and water. "She says you should eat again," the girl said after she'd lit a lantern and looked around the tiny cell. Antonio sat up and hastily tied the bandana around his face. "I never been in here before," she said. "One of the girls told me this used to be a hiding place for slaves they was smuggling to Mexico."

"Thank you. Was your name Josephine?"

The girl gave a short laugh. "My real name's Zorabia, but the mistress said that was so ugly she couldn't even pronounce it, and she told everyone to call me Josephine." She blew out a long breath as though she'd been waiting to tell someone that bit of her history. "She gives everyone a new name when they wash up here. She says it helps to keep one thing that's just for you, and when you leave, you get to leave that whole person behind."

"You're a good cook."

She shrugged. "When you're done I've drawn you a bath. Everyone's asleep now so you'd better hurry on up." She picked up his chamber pot and retched and made a great show of clumping up the stairs with it, pausing every so often to clutch her chest. Antonio swallowed the last of the food and carried his dishes after her. Leaving the absolute darkness of the cellar, he was surprised to reach the kitchen and see daylight. He washed his dishes while the girl dealt with the chamber pot outside, and when she returned she led him up a rear staircase to the second floor. The hallway was bare save for a row of sconces and a series of doors lining either side, each with a plaque hanging on it and a different girl's name written in a looping, feminine scrawl: *Fantasia, Penelope, Frederique, Callais.* Antonio had visited enough whorehouses to know this one fancied itself a finer establishment. The fact the girls were allowed to sleep in their rooms and were not rousted out of their beds for a day shift implied the house made enough money off the evenings to feed and clothe the lot. No one stirred as they crept down the hallway to the last door, which was unmarked. Inside was a room covered in blue and white painted tiles, vases of fresh roses, and a large tub in the center of the room filled with steaming water. And almost as miraculous, there was a fresh set of clothes draped over a chair.

The girl lingered a second at the door as Antonio removed his boots and began pulling the socks off his swollen, blistered feet. "Thank you," Antonio said, and nodded to the door.

The girl shrugged again but otherwise did not move.

"I'd like to get in while the water's hot."

"I want to see what you're hiding under that bandana."

"I had an infected tooth. It's very ugly."

"I seen a whole family of Mormons burnt up in a fire. I figure I seen worse."

"Let me bathe in peace."

"Soon as you take off your bandana."

In this gleaming room with the clear water and the air wretched with the scent of fresh roses, Antonio was grossly aware of his own smell, how his clothes were stiff with sweat and dirt, and he longed to be in that water. He hadn't had a bath since he left Cielita's. The madam trusted the girl, insofar as she let her alone with him. He knew the girl would leave him if he raised his fist in her direction, but he felt sorry for her, spending the dwindling moments of her childhood dodging beatings until she would one day graduate into the far worse existence of whoredom. He decided to indulge her. He brought his hands slowly up behind him and untied the bandana. The girl came right up to him with one hand outstretched, and traced her fingers along his cheek in a motion that was tender and curious.

"I didn't notice last night, but your eyes are green as grass," she said with some awe. "I never knew a Mexican could have green eyes."

Antonio took her small, calloused hand off his face, brought it to his lips, and kissed it like a gentleman, like he knew a man would never, in her lifetime, kiss her hand again. "Leave me," he said. She blushed as she withdrew her hand and she closed the door quietly behind her.

After he finished his bath Antonio went to the window wrapped in a white towel. From there he could see most of downtown Valdez: a bank, a store, a couple of false-front saloons. The time on the courthouse clock tower read a quarter to noon. The people below moved slowly through the hot and cloudless morning. There were a lot of men who looked like him, who walked with their heads up and their hats low, wanting to see but remain unseen. And there were others, white men, who leaned against telegraph poles and watched the passersby with malice, one hand resting on the butt of their holstered revolver. A group of men exited a hotel across the road and headed toward the train depot at the far end of the street. And at the head of the pack, moving with unearned swagger, was Captain Fish.

A train whistled far off and Fish pointed some of the men in his entourage in its direction. Others he dispatched elsewhere, aiming his finger like a gun and firing men up and down the street. But where was Casoose? Antonio scanned up and down but didn't see the ugly brute. Fish looked down toward the depot, checked his watch, squinted up at the sky, adjusted his belt—Antonio watched it all with great anticipation. Where would he go? And with nervous excitement, Antonio saw Fish turn around and head straight for the brothel, passing practically under Antonio's feet on his way to the front door.

He had his clothes on and was strategizing his attack—surprise him from the stairs or go around the back and through the kitchen and catch him in the parlor?—when Peter opened the door and strode into the bathroom in his drawers, a clean suit on a hanger swinging from his hand.

"There you are!" Peter exclaimed, loud enough to wake the entire building.

"Fish is here," Antonio said in a rough whisper. "Right downstairs. It was nice knowing you, whitey."

"Just a moment," Peter said, dropping his voice. "Here as in, he's taking tea with Lenore as we speak?"

"Give me your derringer."

"You can't shoot him in here."

"Give me your derringer."

Peter's face hardened, and for the first time he looked really angry. "You will not shoot an officer of the law in here. Lenore is a dear friend and I will not allow you to destroy her livelihood. What is your obsession with the Rangers?"

Antonio felt heat in his fists. He pushed his chest out and got so close to Peter the Englishman had to take a half step back. The two men stared each other down, Antonio curling and uncurling his hands. The room was humid and close; he could smell bergamot on Peter's breath.

"They killed my brother," he finally said.

Peter's face didn't move, but Antonio saw his eyes soften. "I'll go downstairs and speak to Lenore," he said quietly. "Stay here and don't move."

"Don't give me orders. I told you I'm not one of your little cotton pickers."

Peter gave him a frustrated look and then turned around and left. Antonio paced from one end of the room to the other, deciding what to do. No telling who was downstairs. The madam might have more than just the two goons he'd seen last night. And while he and Peter were arguing, Fish could have left. He finally posted himself again at the window to see if anyone came in or out.

After a while Peter returned, and Antonio could tell the Englishman had nothing good to report because he wore a schoolboy grin like he'd just nicked a pie from a windowsill.

"It's a good thing you bathed, because we have been invited to a party."

Antonio watched him without expression.

"Lenore's preparing an absolute bacchanal. Just for us." He looked down, slightly embarrassed. "The last one of Lenore's parties, there was this Argentinian girl. She started with a handstand—"

"Are you fucking stupid?" Antonio was beyond the end of his patience with the Englishman. "You're like a child playing pretend." He'd been so foolish, *so foolish* to have let himself fall in with this playboy. "Get out of my way. I'm going after him."

"I'm sorry, all right? No, don't run off. Listen, Lenore's spoken to your Ranger captain and he's promised to come to her little affair tonight."

"It sounds like a trap."

"Because it is. But it's a trap for him, not you. He's here looking for you. He suspects you're in the area. But believe me, the absolute last place he'd expect you to turn up is in a whites-only brothel."

"I can't go to a party, you jackass."

"You're worried about being identified—that's not a problem. Lenore's parties tend to be quite spirited. No one's eyes are on the men, if you catch my drift. And besides," he said with satisfaction, "we'll all be wearing masks."

Antonio put his hands up to his face and pressed down hard on his eyelids. "This is crazy. It's idiotic. I should have left you to die out there."

"Live a little, won't you? Come to the party, have a couple of drinks, and once you've sighted your man, you get him cornered—*outside*—and bang. Speaking of which . . ." Peter handed him a nicely polished Remington.

Antonio looked at the pistol a few seconds before he took it and shook his head. He needed to get away from Peter, away from the cloying smell of roses, away from this prison he'd built himself brick by brick out of so many compromises.

That evening Peter appeared in his basement cell with a candle, two glasses of tequila, and two masks tucked under his arm. "I prefer the dog," Peter said, holding them out for Antonio to see in the feeble candlelight, "but I suppose I could be the rat if you really insist."

Peter was dressed in another gray suit, a sprig of mountain laurel pinned to his lapel as though he were attending a wedding. Antonio looked at him with annoyance, but he reached out and took the rat mask. It was elaborately painted all over with gray fur, rosy-pink cheeks, and large arching eyebrows.

"Splendid," Peter said, clinking glasses with Antonio and throwing back his drink. Antonio just looked at the tequila. He'd lived his entire life following his instincts and he'd survived where others had fallen. This town, this brothel, this mask, this Englishman—they all belonged to a world he'd stepped into unwittingly and hadn't asked to see. He felt that his only way out was now on Peter's terms, which unsettled him greatly. And still, the Englishman was right: Antonio might have Fish cornered here, caught unaware. He shook his head. A goddamn whites-only party.

"God forgive me," Antonio said and he swallowed the drink. He became aware of a repeated sound coming from above, the sort of background noise that could have started just that moment, or could have been thudding down through the wooden beams of the house for hours. It was a lively bass—*pum, pum, pum*—similar to but a lot faster than something Comanches would play over a canyon to signal a fight. The bass was joined by other percussive sounds, then trumpets and tubas and other instruments, until Antonio was sure the madam had an entire orchestra up in her parlor.

Peter let out a whoop. "What did I tell you, old boy? Lenore's a mean piece of work, but no one throws a better party." And he put on his mask and bounded up the stairs, clapping his hands to the drums.

Antonio was left with nothing to do but follow. He looked at the rat face again, and its black eyes and simpering smile were spooky in the dark room. "Pinche rata," he said, putting on the mask.

He followed the noise through the house to a pair of doors painted all over with cupids. There were three chandeliers in the hall where he stood and they rocked in time to the seething chaos beyond. He took a deep breath, told himself he was a damned stupid fool, and turned the door handle.

Mirrors—mirrors on every wall, mirrors on the ceiling, mirrors even on the tables—that's what Antonio saw when he entered the room. And contained within every prism and reflected infinitely into every dimension was a heaving, sweaty mass of bodies gyrating to music that was so loud Antonio could scream and not hear himself. Two naked women were perched like plucked canaries on giant swings above the room and they rocked in tandem, illuminated by electric spotlights that traced two arcs back and forth. Antonio looked again and corrected himself. They weren't completely naked—they wore identical feathered masks with blue and green peacock feathers fanned about their heads. There was a marble-topped bar behind which a grinning man spun two bottles around his torso before catching them in midair and pouring the chartreuse liquid into dainty crystal glasses. The bartender then shot a flame out of a small canister, and all the little glasses were at once alight, the burning green drink producing a steady blue flame. Eight men and women standing near the bar picked up the glasses, clinked them, and swallowed them down, fire and all. And as soon as the empty glasses had been cleared away, a troupe of young men in red satin bloomers and white masks ascended the bar and began a choreographed dance. It was at this moment that Antonio felt that, to survive the night, he needed to either leave or get knee-walking drunk.

He put on his Texan accent and asked the bartender for whiskey, though he agreed with Peter that no one was likely to take notice of him in all that bedlam. Everyone wore a mask save the bartender, and as Antonio surveyed the room he saw a zebra, an antelope, many laughing harlequins, and the madam herself bustling through the fray in a bejeweled devil's mask, the curling horns of which stood high and threatening. Who were the men inside those disguises? Marshals? Outlaws? And which one was Fish? Men staggered around with girls on their shoulders, men straddled girls like horses and whipped them with ostrich feathers, and a small crowd of men were gathered in a corner, where two women writhed kissing and stroking one another atop a chair shaped like a pair of lips. Antonio had visited many whorehouses but never one with such Caligulan pretensions. And as Antonio was seeing everything under the strange blue-white glow of electric light, the scene took on an extra nightmarish sense of surrealism, that his very perceptions of light and color could not be trusted. The glut of feathers and jewels, satins and silks, made him bitter and ashamed that the finest thing Jesusa owned was the red rebozo he'd brought her from a trip to Monterrey. He doubted the poor girl had ever even touched velvet, and he vowed there and then that the first chance he got he'd steal her something magnificent.

The band had finally stopped to take a break and the room erupted in all the pent-up conversation of the last half hour. Antonio looked up and saw the rat face looking down at him from the mirror on the ceiling, its smile seeming wider now, grinning ear to ear.

"Woof, woof." Peter clapped Antonio on the back. He was joined by two swans, one white, one black. He had an arm around each and they took turns petting him on the top of his head and his stomach.

"Good doggy," one said.

"Nice puppy," said the other.

"Ladies, this is my very good friend, Mr. Rat."

The swans curtsied together as if on cue.

"I have some business to discuss with Mr. Rat," Peter said, releasing the women and lifting up his mask to give each of them a kiss, "but I promise I'll find you when I'm ready for a treat."

The black swan produced a long cigarette holder and swatted Peter on the nose with it. "Bad doggies don't get a bone," she said and walked back into the crowd. The white swan, apparently out of dog-related quips, shrugged her shoulders and followed.

"What did I tell you?" Peter slapped the bar and ordered two whiskeys. "I've fallen in love a half dozen times in this place and I may do it again tonight. I never asked you: Are you married?"

Antonio nodded. "And two children."

"If I was going to marry I'd choose one of these sporting ladies here, if for no other reason than to imagine the look on my father's face."

Antonio shook his head and concentrated on his drink. "I guess when you're rich you can play pretend forever."

"You think all this is foolish." Peter bristled and Antonio could see he'd touched something. "This is what's real—loving with abandon, enjoying what God gave us to enjoy. Out there, where everyone puts on a tie and calmly reads about atrocities in the newspaper and then compliments the mediocre soup—that's the mask. That's the fantasy."

Peter was very drunk and winding up to that particular clarity that only comes after a long soak.

"The whole facade of polite society was built to hide the fact that underneath we're a sweaty mass of lust and jealousy and greed. When I saw your face that first night out in the water, I didn't see a monster. I saw a man—a *real* man, one for whom all artifice has been scrubbed away. And in that respect, I envy you.

"Lenore and all the women like her do us the enormous service of allowing us these little glimpses of reality, just enough to sustain us while we put on our disguises and step back out into the world. So yes, if I could marry one of these girls and 'play pretend,' as you put it, for the rest of my life, I'd do it gladly."

"You and I have different versions of reality," Antonio said. "And if you want me to shoot you in the face, I can arrange it."

"Ah yes, there's the tough-man bravado. For what would our sex be without our posturing?"

"You talk like someone who's never had his ass kicked, like someone who walks around with one eye closed, seeing only what he can see from his fancy carriage rolling over the mud."

"Oh, you're going to bring class into it? How unexpected." Peter tapped the bar for two more drinks and looked sullenly down into his empty glass.

Antonio chewed the inside of his cheek, not sure why he'd gotten so riled up in this argument. What the hell did he care what the Englishman thought or believed or did or said? Still, some of what Peter had said was true. He'd left Jesusa and the children because he felt that domestic life was not only boring but oppressive in its falseness. Perhaps he hated feeling like Peter understood anything about him, could read anything at all into his experience.

"All right, so which one is Fish?" he demanded, changing the subject. "The elephant? The clown?"

"Oh, yes," Peter said, as though he'd forgotten entirely that they had any reason for being at the party. "I don't know," he said, looking slightly deflated. "But I did hear that they got a tip that you're at Rancho Los Ybarras. They heard you had friends there and were planning to cross into Mexico at their ranch." Peter looked around them to be sure they weren't overheard. "They can't pursue you across the border, can they?"

"They can do what they want until someone stops them. But I need to know which one he is. He's consumptive. Have you heard anyone coughing? I'm going to walk around and see if I hear his voice."

But Peter wasn't listening. The band was beginning another set. The drums were going: a long roll and a quick procession of bass notes. A gazelle in a flimsy harem getup stood in the center of the room and spun a large wooden hoop around her neck and torso.

"I bet that's where Casoose went. Rancho Los Ybarras isn't far from here. With a couple of good horses we can be there tomorrow afternoon."

"Tomorrow," Peter slurred, waving him off. "We'll leave first thing in the morning. Now, where did my swans go?"

"The hell we'll leave in the morning. We leave as soon as I find that son of a bitch and drive my knife through his throat."

"I'm piss drunk," Peter said. "I can't ride a horse, much less steal one. Now, as soon as I find the white swan you can have her. The black one's got a violent streak in her I quite like."

"Then stay here," Antonio said, moving into the crowd.

"Don't be like that!" Peter reached out and caught Antonio's shirt, but Antonio jerked himself free. "Come on," Peter shouted, "I thought we were friends!"

Even amid all the music and whiskey and frenzied dancing, people were turning to look at them. Antonio had the uneasy, extrasensory feeling that something was afoot. The electric currents running through the walls made him intensely aware of everything in the room like a spider feels a fly struggling in her web. He pushed through the crowd toward the mirrored door, his hand almost on the doorknob, when a rangy wolf materialized in front of him, barring his way.

"Let's take off that mask, Antonio," the wolf said. "Slow, and won't nobody get hurt."

Antonio turned around and saw that the entire party had ceased moving. The band was quiet; the men in red bloomers had paused their dance and stood atop the bar watching him. Antonio felt he was onstage, curtains pulled back, floodlights blinding him.

The only person not watching him was Peter, who stood on tiptoe to peer into the crowd for the two swans. "There you are!" he shouted, pointing at Josephine, the kitchen girl, about to slip out of the party through another mirrored door. She brought up her face to see who had called out to her, the white swan mask in her hand, and the crowd pivoted to watch her, now the object of their attention.

"Captain Fish, please don't harass my guests." Lenore was pushing through the crowd to where Antonio and the wolf were standing. "Everyone is behaving. Why do you want to go and spoil a good time?"

The wolf took off his mask. The bastard was only a breath away from Antonio, his knife singing, screaming to do its duty. "That little girl over there says this is a wanted man. Says he's *the* wanted man. She says you've been feeding and harboring the most wanted man in Texas for twenty-four hours, and if that's true, miss, I'm gonna do a lot more than spoil everyone's good time."

Lenore still wore her devil's mask, so her expression was inscrutable behind the grinning, glittering face, but she laughed loudly, which caused others in the room to laugh as well. "That girl's imagination is the only thing on her that isn't lazy," she said. "I'm afraid she's been telling tales."

"She's lying!" Whoever had been manning the spotlights that followed the two women on the swings now fixed them both on Josephine, whose young face under the mask had been garishly painted in white and pink and was now melting like icing. "Take off his mask. He's the one y'all been looking for and she knows it." She threw an accusatory finger at Lenore. The madam's devil grin was beginning to slide, frowning down into something hate-filled and furrowed. It was not hard to understand why the girl would want to see her mistress hang.

"In position!" Fish shouted, and thirty men surrounded Antonio. The spotlights were on him, boxing him in, too. People stood on chairs and tables to get a better view. No one breathed. He looked for Peter, but he was nowhere, probably off in some corner slobbering over the black swan.

"Take it off slow." Fish had his right hand out to the side and slightly raised, waiting for a reason to pull his gun.

Antonio let out a quiet breath and tried to count his options, but there were none, a fact all the more vexing for his having known not to come to the party, not to show his face, not to ride into Valdez at all. Would they hang him then and there, or haul him up to Houston and make a day of it?

"Mr. Rat!"

The room turned as one to Peter standing near a metal box on the wall behind the bar that contained many small knobs and switches. The spotlights pivoted to him as well, just in time to catch him swinging a full whiskey bottle at the box. There was a sound of breaking glass, a minor hail of orange sparks like worms that rose into the air and disappeared, a hiss and a fizzle, and then darkness.

Antonio was out the door while the big brown bottle was still sailing through the air.

Horses weren't hard to find. There were a dozen of them tied in front of the brothel. As Antonio was mounting one, Peter came streaking out, screaming for Antonio to wait for him. Antonio untied the horse next to him and the two men, now unmasked, galloped away down the street.

"I hope it doesn't burn," Peter shouted over the galloping hooves. "I feel dreadful. I only meant to take the lights out."

Antonio said nothing, leaning farther down on his horse. The first bullets were wide, but not short. Peter brought out a pistol, but in the dark, firing backward on a galloping horse, it would be a waste of a bullet, and so he put the gun back under his arm and bent low over his horse as well.

Antonio kept them on the road, wanting to put as much distance between himself and Fish as he could before he broke off into the chaparral. It was tricky business to navigate the brush in the dark and Peter, despite his quick action at the brothel, was stumbling drunk. Their horses seemed to be in good shape, and after twenty minutes he let them slow and catch their breath.

"You don't think Lenore's in any trouble, do you?" Peter was agitated and his voice shook and he kept sniffling as though he'd spent the ride crying. "No one actually saw your face. It's that girl's word against Lenore's."

Antonio refused to speak. He'd been so stupid. He'd allowed the Englishman's predilections for women and soft sheets to almost cost him his life, and if he died in vain, then so did Hugo.

"The electricity was my idea. I paid for the whole system." Peter's voice broke and he started to cry in earnest and Antonio wished he had a whip so he could strike the man with it. But all he had were his fists, so he brought his horse alongside Peter's and gave him the back of his hand.

"Why?" the Englishman howled. "What have I done?"

"If I'm going to die, I want to die on my horse like a man," Antonio said. "Not in a goddamned feather bed."

"I saved us."

"You almost got us killed."

"Isn't this all part of the adventure?" Peter had stopped crying and was now angry himself. "The thrill of the outlaw life? If you're averse to taking chances, this is the first I'm hearing of it."

Antonio said nothing because there was nothing to say to the Englishman that would make him understand that, for Antonio, traveling across the river to buy soap and flour was an adventure when Mexican lives were worth less than the boots on their feet. The horse had regained its breath and Antonio spurred it into a lope with Peter not far behind.

After another twenty minutes Antonio stopped and listened. He could hear nothing, which was worse than hearing them close behind. The sky was losing some of its indigo. Sunrise would begin in another hour, and so Antonio led them off the road into the brush, picking through the overgrowth in search of a trail.

Peter waited an hour, until the sun was colored orange marmalade, to tell Antonio he thought it was a bad idea to ride straight to Casoose.

"It's suicide. They laid that bait hoping you'd bite. For all you know they've got a hundred men waiting for you. They could have called up an army regiment. You haven't thought anything through."

"I'm through listening to you," Antonio said.

"I'm thinking of myself here, too. I don't particularly feel like facing down the United States government. I'm not even really supposed to be in the country."

But Antonio had heard as much of the Englishman's talking as he could take, and he drew his pistol and aimed it at Peter's stomach.

Peter's mouth hung open and his hands flew instinctively up above his head. He seemed about to speak again and so Antonio preempted this by pulling back the hammer. Peter's mouth closed and they continued in silence for the rest of the morning.

It felt exactly like a trap, with Fish behind him and Casoose in front of him, two metal jaws closing down on his leg like he was some wild coyote. When they neared the barbed-wire fence around the pasture of Rancho Los Ybarras, Antonio saw it had already been filed down. Beyond the fence the brush had been cleared and the land was more contoured as it neared the frontage along the Río Bravo, with gentle rises and falls like a body under a sheet. There was nowhere to hide and so they continued west, Antonio all the while watching the horizon for signs of Fish or Casoose. How would they come? he wondered. Man-to-man or leading an army?

As soon as they spied a few cattle Antonio rounded them up and drove them in front, the two men appearing to anyone watching from afar to be just a couple of workers. But the cattle were thin with runny eyes, and a spindly calf among them showed signs of scours. There was no one about. Even on a big ranch one would expect to see people.

Peter, forgetting Antonio's prohibition on talking, pointed to a pig on the far side of an oak. "He's got a chicken in his mouth." Antonio looked and the pig was indeed in the middle of killing a chicken. It savaged the bird with what looked like joy, sowing white feathers on the brown dirt like snow.

They continued unimpeded, and before the sun had reached its zenith they were standing in front of the outbuildings and could see the ranch house sitting on a little rise overlooking the river. Antonio heard the drone of flies as they approached the first building. He turned away when Peter nudged open the door of the first bunkhouse and stuck in his head. Peter jerked back with a cry and vomited into the grass. It was the same at the store, the schoolhouse, the tannery. Every building contained bodies, with more prostrate on the ground. The worst was what they discovered at the ranch house: the entire Ybarra family hung from a pecan tree, father, mother, children—Antonio stopped counting victims at seven. From the graying fingers on one child's hand Antonio thought they'd been dead maybe a week. He turned away, screwed shut his eyes, even covered his face with his hands, but he could still smell them, could hear the weight of their bodies creaking the limbs of the mighty tree, so many lives suspended.

No mires a otro lado. Antonio blinked, but it was still there. *Don't look away,* scrawled in black paint on the front of the ranch house, the handwriting, the hanging, the entire massacre a gesture only a maniac could enact. And until now he'd been unsure, but the painted command made it clear—Casoose had done this, and done it for Antonio. For what reason, whether to frighten him or punish him, he didn't know. But Antonio could intuit that in the Ranger's twisted mind, massacring a ranch's worth of innocent victims was appropriate retribution.

"It's bloody savages who've done this," Peter said, looking pale and green. "But nonetheless, you seem to have a guardian angel up your arse."

"This is revenge. It's—" But he came up short, no words ever able to express the inexpressible unsewing of God's created world when a child was murdered. "The Rangers did this. This is why I have to stop them."

Antonio dismounted and led the horse down to the river to drink. Then he took out his knife and began sharpening the blade against his belt. Overwhelmed with the weight of it all, he could think of nothing but to put himself to work.

"No." Peter was shaking his head. "No. Look where we are!" And he pointed at Mexico on the other side of the water. "We made it. We got away. A quick dip and we're gone like smoke." He looked at Antonio and his face was pleading. "How many reprieves do you think you get?"

Antonio spit and continued sharpening his knife. When he was done with that he would clean his gun. Then he would scrounge around the ranch for tools and provisions, and then he would set off, alone, to find Fish and Casoose.

"Listen, I've got a little land in Manzanillo. It's not much, but it's right on the Pacific. The fish I've pulled out of the water down there are as long as you are. We can cross right now, grab your wife and children, and all go down to Manzanillo together. Or leave the señora at home and you can still come. It's a fresh start in a tropical paradise, none of this mucking about with boll weevils and droughts. You'll fatten yourself eating bonita and mangoes all day and watch the sunset melt from the deck of an oceanside villa. How could you possibly say no?"

Antonio put the knife back in his boot and moved on to the pistol, taking it apart and wiping it carefully with his shirt.

"And the women, my God. They've got these short, round little bodies. How they look at you when they're walking down the beach . . ." Peter stopped talking and looked sadly at Antonio. "You're a fool," he said. "It's vanity keeping you here. Don't mistake it for heroism."

"I could have been you," Antonio said. The gun was empty, but as he cleaned it he swung it in Peter's direction. "I've had money, could have had a big house. I've carried so much gold I had to drag it along the ground. But that's not living. Living is this"—he looked at Peter down the barrel—"seeing yourself on the other end of the gun."

"It's not you I see on the other end of that gun. It's your children."

Antonio did not answer, nor did he put down the gun.

"Forgiveness is better than revenge," Peter said.

At that Peter stood up and walked into the water. His horse was already in the river up to its knees and he took it by the reins and led it deeper until neither could touch bottom and then they swam.

Antonio could hear the horse breathing, *huff, huff*, next to Peter's fluid strokes. He told himself he did not care to see if Peter made it safely across to Mexico, so Antonio retrieved his own horse from the water and began to coax it east.

He tried to convince himself that he did not know any Englishmen; he had no ties to any such person, even as a strange and sudden regret he could not completely understand welled up inside him. Antonio swallowed something of himself down as he mounted his horse and spurred it into a trot.

The two men, cocooned inside their own private pains, did not see that a slim shadow had darkened the far shore. Nor did they see as Remedio took shape, stepped into the water, and began crossing to the United States.

THE SONORO FAMILY

BY MARIA GASPAR ROCHA DE QUIROGA
Published 1783
Sevilla, España

It is understood by all intelligent men that time moves forward in a linear fashion, one moment followed by another, the events of the past firmly situated in the precedent, and as unreachable to modern men as the sun is to the moon.

And yet I observe a disquieting pattern when I construct the lineage of the Sonoros, as I find myself seeing not a line but a recursion. Or, perhaps this is not the correct word. Reversion? I see a return, a perpetual collapsing in of the story: pain begetting pain begetting atrocities begetting recriminations begetting pain begetting pain . . . It is a terrible privilege to see the workings of the world at a remove, at a perspective sufficiently high as to comprehend the grisly mechanics of the whole machine. It is as though a seam had opened up in the thin air and I could glimpse at once the forbidden inner workings of the universe, the world at last unmasked. It is a writhing snake-knot of lies necessitating hierarchy, and rewarding only exploitation, exclusion, and bloodshed. And at the heart of the knot, and written into the instructions for every iteration thenceforth: the Sonoros.

Perhaps then *recursion* is the correct word. The Sonoros are a recurrence throughout time, a malady written into the souls of men, reflected and rotated, but always there and there and there and there.

Time does not move forward. It circles, spirals, pivots, and repeats. Echoes of another's memories live within us, impelling us around and around, ensuring that the story closes itself, that the pattern resounds, that the picture from up high is a shape infinitely repeating.

SEVENTEEN

Out of the corner of his eye Jaime saw walls slide apart like doors, figures dart behind bushes through the open windows, men shrink back into the furniture every time he entered a darkened room and turned on a light. Remedio was gone, but the feeling of him remained. The children complained of nightmares. Elena was in and out of bed with headaches. Before Jaime could stop her, Ignacia brought around a woman from her neighborhood who sprinkled holy water throughout the house. Only Juan Antonio seemed unaffected, apart from the poorly concealed joy he took in Remedio's banishment as well as his own rightness in having prescribed it.

Jaime cursed his foolishness in having let the man into the house, though he forgave himself just a little as he gradually concluded that Remedio had played some sort of trick on them, hypnotizing the entire family. He was not so absurd as to call it a spell—for God's sake, these days they were sending men into outer space—but something about the whole visit was so strange, so outside their normal lives, that it brought Jaime as close to believing in superstition as he'd ever crept. Coupled with the image of the shadow man from Rocha's book, it made his skin crawl to picture Remedio carrying Mito in his arms at the park, to recall him sitting at his dinner table clinking glasses with Elena and the children. He woke often in the night and would make a circuit through the house, testing doors and peering through windows. But though nothing had changed that he could see, the sense of violation would not leave, no matter how many times he reassured himself they were safe.

It was on one of these nightly rounds that he found himself standing in sock feet before the door to his office. The knob turned with a sound that seemed to fill the sleeping house.

He brought the book into the garage and wrapped it in a paper bag. After removing all the garbage from the can, Jaime laid the book carefully at the bottom of the bin and replaced all the other bags on top of it before carrying it out into the alley. He made the sign of the cross and told himself, yet again, that nothing had been right since the book had come to the house, that however much he wanted to finish it, he needed to get rid of it before it could cause any more damage.

But the next morning on his way to retrieve the newspaper, he passed his office door and could tell by the smell that the book was back. He peered inside and saw the damned thing under his green desk lamp, a pad of paper and a pencil beside it.

And so that night Jaime took the book away again, this time walking it six blocks to a greengrocer and tossing it with vengeance into the large dumpster behind the store.

But again the book denied its disposal. Jaime woke early to find it back on his desk under the reading light, his chair pulled out and a pack of Elena's cigarettes open next to a clean ashtray. *Well, why no scotch and slippers?* Jaime found himself asking.

The word *Ignominious*, baroque and gilded, seemed to glow even in the dim early-morning light. The longer he looked, the more it seemed the book watched him. Two almost symmetrical tears halfway down the front cover could be eyes, the publisher's mark in the center could be a nose, the—

Stop it, he told himself. *You're getting silly.*

He didn't try to throw it away again. He woke up Ignacia and told her to put the coffee on and he sat down at his desk, rededicating himself to finishing it with a grim anticipation, a man digging down into a deep hole knowing it contained bodies, but maybe also treasure. And as he read, Jaime also thought of his father sawing their branch from the family tree, and how the old man must have seen the futility in his efforts the day the book arrived.

He finished reading late that night, closing the cover one last time without cheer or satisfaction, but a feeling more like dread. The woman had ended the narrative on such a grim note—without summation and without redemption, an ending so unlike what he had hoped for and had, through decades of film-going, been trained to expect—that Jaime sat in his desk chair and, for once, lit one of Elena's cigarettes and pulled on it long and hard, wondering what the point of it all was.

"I told you not to read it," Juan Antonio said the next morning at breakfast, Jaime's disappointment a gray murk in the dining room. "I hope you're satisfied now."

Jaime half heard him as he pushed his fork through his eggs, but couldn't bring himself to eat.

"It's almost as though she died midsentence," Jaime said later that morning to Elena while she thumbed through magazines. "If you could read the last page—it's like someone watching the light disappear from the world, knowing it'll never return. I just keep thinking about how she seemed so different from the beginning of the book to the end. How she seemed to have lost something of herself, or how the story had become so perverted, she was unable to wrestle it back into whatever she'd intended."

"And what do you think she intended?"

Jaime sighed, because he thought he absolutely understood her intentions. "She wanted to understand evil. And she wanted to know if people can be better than they are. But she never could answer these questions because they're too large. She was like a painter trying to make a picture of all the known world."

"Then how do you think she should have gone about it?" She paused a second before she continued. "Do you remember when we visited the Orsay? How you found me crying over the Morisot painting of the mother with her baby? I found such loneliness in that painting, such—such—disconnection in the eyes of that woman looking down at her sleeping child."

Jaime could hear her throat clench with the effort of not crying now, and he put his arms around her and kissed her warm cheek.

"It felt like that one small thing was standing in for everything," Elena continued. "That was apparent to anyone with their heart open enough to receive the message."

"So what are you saying? That I should try to adapt a little piece of the book to the screen?"

Elena was quiet a moment. The morning sunlight backlit the serene contours of her face—her upturned nose, the perfect curve of her full lips—and he was struck as always by the wisdom that lived inside her. "Would you say your father is evil?" she finally asked.

"No," Jaime said with a little shake. "No. Stubborn, closed-off, old-fashioned. But not evil."

"Well, something prevented the transfer of evil from one generation to the next. It's as though the disease was stopped in its tracks. But why?"

Jaime chewed the inside of his cheek. "Rocha ended her book on such a bleak note because she couldn't see far enough into the future. She couldn't find a resolution because she didn't have enough time."

EIGHTEEN

You had him. You had him. Every one of the horse's footfalls beat a rhythm in Antonio's mind, one refrain repeated kilometer after kilometer: *You had him. You had him.* The farther he rode from Mexico, the more Antonio began to worry. Something sat in his stomach, gnawing, telling him he'd made a grievous error.

He waged war inside of himself. He was still riding in loose, looping circles, both searching for signs of the Rangers and trying to avoid detection himself. He stuck to a game trail that was also used by spotty bands of Mexican Kickapoo. They were happy to trade gossip and guns for food, though Antonio soon learned the truth was hard to pin down: According to rumors, the Rangers were looking for him in Austin, in Brownsville, El Paso, and New Mexico. He was told the posse numbered five hundred, seven hundred, even a thousand men, that the reward for his capture had jumped to thirty—no, forty—no, fifty thousand dollars. The posse was just here; the posse was headed south. It began to seem that giving Antonio conflicting accounts of his own pursuit was some sort of ongoing entertainment to the hunters before they retreated into their winter wickiups. But one thing was clear: The massacre at the ranch had been pinned to him. He was now a train robber, an arsonist, and a child murderer.

"But no one from around here would believe that," one man told him. He introduced himself as Shem, he wore dungarees patched with fox fur, and he spoke with a soft and sympathetic voice that reminded Antonio painfully of Hugo. "The Babbotts—they've been after that ranch for years. Looks like they finally paid someone enough to get the family off the land."

Shem looked at Antonio with pity, and he offered him a corn-husk cigarette, which Antonio took with great appreciation. "Yeah, man, you're pretty much fucked," Shem continued, lighting his own, "if you got that lunatic Casoose after you.

"They call him the Bandit Butcher," he said. "He used to be a rancher down around Matamoros, see. A while back he came home to find his wife and his daughters murdered—all of them. He didn't move or talk for weeks. Everyone thought he would stay like that forever. But then one day he got on his horse and disappeared. No one heard from him, see, until stories started to come out—horrible stories of men strung up in trees, their heads cut off and their bodies hung along the road. They said he was poisoning water wells. Everyone's horses and cattle started breaking out in boils—Old Testament stuff, you know? He wanted to punish not just the men who murdered his family, but everyone. Everyone had to pay. The Mexican government tried to catch him, but he was too good. Then when he came into Texas to buy guns, who do you think courted him to join the Rangers? So now he's official—gets to kill people for a living. But he's never stopped making everyone pay." Shem took one last draw on his cigarette before he pinched it out. "If he's after you, it's like I said: you're fucked."

Antonio gave him five squirrels and rode away burning. So he was enemy number one, the boogeyman embodying Texas's collective guilts and fears, and it was all a cover-up for a land grab. And Casoose—his reasons be damned—was no more than the white man's enforcer.

But as he rode, as the game trail petered into nothing, as the hunters disappeared along with the roads and he found himself alone and armed in the vastness of western Texas, the flame inside him that he stoked regularly with appeals to honor and vengeance, justice and manhood, and always, and always, violence, began to flicker and wane. Days bled into one another. The sun grew redder and the nights longer and sometimes if he crested a brief hill at just the right moment of sunset the whole world would look like molten gold, like Cibola in the eyes of Coronado. Then the earth would turn and the sun would sink and the entire sheen would disappear—the sky was gray and the dirt and the trees were gray and he would sink into a bitter depression. He'd wake up and find himself still on the horse, still moving. He thought he'd been in Texas for years, that he'd always been there, that the entire state was a figment, a puzzle, a giant labyrinth designed to keep him circling forever, running again and again into dead ends, all slightly different, but every one terminal.

He felt like tearing his hair out when he finally reached a road and saw a sign pointing to Eagle Pass and discovered he was little more than a day's ride from the border. He'd completed a giant circle, northeast and then south again, ending up almost back at Rancho Los Ybarras. He was too tired and afraid to attempt a guess at how long this diversion had taken him. A few days, a few weeks? When he didn't know where he was going or who he was following, he supposed it made no difference.

It was here, paused on the road, that he saw the first newspaper. The broadsheet was blown against a rock and urgently flapping in the prairie wind. "Wanted!" it screamed in letters a hand tall. Beneath the fold was a badly drawn caricature of him, a snake-eyed villain with a hideous scar who was described as having not only murderous appetites, but an insatiable craving for the white flesh of "Caucasian lovelies." Antonio laughed without cheer and crumbled the paper and dropped it to the ground, only to find five more blowing about the brush before sunset. The next day the newspapers were everywhere, stranded in trees, tangled in branches, nailed to fence posts. The closer he drew to Mexico the stronger was the wind, and it blew in more and more newspapers to twist around the horse's ankles and slow his progress.

Antonio had almost reached Eagle Pass, planning to find someone there who could give him information, hearsay, any kind of clue that he could follow, when the horse stepped over a rotted log and put his two front feet in a writhing nest of scorpions. The horse shrieked and reared, and Antonio jumped off before the animal could throw him. He ordered the horse to settle, but it was only growing wilder. Its gums whitened, its upper lip curled, and its eyes widened in fear. Finally it bolted, leaving Antonio in the brush under the rattling leaves. A mockingbird alighted on a palo verde and sang its indifferent song, *Chee dee, chee dee.*

He peered over the rotten log at the scorpions and cursed the damned horse for not having stepped a meter to the right or the left. *Chee dee, chee dee, ree lever, lever, lever.* He felt a tickle on the back of his neck and brought up his hand to scratch it, when something spiteful bit him and for a second the pain blinded him red. A scorpion had dropped down on him from a tree. Antonio responded by drawing his gun and firing five, six, seven times into the nest before he staggered away and tried to find somewhere safe to rest. He ended up next to a boulder and some scrawny mesquites, and he checked the ground for signs of snakes or other nasties before he sat down. The back of his neck throbbed with surprising pain, and the bite being where it was, there was nothing Antonio could do but wait for it to subside. He sat there growing drowsy in the midafternoon sun, and was buffeted by more newspapers, which seemed to issue straight from a printing press to him, their urgent message flung by the wind again and again at his body. *Wanted! Wanted! Wanted!*

He wasn't going to let this stop him. If he didn't have a horse, he'd crawl to Eagle Pass. He got on his hands and knees and tried to ignore the pain in his neck, spread now up the base of his skull and down to his shoulders. It felt like he crawled for hours before his arms gave out. The mockingbird had changed its song. Before Antonio closed his eyes, it whistled low and sang, for Antonio only, *You had him. You had him.*

NINETEEN

When he awoke he thought it was night, but on pushing himself to sitting, Antonio discovered it was still day and that in his sleep he'd been completely papered over. "The Most Dangerous Man in Texas!" the newspaper now screamed. "Armed and extremely violent, any citizen suspecting they have run into the dread Tragabalas is advised to take cover immediately and alert law enforcement. If necessary, lethal action is authorized. 'We figure he hid out at the Ybarra ranch and then killed those poor people when they discovered him on their property,' said Captain Cyrus Fish, commander of the Frontier Battalion. 'We need to eliminate this predator. Every day he lives and roams the streets of Texas is another day the men, women, and children of this state are unsafe.'" Antonio skimmed the rest of the article, about to wad it up and leave it to bleach and dissolve in the sun, when his eye caught on a final quote from Fish: "'. . . rumored in the vicinity of Espantosa Lake, and so that's where we're headed. By God, if he's out there, I will catch him.'"

Antonio had to read the line several more times before he dropped the newspaper onto the ground. The lake was close—a day, a day and a half at most. He was only one man, and lightly armed at that, against who knew how many men besides the Ranger, but Antonio was not overly worried about odds. This was his chance. Providence had, at last, pointed him in the right direction, though he had to wonder at the strange machinations of fate—Espantosa Lake was, other than the Río Bravo, the only body of water he could recall that was known for a fact to be haunted. The name, Espantosa, meant "haunted by horrors," and had been called thus by some Spaniards who'd camped there two centuries before. Legends abounded of phantom wagons and wolf-girls, but another less-known story held that the bottom of the lake was an entrance to Hell, a side door for the devil as he rounded the globe collecting souls. Of course the supposed mouth of Hell would be somewhere in Texas, Antonio thought with bitter humor. And of course his journey would take him there.

He'd walked a couple of kilometers in the direction of the lake, following an overgrown trail that skirted an enormous stand of nopales, when he rounded a bend and found a giant white mare quietly chewing tunas and blocking his path. He jumped back upon seeing her, mistaking her for a bull. She was squat and thick and muscled beyond anything he'd ever seen on a horse. Her legs looked like they could not possibly support her bulk, which bulged and bunched about her chest and upper thighs, her skin glistening like a cooked turkey. He doubted she could move with all that girth, though when he patted her gently and climbed on her back and she trotted off down the road with him holding gently to her mane, he saw that her gait was smooth and had a slow cadence like a horse half her size. And because of her bulk he found it was not too uncomfortable to ride her without a saddle. He took the prayer card that Cielita had given him out of his pocket and kissed it.

She was well-fed and clearly had been worked and trained by a skillful owner. Antonio decided she must be a draft horse of some exotic European breed, though it was curious that she had no brand, no bridle path, no sores or markings, no indication of having ever worn a saddle or a bit or a harness or anything. She seemed as brand-new as if she'd simply appeared there in the brush, quiet and still, for the sole purpose of ferrying Antonio more quickly to Espantosa Lake. And upon realizing this he stopped the horse and climbed down off her back.

"No hay manera," he said out loud, backing away from the mare and brushing himself off in case some of her dark magic clung to him. "The devil sent you to bring me to him. Well, no thank you. I'll walk." He set off and could hear the horse following him, and so he turned around and swatted her with a broken branch and shouted at her to get away and find someone else to haunt. The horse only looked at him with sweet brown eyes under long lashes. He struck her again, but she would not budge. "¡Vete a la chingada!" He turned around again, but as soon as he started walking he heard the heavy beat of her hooves behind him. He pulled out his gun and shoved it between her eyes. "I'll do it, by God," he whispered. "I'll send you right back to your master." But after a few seconds of horse and man blinking at one another, he put the gun back in his belt, for he was afraid to see whether the bullet would enter the horse's skull, or not.

Well, I am haunted by a ghost horse, he thought grimly as he mounted her again. *Perhaps I won't have to worry about her stopping to eat.*

But she did eat, and quite often. She would lope for a couple of kilometers and then stop to munch brown buffalo grass. After doing this several times, Antonio kicked her and told her she could eat later, but she only flicked her egg-white tail at his words and continued her meal, and after several attempts he gave up and decided he didn't have the energy to correct her bad behavior. It was better than walking.

He eventually saw the virtue in her method, though, as she continued carrying him at the same jaunty pace all day. "I'm going to call you Candida," he said after a while, choosing a flouncy, romantic name that seemed wholly at odds with her bulky frame, and the juxtaposition amused him.

After a while the land finally dipped down toward a shallow creek. Antonio let Candida drink and he took off his boots and waded in up to his knees, splashing himself all over with water and feeling how good it was on his chapped lips, his dust-matted hair. For just a second he watched the sunlight dapple the leafy water and he could forget where and what he was as the light gathered and split apart in the gentle current, a hundred tiny explosions like little stars living and dying, born and born again, the cycle never ending.

There was a groan of wagon wheels and Antonio pulled himself and the horse into the trees and watched, his hands ready, but it was just an old farmer returning from market, his wagon emptied of whatever he'd gone to sell, and now freighted with only burlap sacks and a couple of clucking hens.

"Despierta," the farmer said, clapping his hand against the side of the wagon. Someone stirred inside the bed—a gray hat, a faded bandana worn high up over the man's face, and a dandy tie, red as the dawn.

Antonio watched Peter Ainsley shake himself awake and, after yawning and thanking the farmer, climb down out of the wagon and saunter over to the creek.

"Hey, idiot," Antonio said, stepping carefully out of the trees, "anyone ever tell you that tie looks like a big target around your neck?"

"By God, by God!" Peter exclaimed. He clasped Antonio and Antonio allowed it. The strength of Peter's arms and the urgency with which he held him touched something in Antonio he hadn't realized was there.

"I've been in and out of the damned brush looking for you for weeks," Peter said. "That family at the ranch—I couldn't get them out of my head. I spent two nights in Mexico, but I had this awful feeling those bastards were going to fix the crime on you. Have you seen the papers? It's damned insanity. You're enemy number one."

"Don't mean nothing," Antonio lied.

Peter looked somber. "You were right," he said. "I have been playing pretend. I've been running around having my fun, and when things got grave my instinct was to dash off to the next good time. It was unforgivable and I am sorry.

"You were also right about going after the Rangers," Peter continued. "Until I saw those children, I just didn't—well, I've been a fool. And it's grave out there. In Eagle Pass they shot and killed a man coming out of a cantina because someone thought he looked like you. Same thing in San Antonio. This madness has to end. When I read in the paper that Fish was headed to Espantosa I knew you'd be on your way there, posthaste."

He held out his hand to Antonio, who looked at it, pale and clean. "I'm sorry. I'll not desert you again. We are brothers," Peter said. "Until the end."

Antonio hesitated, his mind stuck on *brothers*. So much weight for such a small word.

"Hasta el final," Antonio finally said, and he shook Peter's hand and pulled him close for a second embrace, enjoying this brief comfort, knowing he was not alone.

He whistled to Candida and as the horse emerged from the brush she gave Peter such a start that he almost stumbled back into the shimmering creek.

"The bloody hell—" Peter began. "That thing looks like she ate two horses."

"She's ugly, but she can move."

"I suppose I'll be needing a horse as well . . ." And Peter and Antonio looked over at the farmer, who'd fallen asleep sitting up in the wagon's seat, his open-mouthed snores soft as down. Without waking the old man, they unharnessed one of his horses. Peter placed thirty American dollars in the farmer's front pocket, and under cover of birds singing to bring the night, they went east to Espantosa Lake and whatever waited there, man or devil.

TWENTY

It was while playing his guitar, tinkering up and down with a little melody—a question that opened with A minor, grew sadder and less resolved in D minor, climaxed at E7, and then finally was resolved back to A minor—that Jaime finally had an idea.

Beyond the iron gates of Estudios Churubusco, beyond the sound-stages and administrative buildings and a water tower the color of boiled corn, was a squat concrete building where the studio housed its film archives, as well as old newsreel footage, trade magazines on microfilm, and a small library containing histories of costume design, the works of Shakespeare and Euripides, books of formulas for explosions, fake gore, miracle hair remover and, to Jaime's interests, songbooks containing corridos from all over the country, going back to the War of Independence. He'd used them on occasion when he wanted inspiration for a particular character—the old songs could sometimes provide unique turns of phrase, or describe certain attributes of bygone folk heroes. All of Mexican history was contained in these songs, passed orally through communities until someone bothered to write them down. As Jaime ran his finger up and down the browned and broken spines, he thanked God for the dull little chap in spectacles who must've long ago thought it might be a good idea for the movie studio to have a complete record.

There were several volumes of Tamaulipan music from before the Revolution, hundreds of pages of ballads to beautiful women, brave bull-fighters, devoted mothers, and dogged mule skinners. There were songs about smugglers and bandidos, too, songs about lost land, broken prom-ises, stealing back stolen cattle, and the brave journey from Texas across the river, lifesaving provisions and medicines in tow. Jaime skimmed it all, hoping for a miracle.

He was starting to get tired and the clerk had just warned him that the building would be closing in fifteen minutes when he finally let out a little whoop: He'd maybe found his treasure.

"El Corrido de Antonio Sonoro, El Tragabalas." It was one page long and contained no musical notation or tablature, listed no composer. It was only lyrics and a crude little engraving of a bandido wearing a sombrero and bandoliers, his face mostly obscured by a wide, black mustache, and a skeleton in an identical sombrero, the two figures with one arm around the other, Tragabalas holding a bottle of tequila, about to take a drink.

> *Where he comes from, no one knows.*
> *Where he's going, he won't tell.*
> *If you see el Tragabalas,*
> *You'd better say farewell.*
> *A friend to the forgotten,*
> *Enemy to the state,*
> *His knife, it brings the sweetest justice,*
> *His hands will seal your fate.*

Could this be it, his Rosetta stone? Was this Antonio el Tragabalas his grandfather? His missing piece? If his grandfather had been a bandido, and a fearsome one it looked like, then that went some of the way to ex-plain why Juan Antonio had kept him a secret—shame perhaps? Fear that Jaime would idolize his grandfather and follow his example?

> *From Del Rio to old Dorado,*
> *The Rangers' guns were all around.*

But their bullets went right through him.
Only his shadow could hold him down.

For a second Jaime went cold all over, his eyes lingering on the word *shadow*. He skimmed the rest of the song, but that was the only mention, the rest of the verses a tribute to El Tragabalas's wiles, his skill with a gun, his general machismo and bravado. It was a story of a man who'd gone to Texas to right a wrong, and there found himself trapped by the Texas Rangers. They had a gunfight; he escaped with only a scar. But while the Rangers continued to pursue him across the state, they burned villages to the ground, lynched farmers in trees, and terrorized any Mexican unlucky enough to cross their path. Still, El Tragabalas sought his vengeance. The last lines narrated his death, a poetic and fitting end to a smuggler's life, drowning while crossing the Río Bravo.

The water lashed; the wind, it howled.
The river took him down to its bed.
Now Tragabalas is just a memory,
With deeds undone, and words unsaid.

Jaime had to sit back a minute and take it all in. There it was, a whole life on the page. How many times had he driven past the studio's archive building, even rifled through these same stacks, not knowing his own grandfather might be lying in wait just inside?

He had the clerk make several copies of the song and he left the library with purpose, making his heels land hard on the asphalt.

That night at home over dominoes, Jaime could no longer contain himself.

"Pop, I need to ask you something," Jaime ventured.

This was their first game since the Remedio intrusion, and Jaime was hoping his father was inspired to good spirits. He quickly recounted finding the song, though he couched it as a fortuitous discovery while doing research for a part—"The luckiest goddamned coincidence," he said. "Is that him? Was he your father?" And when Juan Antonio said nothing,

Jaime pivoted his focus. "So I understand why you wouldn't want to tell me about him. I remember you said once you kept safe by keeping quiet—if you were a killer I don't think I'd be shouting it from the rooftops, either. But I think the story is so much more than that, than him being a bad guy, I mean. It's about vengeance and justice and history and, well, all of it. So I'm asking you, if I adapt this into a movie—I mean, I think I'm pretty set that I'm going to do it—but what I want to know is, do I have the right man? And if yes, do I have your blessing? What do you say? Can I make a movie about your father?"

Juan Antonio had been listening to his son's story with a stone face. Now he finished the cigarette he was smoking and stubbed it out in the glass ashtray. Picking up his opening domino, for he'd been dealt the double five, he looked up at Jaime with the same grim expression he'd been using for over forty years to wield authority over his son.

"If you write this movie, I will never speak to you again," he said, and he laid the tile sharply on the table.

PART THREE

BECOMING LIGHT

TWENTY-ONE

As they neared the lake, signs of the posse were everywhere: hoofprints, broken branches, discarded cartridge boxes, and wads of greasy waxed paper. Antonio stopped often to listen, but he and Peter seemed to be a day or so behind Fish and his men. There was nothing in the air but birdsong.

At sundown the wind changed direction, now blowing down from the north. The moon hung yellow over the landscape, banked by clouds on either side that swallowed the stars and dropped the temperature so abruptly Antonio realized his hands had gone numb around the reins before they even felt cold. Soon he and Peter exhaled white clouds with every breath.

Antonio thought they must be nearly at the lake, when a shrill scream ripped open the night.

"Only an owl," Antonio whispered, though this one had a distinctly feminine pitch to its cry. They went forward a few steps and the scream came again. "Let's tie the horses here," he said. "We can sneak up and see how many there are."

They came on silent feet under the drooping boughs of a willow tree. A wispy fog hung over the water and only over the water, like the accumulation of a hundred nightmares. Under the jaundiced light of the harvest moon everything took on an ominous appearance: the black shore twisted with vines and mesquite trees, fallen limbs that reached out of the water like hands. The scream came again and this time Antonio saw the white body of a barn owl stark against the night sky. And just as quickly as the barn owl flew across the sky, the moon was shoved aside, swallowed by clouds that took not only the light but the sound, and a silence fell over the lake as though every ant and every leaf turned their faces in fear.

He didn't see the posse, but he could sense them, almost hear them, as though the wind blowing through the trees whispered of foreign bodies, resenting the presence of each man within. He signaled with his finger for Peter to follow him, and they slunk behind the broad trunk of a live oak, whose branches thrust low and wild and reminded Antonio of Medusa's head of snakes. They would wait out the posse there, pick them off, hope Fish made a mistake.

While he was squatting and trying to see into the trees on the other side of the lake, something struck the end of Antonio's nose. He reeled back on his heels, for though he might have been expecting a bullet, he was certainly not expecting a fat, cold raindrop. He even brought his fingers to touch the water and see if it was real. He held them close to his face and inspected them in the dark and it was indeed rain, that promise withheld so long he no longer believed it existed. A few seconds after the initial salvo the shower began in earnest, until every sound was the *pat-tat-tat* of water hitting leaves. He put his face up into the downpour and let the miracle fall over him, forgetting the cold for a moment. He hoped the storm had already passed through Dorado, that Jesusa and the children had danced in it with palms open to Heaven.

The rain fell harder. Antonio and Peter were soaked in a few minutes, and Antonio's teeth chattered. There was no shelter to be found other than the trees. Their only option was to try and find a better tree under which to squat, and it was when they were turning and squinting and searching for something to get under, that lightning suddenly lit up the sky and Antonio saw Captain Cyrus Fish, watching him from atop a rock twenty meters away.

He looked like a ghost, his face hollow and pale. Their eyes met in the

instant of the lightning flash, and the Ranger's face was both fearful and resigned. The look on his face said, *Well, here it is.*

Fish whistled as the darkness returned and the trees around Antonio and Peter were ripped apart by bullets. The two men flattened themselves on the muddy ground while the gunfire hailed, but Fish whistled again and ordered his men to stand down.

"Hold your fire!" he shouted into the pouring rain. "Get ready. Aim!"

Antonio scuttled behind a different tree, while Peter plunged left along the shore of the lake, trying to catch the posse from a better angle. Antonio crouched and waited for the next lightning strike, which came a minute later. Fish and his men were also apparently waiting for the lightning—as soon as the light flashed, bullets rained again. Antonio ducked and returned fire, though it was dark by the time he did and he'd just wasted his bullets. He moved a little farther away, hugging the trees, and waited for the light to come again. A flash, shots fired, the rifles spitting orange flame, and then darkness. The lightning strikes were getting closer together as the storm crescendoed. Thunder began to accompany the lightning, starting with a long, crackling slide down into an enormous boom that rattled the remaining teeth in Antonio's head. Bullets flew before him into the trees, and he saw with admiration it was Peter, sharpshooting his way into the posse and bringing them down, one by one. With this cover, Antonio tried sprinting to the last place he'd seen Fish, hoping to catch him from behind. He made it to the rock, sliding beside it just as the lightning came again. But in the queer light he saw Fish was now closer to the lake under a bush, visible by the white peak of his hat.

Thunder clattered like boulders over a tin roof. Antonio figured he would press Fish against the water, and so he moved tree to tree, closer to the shore. Antonio copied the Ranger and slid under a bush and peered out into the rain, but when the lightning came again a bullet struck the ground right in front of his face and temporarily blinded him with mud.

"Come out, you coward," Fish shouted over the storm. Antonio could see him running, hugging the perimeter of the lake, which was long and worm-shaped, and he got up and went after him.

"You killed my private," Fish continued, "blew up a train, burned half the waterfront in Corpus Christi."

"That last one was you!" Antonio shouted. He fired and missed.

"I know it was you who killed the policemen in Houston. You killed the Lozano brothers outside Corpus. And I know it was you at the whore-house in Valdez. How much more hell do you have to raise? How many do you have to kill before you're satisfied?"

A thunderclap crashed, sounding as though the world were being torn in half. "Two more," Antonio shouted, and he clipped the Ranger's hat, knocking it off his head.

"Well then, get it over with!" Fish shouted. Antonio fired at him as he saw him pass between two trees, but the Ranger seemed to slip on the wet grass and he disappeared as Antonio's bullet sailed over his head.

"Not if you don't stand still." He heard Fish cough with big rasp-ing sounds like metal scraping metal. He crept closer to the spot where he'd seen the Ranger slip and fall. He was squinting into the trees through the sheeting rain and wasn't looking at the ground, when he found that the earth suddenly dropped away and he was sliding down to the water. He held his gun tight and didn't drop it when he landed in the frigid lake. He tried to kick his way up onto the bank, but something had his foot.

The lake was chest-deep where he'd landed and the water all around him was jumping and foaming in the rain. There were vines cast across the water with dead branches tangled among them so that he'd fallen into a sort of net, the bottom of which was made of catclaws that were noto-rious for snagging people and drowning them. He tried to jerk himself up out of the water but his right foot had gotten shoved somewhere deep in the tangle, and vigorous shaking and yanking could not free him. The lightning strikes were getting so close together the lake was now lit with an almost continuous artificial daylight that gave everything a hysteri-cal sheen of blue. He held his breath and ducked under the water, trying to reach for his knife, but it was inside his boot and impossible for him to reach. He brought his head back out of the water. In the darkness he couldn't see the Ranger, but what he did see slinking through the water in his direction was a long reptilian body, two wide-set red eyes, a ridged

back, and a long tail that moved like a pendulum and seemed to go on forever. Antonio kicked both feet, and this only lodged him deeper in the tangle, but he wasn't able to think of anything but those red eyes. He tore at vines even though he knew they weren't the right ones, even though he knew he was only a rabbit struggling inside a fox's mouth.

A shot fired and then another. The alligator thrashed its tail but turned around, and Peter's hand reached down to Antonio through the darkness. Antonio was finally able to maneuver the knife out of his boot and cut himself free before he grabbed Peter's hand and was pulled to shore.

"Some posse," Peter said as Antonio caught his breath against the split trunk of an elm tree. "By my count Fish only brought ten men with him. I've hit four, and I'm going to lead the last six away from the lake heading east. That'll give you a chance to finish the captain."

"I'll meet you back at the horses," Antonio said, clasping Peter's hand.

"'Once more unto the breach, dear friend,'" Peter said. "'Once more; Or close the wall up with English dead.'"

"I'll see you," Antonio said, releasing his hand, and there passed between the two men a farewell tinged, in Antonio's heart, with regret, as well as an understanding that each man had chosen his path.

"At the horses!" Peter called as he set off back into the trees, the rain and darkness blotting him out.

Antonio climbed back up the bank and looked around for the Ranger and found him by following the sound of a coughing fit that ended with Fish throwing up on the sand at Antonio's boots. By the white glow of a sideways bolt of lightning Antonio could see that it was mostly blood. The Ranger wiped his mouth on his sleeve and stood up straight to face Antonio. The storm was finally passing, the rain letting up a little and the thunder chasing west.

"I wouldn't have believed in ten lifetimes things woulda ended like this." Fish started laughing, but this segued quickly into more coughing. Antonio pitied the man, though he made no motion to slap him on the back or otherwise help. "Why?" Fish was bent over and struggling to get out the words, but he turned his head and spoke into the rain that continued to fall. "Why are you here? Why didn't you go back?" He straightened and blood dribbled down his chin. "If you'd run back to Mexico I might never have found you. Why are you here? Why?" And at this he grabbed Antonio's shirt and pushed him away and Antonio was embarrassed for him, for how he was diminished. "Why chase me? I've upheld the law. That's all. Is this how I'm repaid?"

"I had to make things right for my brother." Antonio hadn't planned to speak, hadn't felt he owed the Ranger any explanation or due process when he and especially Hugo hadn't received them. Perhaps it was the state of the shriveled, trembling man before him, who looked to be a day or two from going to sleep and never waking. Or perhaps there was some part of Antonio that wanted to hear his explanation spoken aloud, to view it away from the slippery contours of his own mind. He took out his pistol, made sure there was a bullet in the chamber.

If Fish noticed the gun, he gave no sign. "I suppose you're after Casoose next," he said. "Well, I can't blame you there." Fish gave him a strange look, as though even now his loyalty to the star might outlive him. "He's been known to hide up in the caves outside Brackettville," he said. "But if you go up there, don't expect to come back."

Gunshots sounded far off, Peter and the posse exchanging fire. Fish took off his hat and wiped his brow and looked up to the rain, letting it fall across his drawn face. "I haven't seen my wife in four months," he said. "I told her when I left, I said, 'I cannot choose how I am to die, but I can choose where.' And now that I'm here all I want is to be home in my bed." He looked at Antonio and his eyes were deep pockets of grief. "Pride has ruined me far more than disease," he said, "and so I fear it has ruined you as well. I'm sorry. I've made a terrible mistake."

"No!" But Antonio's objection was moot. Fish drew his own pistol and put it in his mouth and fired at the same moment one final bolt of lightning ignited the sky, so that his livid expression as the bullet breached his skull was illuminated and hung in the air even after his body dropped to the ground.

Antonio looked at the Ranger captain in the diminishing rain with fury, hating Fish for using his last moment to rob him of the ability to fulfill his vow. This was the man whose face burned nightly under Antonio's eyelids before sleep? This wet pile of bones and rags? Antonio kicked the body, and when nothing happened he kicked it again, kicking it until it rolled down the bank to the water and the alligators. Fish landed with his head under the water, and Antonio stood over him and waited for his blood to lure the dark-hearted monsters. And when even they failed to give him some kind of conclusion, he was left to turn his anger at himself, for what did he expect? Had he believed Hugo would float down from Heaven and give thanks? No, he told himself, he needed to snap out of it. The Ranger had chosen the coward's way out, but he was gone just the same. He had only one man standing between him and absolution.

The sound of gunshots brought Antonio out of his fury and he followed it up the bank and into the tangled trees. Three, four, five bodies lay across his path, facedown and faceup, their open mouths and open palms filling with rain. A volley of bullets peppered the ground around him and Antonio dove under the droop of a weeping willow. Inside he was unable to tell where the shots had come from, and so he stayed behind the trunk and waited, feeling each heartbeat pulse in his neck and the tips of his fingers.

More gunshots, now farther away.

Antonio crept out from under the willow but stayed inside the cover of the brush, moving slowly and soundlessly toward the battle.

.22-caliber reports, vicious pops dampened by wet leaves and the splintering of tree trunks, tore open the night. Antonio caught a glimpse of an orange muzzle flash. He turned and fired, but his shot was answered tenfold and he had to dive for cover again.

In the darkness, he could make out some rocks, an open space, and what looked to be the remnants of a long-abandoned homestead. Antonio had just crawled to the edge of a dilapidated stone wall, hoping to use it as cover, when Peter's overseer whistle caught Antonio off guard. He was quick to intuit its meaning—he ducked before a tremendous gun blast blew a hole in the stone wall where his head had just been. He crawled through the mud back to the safety of the trees with his ears still ringing.

Before long Peter crashed into the empty space beside him.

"This feels familiar," he said.

"No ice factory this time," Antonio quipped.

"This man's good. I'd say he could thread a needle with that damn Winchester."

"Don't tell me you're outmatched."

Peter gave him an unimpressed look. "I didn't say I couldn't hit him."

"Then what are you waiting for, whitey?"

"I'll remind you we could be in Manzanillo right now. Up to our ears in tits and mango juice."

"Next shoot-out, okay?"

The firefight continued through the black night. One man would fire and two men would answer, on and on. Antonio was getting drowsy, daylight less than an hour away, when he heard a sound across the clearing—leaves quaking, branches snapping.

"Thinks he can climb to safety, does he?" asked Peter.

He fired up into the trees, again and again, two pistols in tandem, slowly emerging from the brush and stepping into the clearing, still firing up into the leaves.

He fired until both pistols were empty and then he stood, tensed, his tie undone and his suit wet and mud-bogged. He cupped one hand to his ear, his other arm outstretched as if he were about to take a bow, waiting for the inevitable thud of a body falling to the ground.

Antonio stood up, about to congratulate him, when a single shot sounded and Peter was struck in the chest—the blow so strong it spun him a half turn sideways before he fell.

Antonio breathed hard through his nose, daring the son of a bitch to come out. But no one did, as if no one was there at all.

After more than an hour with no sound and no movement, Antonio, figuring the shooter for dead, walked to Peter and said a prayer as he stood over him: *He sent more motherfuckers to Hell than even I did. Take care of him.* He cleaned the mud from Peter's face and hands, and folded his fingers together across his chest. Then he broke off a sturdy branch from a tree and took out his knife and started carving words into it. He finished it just as he realized the sun had risen. He looked around him and the trees were lavender, the mud a glittering gray. The birds twittered morning songs in cheerful oblivion. He stuck the branch in the ground next to Peter's body, crossed himself. He didn't figure Peter cared about having his body returned to his family in England, but Antonio knew his friend would want the record straight about who he was. On the branch he'd left but a simple epitaph to be inscribed in granite by whoever found him: *Peter Ainsley: The Gentleman Assassin.*

He felt a shadow pass over him. Antonio stood up with his pistol out to watch two men, their backs to him and one of whom had Peter's same sandy hair, walk straight into the lake. Antonio blinked and looked again, but there was nothing there, not a ripple. Then, at the far shore, one of the men emerged and kept on walking into the trees.

Antonio followed at a run, his pistol still out. The man never turned around or broke his pace. Antonio ran faster, shouting after him, trying to catch up. He didn't feel his boots slipping in the mud, didn't feel the wet leaves slapping his cheeks. He came to the edge of the tree line and stopped abruptly: a vast field of Bermuda onions, rows upon rows of foot-high emerald stalks, stretched from his toes to the horizon with surreal and unbroken exactitude.

The man was already far away, heading east. Antonio pulled the hammer back on the pistol, but he didn't fire, feeling some trick was being played on him, that dealings that centered on him but of which he had no say were taking place above and around him as though he were a child too small to see what transpired at the kitchen table. The enormity and the greenness of the onion field, after six years of drought, made him sick. In that moment he felt lost and alone and far from home. The world he'd known, the world his ancestors had seized and shaped and hammered into submission was being seized again and erased and remade under his feet, and he could do nothing to stall its progress, only stand and wait for the tide to carry him away, too.

TWENTY-TWO

"Do you know how many people he killed?" Juan Antonio's voice, though quiet, shook with rage, rage that Jaime felt was directed not only at him for daring to push the issue, but back decades at Tragabalas as well. "He shouldn't be glorified—he should be forgotten, forever. Do you hear me, boy? I will not forgive you if you do this. There will be no going back."

"But if you'll just listen to what I have in mind—"

"If you think you're going to use our family to get rich, or to get out of your little comedies—"

Jaime's eyes went wide. "My little comedies?" he repeated, and he sat back against the plush dining room chair and avoided his own gaze reflected in the patio doors.

"You think I don't know you want to be like Infante? Negrete? John Wayne? What was that last picture you made? *The Rooster Goes to Mars*? And the one before that? About the witch with the lasso?"

"*The Rooster and La Malina's Curse*," Jaime muttered, hearing the inanity of his movie career in every syllable.

"This is the life you built for yourself," Juan Antonio said, derision in his voice. "You make silly movies that people obviously like. And now you live in a big mansion and drive a new car and you make your children learn to speak French so they can recite poetry with the other eggheads. You have everything you ever wanted. Why change things?"

Jaime excused himself and, after grabbing a bottle of whiskey from the cabinet in the kitchen, went upstairs to bed, swallowing two aspirin down with the Cutty Sark. What hurt as much as his father's scorn was his absolute discernment of Jaime's motivations. It was true: Jaime often felt like a hack, and he looked upon this story as a way to make himself a more credible actor, to leave behind at least one film of import, something that might outlast fickle public infatuation. And Jaime felt profoundly silly, a feeling all the more penetrating for knowing his father believed him silly, too. He fell asleep open-mouthed with his clothes on. The mostly empty bottle was upright on the floor, and the bedside lamp shone through it to create a gold coin reflection on the snowy carpet.

The next morning Jaime took four more aspirin to quell his headache, and sat down at his desk, the old man be damned. In an hour he had a good outline: three acts, forty scenes, a heroic ride into the sunset on the final page. His Bullet Swallower was handsome and heroic, funny and smart. He had the bravado of Pancho Villa, the doggedness of Gregorio Cortez, the dauntless energy of Juan Cortina, and he owned the hearts of the people like Emiliano Zapata. The picture grew clear in his mind as though he watched it on-screen. Tragabalas was vain but selfless, cruel but judicious, braggadocious but knew when to stay quiet, a virtuous hacendado who'd lost his fortune and subsisted in noble poverty. And the cast was all there—a hero, a villain, a bruja, a sidekick, a sacrificing wife—everything required for a satisfying story. He pulled the cover off the type-writer and began.

```
In a little village on the banks of the Río Bravo, at
a time when men were fierce by necessity and women
loved just as fiercely . . .
```

Jaime had been in the movie business a long time and he knew what would make an audience fall in love. The secret, he knew, was that people watched movies to see themselves up on the screen. Jaime put himself into every character, every line, knowing that if he made the movie a true reflection of himself, it would in turn reflect a little bit of everyone else, too.

When he was finished for the day he took up his guitar and began playing with the corrido, fitting the words to the chords and changing them as needed to better reflect the events of his story. When he came to the word *shadow*, his finger slipped on the B string and it snapped and bit his hand. Looking down at the broken string curling in on itself, Jaime remembered—Maria Rocha had said it, hadn't she? Time moved in a spiral. Not a line. A spiral. Meaning Remedio could be following Jaime in Mexico City in 1964. And at the same time he could be following Antonio decades before.

Jaime stood up so quickly he dropped the guitar on the floor, where it landed with an off-color twang. He recalled Rocha's words about a seam opening up in the universe and through it glimpsing something forbidden. His eyes swam at the truth he was trying to apprehend. Remedio was following Jaime and Antonio simultaneously, flitting from one time and place to another like a bird hopping branches. And he'd maybe been doing this for thousands of years, maybe for all of time. But in the entire recounting of the Sonoros' story, Rocha never mentioned Remedio's name, nor did she ever write of him introducing himself or making himself known in any way. He was a lurker, a dim shadow. Why, then, make his existence known to Jaime?

Jaime reached up to the air in front of his face and moved his fingers gently through it, without understanding what he was even feeling for—perhaps a curtain to withdraw and see Antonio staring back at him? He looked around him as though for the first time, the world at once seeming so thin, so built on illusions. *Maybe this is the key to the Sonoros' evil*, he thought, *that they apprehended what was happening around them. Maybe they figured out the game was rigged and they'd better get what they could, when they could.*

Meditating on this he took his place at the typewriter again, getting back to work.

TWENTY-THREE

North of Brackettville, Antonio saw two large hills in the distance, a mother and a baby one next to the other, and he went there, figuring he must be nearing cave country. The land began a slow ascent as Antonio and Candida mounted the plateau that defined the center of Texas. The trees and shrubs abruptly shrank, mesquites were replaced with ashe junipers, and the air cooled even more. The sun was low and orange, but he had another hour of daylight, and so he spurred the horse on, hoping to camp at the base of the two hills.

There was a driving, bitter wind bearing straight down. His cheeks were numb, his eyes watered, and he'd given up trying to stanch the steady flow from his nose, letting it run down over his mouth and into his patchy beard. He rode like this for as long as he could, focusing on the two hills until his eyes burned from the relentless wind. He turned the horse around so the wind could be at his back for a few moments and that's when he saw the black dot behind him, what looked like a soldier ant marching over the rocky soil. He squinted in the low light but couldn't make out anything other than that the black dot was gaining on him.

Antonio spurred Candida first into a jog and then a run. The wind was blowing so hard he felt they were barely moving and yet eventually the hills grew large before him and when he turned around the black dot had turned from a soldier ant into a flea. He could be anyone, though as Antonio watched, the rider hastened. Antonio apologized to Candida and rode her past the hills. His plan was simple: he'd find a good place to hide and then shoot whoever it was when they came past. Except finding a spot proved difficult. The trees were too short and barren, and after about fifteen minutes, Candida slowed and then stopped. Antonio coaxed her back up to a jog and she obliged for a few minutes, only to stop again. Antonio was close to dismounting and making his stand from behind the horse when they finally reached a little copse of trees that was dense enough for Antonio and the horse to slip inside. It would be obvious that Antonio had chosen to conceal himself there, but he did not have the luxury of surprise.

He left the grateful Candida to eat and chose a good spot behind the forking trunk of an old oak and waited. The sun had set and the sky held only a persimmon glow on one side, a deepening blue on the other. He'd lost sight of the rider, but he was sure they hadn't lost sight of him. The wind slowed and, for the span of a couple breaths, stopped altogether. Antonio sniffed the air to see if he could catch anything—burning wood or gun oil—but there was nothing. He shivered, for the wind was blowing again and without the sun the night was brittle as a dead branch. He held his gun in his lap and stared out into the darkness and flexed his hands to keep them ready.

About twenty minutes after he reached the trees he saw movement to his right and he pointed his gun in that direction. But when he looked through the leaves, expecting to see a man creeping toward him, all he saw was a skinny paint lumbering closer, still wearing his saddle and dragging his reins along the ground.

It was like something bit him in the left shoulder just as he heard the gunshot. Candida whinnied and took off. The tree trunk above him exploded and he threw himself on the ground. He crawled on his belly to another tree and peered out into the darkness, but there was nothing to see. Three more gun blasts, none of which were intended for him. He hoped the horse had enough left in her to run off. Antonio was so angry now he had to force himself to think rationally rather than run screaming out of the trees, firing wildly into the dark. He crawled to another tree near the west-facing edge of the copse. Antonio found himself wishing Peter was with him, offering arrogant assurances. He even wished Hugo was there, giving benediction over their soon-to-be-extinguished souls. He had to run, but where? The darkness promised nothing.

The branches above him rustled and he looked up to see many small gray bodies soaring above. It was a hundred bats out for their hunt. Antonio watched as the bodies kept coming like a river, and he let his eyes follow their path down to a point in the ground that didn't look too far away. He didn't think or even look—he had only seconds and his best hope was that he'd only be shot in the leg. He bolted, sprinting for the place where he'd seen the bats emerge. But the ground was uneven and rocky. He stumbled and almost fell, and when he righted himself he looked at the terrain and could no longer see from where it was he believed the bats had escaped. He heard the blast of another gunshot. Something bit his leg, but he kept running, eyes wildly sweeping the ground for any sign of an opening. More gunshots, but they were just firecrackers against the driving wind. *Pop, pop, pop.* Something pale loomed in front of him that he couldn't see clearly. It looked like a giant tortoise, bigger than a house, lying prone on the ground. He ran closer and felt the beat of wings against his face and ears and suddenly there were so many bats that he had to wave his hand as they battered his eyes, his nose, slamming into him with their warm, lithe bodies. The great tortoise became a giant limestone outcropping under which was the mouth of a cave. Antonio sprinted the last few steps and then dropped and slid the rest of the way, entering the cave feetfirst and terrifying the remaining bats so that for several long seconds he dared not open his eyes or breathe until the frenzy of bodies stopped screeching and scratching him on their way to the night.

It was tar-black inside the cave. Antonio felt around and determined he was on a ledge, though he couldn't tell if the drop off was one meter or a hundred and he couldn't risk lighting a match. He found a small rock and tossed it over, but there was no sound of it hitting the ground. The roughly elliptical opening through which he'd slid was quite small and now he could enjoy the advantage of being unseen as he peered through it, searching for his pursuer, daring him to come anywhere within firing range. He stood there a long time, but nothing stirred.

Gradually his heart slowed and he felt comfortable shifting his weight from one foot to the other and rolling around his stiff neck. And as he relaxed he became aware that the bites in his shoulder and leg were growing from little stings to spreading aches, and that one sock inside his boot felt wet and sticky. He'd been so little aware of his body that he was genuinely shocked to feel around his leg and realize he'd been shot, that there was a .22-caliber bullet inside the fleshy part of his left calf. His shoulder, too, had taken a glancing blow and was bleeding freely.

He was reluctant to pull his eyes from the cave opening, believing somehow his shooter would know he was not watching, but the wound couldn't be ignored. He lowered himself to sitting and gingerly rolled up his pant leg. The wound throbbed, but he ignored it as there was nothing around to make his task easier. He began tugging at the toe and heel of his boot, and this caused him jolts of pain that were so lightning-hot he had to stop and take several breaths before he could begin again. Slowly, slowly he worked the boot down off his leg so he could brush his fingertips around the place where the flesh was peeled open. Taking off the boot had prompted more bleeding and he could feel it running warm down the back of his ankle. He took a deep breath and then stuck a trembling finger into the wound to try find the bullet. It was there, not too far in, but his index finger was too large to coax it out. He dropped his head against the cave wall and breathed quickly through his teeth, and soon, before he could do anything about it, he was crying.

They started as hot, half-formed tears, just water in his eyes. It was nothing, he told himself. His leg hurt like the devil—why wouldn't he cry? But the tears kept coming along with unbidden other things, a thousand bats leaving the cave at once, so fast they were a churning, gray blur. Jesusa came to him and he wept for her because she seemed that she could withstand any blow, but he knew how she cried when she thought he was asleep and it ate at his heart because he was the cause. He wept for his Nicolás, for how he shouted and struck him because Antonio was hard and not soft and anger was easier for him than pulling the boy close and kissing him. He wept for Aura, for how he would one day give her to some other worthless bastard, that her life, like her mother's, was no more hers to direct than a leaf directs the current. He wept for Hugo, how he'd caused such a bright light to extinguish. And he wept for Peter, whose death also hung heavy around his heart. He was so profoundly alone, and it was all of his bitter choosing.

With trembling fingers he brought his hand again to his leg and used his little finger to tenderly dig out the bullet, letting it fall with a tiny clink against the limestone. He tied his bandana around his leg and closed his eyes.

When he awoke the world outside the cave was a shade lighter. Before he stood all the way up he got out his pistol. He listened, but no sound came other than the steady drip of water far down in the cave. As his eyes just cleared the edge of the hole, Antonio saw a pair of gray boots, two grinning eyes, and the sawed end of a massive log.

Before he could even apprehend what was happening the log came swinging. He was struck in the face with a blow that knocked the color from his vision and turned the world blinding white. He was only somewhat aware of going down, downer and downer.

Antonio knew his arm was broken before he opened his eyes. It felt as though an elephant was sitting on his left arm and, with each heartbeat, grinding itself farther down. But despite this he was grateful, firstly because he was alive, secondly because a broken arm could be dealt with, and thirdly because it was his left and not his right. Casoose was a crazy fool to shove him down into a hole and expect him to die.

But when he opened his eyes it was Casoose's two glittering black pupils that greeted him, and a cheerful mouth of white teeth out of which poured a smell like a brimming chamber pot. He was wearing a wolf skin, the animal's head nestled next to his own, with its mouth open in a final, toothy howl. Flies orbited both heads.

"Where's your master?" Antonio asked in Spanish. If he couldn't fight at least he could humiliate him.

But Casoose refused to play. "Get up," he said in English. "Start walking."

Antonio rolled onto his right side and struggled to his knees, for he couldn't let Casoose see how he hurt, and said in a voice that was muy chingón, "Did you forget how to speak Spanish?" He stood up and the pull of gravity on his broken arm sent all new kinds of pain screaming through him. He bit his lip and took a step, grateful he could do that much.

"Mexicans are children of a whore," Casoose said. "God willing, those volcanos down south explode and drown the whole country." He lit a torch and shoved Antonio's bad shoulder toward a chamber to his right.

Antonio hissed, but did not cry out. "And you'll watch from this side of the river, I suppose. What the hell kind of name is Casoose? Is your name Jesus and the idiot Rangers couldn't pronounce it? Speaking of them, where is your jefe?" Knowing the Ranger disavowed his own heritage meant Antonio took extra pleasure in speaking to him in Spanish. "Or didn't anyone tell you? What was his name? Guppie? Carp? I followed that bled calf down to Espantosa and I watched his brains paint the ground."

"You chatter like a woman," Casoose said. "Someone must have told you a long time ago you're funny."

"No, 'mano," Antonio said, sliding into a familiar tone to get Casoose to talk more. "Handsome, I've been called, virile, but not funny."

"Then you must be nervous. You're wiggling like a little finger that's about to get chopped off."

"Where are you taking me?"

To this Casoose only made a series of gentle grunts that Antonio realized was laughter.

"But seriously, what happened between you and the captain? He said he hadn't seen you in a while. Did you two have an argument? I can't see your pretty little badge under that wolf skin—did he let you go? Did the white man finally get tired of looking at your ugly brown ass?" Casoose was silent. His breathing was steady behind Antonio as they walked, like a locomotive chugging at his heels. "I bet you miss his voice at night. I bet you miss his mustache against your cheek." Casoose said nothing to this either, but Antonio continued, figuring he'd talk until Casoose cracked and either responded or shot him. "When I'm done with you, 'mano, they'll never find you down here. But don't worry. I'll take your badge.

You just tell me where to mail it. Do you have children? I heard what happened to your family in Matamoros. Maybe if they were as ugly as you it was better someone put them out of their misery."

The last comment did it. Casoose didn't even stop walking. He swung back his brutal hand and struck Antonio in his broken arm, crumpling him and whiting out the world again.

He could open his eyes a while later, and as he got to his feet and started walking, he closed himself off to the pain, focusing all of himself on his victory, for he'd succeeded in aggravating the man, and angry men make mistakes. And he hadn't been shot, suggesting the Ranger had some grander plans. He would keep poking his finger into the wound.

"You didn't like that, huh, 'mano? So you got a woman to lay down with you. Pah, I've seen women do more desperate things than that," and he made sure to perform an exaggerated look up and down Casoose's body, "though not much. How many children did you have? A pair or a whole litter? Did your girls come out with beards, too, or just the boys? No, wait—I bet they had tails like their mamá."

Casoose sighed and Antonio felt he was getting somewhere. He tensed himself, ready for another blow, but instead the Ranger started speaking, and this time he chose Spanish.

"You speak ill of the dead, señor. As you'll soon be with them, I'd advise you to say nothing more."

"I see," Antonio said, keeping his voice upbeat. "These things happen. I myself lost a brother."

"You didn't lose a brother. Another sinner met his Lord. Praise God, I hope to see you all burn."

Antonio pushed this comment aside and continued. "So tell me what happened. How did they die? You piss off the local badass?" Antonio turned around to leer at Casoose, but the Ranger was looking ahead of them both and he clamped a fleshy hand down over Antonio's good shoulder. Antonio jerked, but he couldn't shake the Ranger and, looking down, he was startled to see he'd almost walked straight into a hole, another cavern God only knew how deep.

"I remember," Casoose said, and he was no longer speaking to Antonio

211

but continuing some conversation always playing in his mind. "How they looked down on me from the rafters and I could do nothing but look up and look up and look up and . . . The Lord says, 'It is mine to avenge.' That's my forgiveness."

"What the hell are you talking about?"

"You killed them." Casoose's fingers dug so deep into Antonio's shoulder, he thought if Casoose really wanted to he could tear him apart like a boiled chicken. "You killed them," Casoose said again. "My wife, my daughters. My little baby girl not three years old. It was you." His fingers went deeper. Antonio dropped to his knees, but Casoose only squeezed harder.

"It wasn't me," Antonio said. "You're crazy, man." He tried not to peer over the edge of the hole. So many ways for this maniac to kill him in these caves—which one did Casoose have in mind?

"You threw my daughter into a fire and laughed. I see it whether my eyes are open or closed."

"It wasn't me. I'm not a fucking lunatic."

Casoose's fingers had inched up to Antonio's neck and now Antonio could barely speak. In any second Casoose would snap his windpipe. He could feel his good arm twitching and the dim view of the cave was starting to blot out as he slid toward unconsciousness.

"I know," Casoose said, finally loosening his grip. "But you're all just fingers on a great big hand. You cut one off and the others feel it. And I'm gonna keep cutting you off 'til there's no more fingers left. 'Til I have them all."

He pulled Antonio to standing once again and led him down a narrow passage that veered away from the cavern. They rounded a bend and Antonio could see light ahead. A minute later they reached a chamber that was open to the hillside and Antonio had to close his eyes because the morning sunlight was blinding. Something slipped around his neck and, before he could protest, that something snatched him at the throat and he was hoisted up into the air. The world spun, becoming a sickening blur of brown, white, black, brown, white, black. Antonio writhed and realized he hung at the end of a noose. He was not far off the ground, though his feet kicked wildly, sending him into tight revolutions. Casoose had brought him into a chamber where he'd already slung a rope through an obliging hole in the cave's ceiling, creating a short gallows. Antonio hung there now, too surprised and incapacitated to do anything but spin. And then, as suddenly as he'd been raised, he was dropped, his relief at being able to breathe immediately drowned out by the pain of his bad arm hitting the ground. He might have cried out. He couldn't be sure because he was no longer in control of his body, which was now no more than a constellation of impulses that all shrieked at once. He had time to take exactly three breaths before he was raised again, slightly higher this time. He spun a little slower now so that as he turned he could see Casoose grinning at him, gathering strength from Antonio's pain. He was dropped again, and was given a little time to gulp air as Casoose stretched his arms and his back.

"Wait," Antonio gasped, and his voice was made of broken glass and belonged to someone else.

"No waiting," Casoose said and brought him up again. "I like the way you all dangle. Everybody does it a little different. No two men die the same way." Antonio was able this time to bring his good hand up to clutch at the noose, but it was useless. Casoose even laughed and wagged a finger at him. Antonio dropped his hand and stars in every color exploded before his eyes. "You think you're funny," Casoose said, "but I know a funny joke, too. Here's a riddle: How many people in Dorado have to die for Sonoro gold?"

Antonio's eyes widened at the sound of his home in the Ranger's mouth and Casoose laughed that horrible grunting laugh that sounded like an animal in pain.

"You couldn't find your way back across if you tried," Antonio managed to get out when he found himself on the ground again. "You fucking traitor."

Casoose raised and dropped Antonio again. Antonio clawed at the noose to get it away from his throat, but it seemed to have worn its way into his flesh and burrowed there. The joy on Casoose's face was almost as unbearable as the pain in his arm and his throat and Antonio shut his eyes, a thousand inchoate thoughts flying through him: Jesusa, the children.

"*You have to leave the shotgun with us.*"

"*I'm the man around here now.*"

"*Questing como Don Quixote.*"

"*Fighting and drinking and fiddling with whores—those don't make a man.*"

The world was going spotty, chunks of it disappearing behind dark gray splotches like hovering stains. Or maybe they were demons waiting to drag him away. And just as he had that thought, he saw what looked like a man standing behind Casoose calmly watching him like someone would watch ducks skimming a pond. He tried to call out for the man to save him, but no sound came.

Antonio knew he didn't deserve any favors from God or man and so he turned his face away from the shadowy figure and said a prayer for Jesusa, begging God to give her the strength to care for herself and the children without him. He lost count of how many times he was brought up and down. He was slipping in and out of consciousness and was mercifully even starting to lose feeling in his body. He opened his eyes at one point and saw that Casoose was tying the end of the rope onto the base of a spindly rock that rose out of the ground. Antonio was aware of his body jerking, arms and legs dancing like a marionette. Everything slowed down, even to the point that Antonio could see where Casoose would walk next, that his steps were exaggerated as though he treaded through water. He tried to breathe, but his lungs were two crumpled paper bags. The sun was very bright and growing brighter, turning different colors that glowed with such intensity Antonio knew he must be dying, for nothing on earth could be so vivid. *I cannot be afraid*, he thought, *for I've already died once.* He let himself be swallowed up by the lights, to be slowly disassembled into a million fragments and absorbed. And he didn't so much think his final thought as he knew it instantly to be true: Death is the process of becoming light. Red, orange, yellow. He let himself be refracted. Green, blue, indigo. The last thing to be dissolved would be his consciousness and this he allowed, turning himself into the purest shade of violet, a late spring jacaranda petal borne on a warm wind into a darkening sunset. He flew directly into the light, adding his purple to the multitude residing there, and he was pleased that he could make the colors richer for those he left behind.

Except he was not completely dissolved. He could still smell the reek of his death. And the pure purple light to which he'd given his whole self was beginning to break apart, penetrated and bisected with shafts of brown, white, and black. His eyes were open. He didn't know how long they'd been open, but he could see. He was still in the cave, hanging just above Casoose, who was very close to him.

Casoose was in fact so close he couldn't see Antonio's face. He was leaned into Antonio's shoulder, patting him down and checking his pockets while whistling a cheerful song, sucking air in and out of his perfect teeth, each note echoing far back into the recesses of the cave. He moved with ease about Antonio, causing one thought to ring in Antonio's mind: *He thinks I'm dead.*

Something glinted. It was the hilt of his own knife dangling from Casoose's belt. Antonio wiggled the fingers on his right hand to see if they worked, and to his surprise they did. He reached out slowly, slowly, for he could move no other way, and plucked the knife off the Ranger's belt. As he brought his hand up toward Casoose's neck, the Ranger sensed something. He straightened and Antonio brushed his arm. Casoose looked up at Antonio in surprise, and Casoose had enough time to pale before Antonio ran the knife into the side of his neck.

Antonio pulled the knife back out before Casoose fell heavily out of his line of sight. With his final bit of strength he brought his arm up above his head to the rope and ran it over the fibers in a steady motion—as each severed, he could feel it in the base of his spine. At last the rope broke and Antonio crumpled to the ground beside Casoose, gulping in air in a moment that was almost as prolonged and euphoric as the sensation of dissolving into light. Death had been the process of splitting apart, and so life must be the process of being made whole. He hugged his good arm around himself, taking stock of his wholeness again and again, feeling his solidity, his mass. After a long time he looked at Casoose dead on the ground. His eyes were wide open and Antonio wondered what color the Ranger had chosen for his own death.

He lay on the ground long after the sun went down, sleeping a little and waking, running his hand up and down his body to remind himself he was still there, and willing himself to get up, get up, and run. But sleep took him.

Upon waking, his thoughts were slippery black fish too nimble to catch. His left forearm was broken. Luckily the bone hadn't pushed through the skin, but nonetheless it swelled large and warm. When he could sit up he took the dungarees off of Casoose and cut them into strips and bound them tightly around his arm to keep it immobile, and he made a sling from Casoose's shirt. The bullet wound in his leg had scabbed and was healing, and Antonio could stagger a little on his feet. His neck was open and weeping and left his fingers smeared with yellow and red whenever he dared touch it. He didn't know how long he'd lain there in the cave tortured by everything he was, everything he'd ever chosen, but as soon as he could stand and drag himself to the mouth of the cave, he did, and he stood watching dawn break across Texas, the purple darkness overtaken with light. He left Casoose's weapons with Casoose, his own spent pistol there on the cave floor. He kept the knife with him, but he knew it no longer sang for blood.

He took a few tentative steps out of the cave, when he felt a nudge from behind and turned around to find Candida with her mouth full of artemisia. He fell upon her as upon an old friend and cried tears of gratitude. He climbed on top of the horse and pointed her in the right direction. He would not stop until the mare's feet had reached the other side of the river. Then he would climb down off her and swallow a mouthful of Mexican soil.

PART FOUR

WHERE THE RIVER SPLITS

TWENTY-FOUR

THE END

Jaime let his finger rest on the D key a second longer before he rolled the sheet up and out of the typewriter and held it to his face, inhaling its warm, inky tang. He placed it facedown on the stack on his desk and leaned back in his chair, feeling uncertain. It felt like a satisfying story, one of discovery and redemption, and it was something he felt sure an audience would find meaning in. But now that it was all told and printed in black and white, he felt a strange disappointment. He'd told *a* story, but was it *the* story? He'd narrated a life, but what on earth did he really know about Tragabalas? What on earth did he know about killing and being shot at and true, soul-shattering loss? For all Jaime knew, he'd missed the point entirely. He worried his entire act of creation might only be an even bigger act of destruction. He rested his hand on Maria Rocha's book and he knew, truly, what she'd felt when she'd laid her pen down for the last time.

He put the script in a leather portfolio and phoned the studio to have a courier pick it up. It was in God's hands now, or, more precisely, with the studio heads.

219

During dinner the following week Jaime got a phone call from Churu-busco saying they loved *The Bullet Swallower*, they'd be thrilled to film it. They were scrapping the pirate adventure he'd agreed to—the wave machines hadn't arrived from California and the director was stuck in Cuba anyway. "We can start shooting in Valle de Bravo next month," the man from the studio said. "What do you say?"

And what could Jaime say?

The matter of telling his father that not only had he written the script but that the movie would begin filming imminently made an immovable clot in Jaime's stomach. He would have to tell him, there was no way around it, though part of him fantasized that he could just go to work, film his scenes, hope his father didn't notice the entire capital being papered over with posters advertising *The Bullet Swallower*, and live out the rest of his life in cowardly bliss. For days, whenever he saw his father Jaime cleared his throat, the words sitting on his tongue, before backing out at the last second.

"Is your throat sore?" the old man demanded. "Stay away from me if you're getting a cold."

Inside Jaime the battle raged, between filial piety and personal fulfillment, obedience and destiny, integrity of one kind, and integrity of another.

His fears were realized, though, on the day the studio sent the makeup and wardrobe women to his house along with a photographer to shoot publicity stills.

"They said you were expecting us," cried the photographer. "I'm so terribly sorry, but since we're all here . . ."

And so it was that Juan Antonio learned Jaime was going to star in *The Bullet Swallower* when he returned home from a walk and saw his own father, scar and all, glaring and pointing a prop gun at him in the living room.

"Pop!" Jaime shouted, chasing Juan Antonio out into the street. "I'm sorry, okay? I know you said not to, but I had to. *I had to*."

"You idiot," Juan Antonio said, so overcome with rage and fear and sadness and disbelief he was practically laughing, "you ignorant little fool. I thought I could keep you safe. Keep you out of it. And every time I turn around, there you go running right into it." He grabbed Jaime's shirt and pulled him close. Jaime looked so much like Antonio. "I thought if I moved you away, if I didn't tell you anything and brought you up to be good and honest that I could keep you safe, keep you from being like the rest of the Sonoros. But when that man appeared, I thought, 'That's it— we're ruined.'"

Jaime shook his head, comprehending and not comprehending. "Remedio? He's after our money, Pop."

"You fool. This isn't about money. He came here to bring you to Hell," Juan Antonio said. "You, me, the kids. All of us."

TWENTY-FIVE

Antonio reached the border south of Ciudád Porfirio Díaz. Before he crossed he saw a bulletin nailed to a tree trunk announcing the death of Antonio el Tragabalas. "Discovered killed in a cave outside Brackettville, the citizens of Texas may breathe a sigh of relief knowing this brutal killer is no longer among us. Governor Culberson thanks Captain Cyrus Fish, killed in the line of duty, for pursuing this murderer to the bitter end."

Antonio shook his head. The Americans comforted themselves with lies like a child sucking his thumb and stroking a soft blanket.

When he reached the opposite shore of the river, as he'd promised himself, Antonio scooped up a handful of the cold, chalky soil and put it in his mouth, chewed through the gritty earth, and swallowed it down, where it made a lump that sat in his stomach like a fist.

In Mexico the sky disappeared under vindictive clouds, and the pummeling wind drove sleet down from the north and froze the hair on the back of his head. The sleet continued day and night as Antonio and the mare traveled south. Soon he was sick with a fever and chills that made his teeth chatter along one side of his jaw and his gums smack along the other. With no reason to hide, he took the main road that connected the dozen or so villages that fronted the river, and Antonio saw many homes aglow with lantern light, burning mesquite logs that sent sweet smoke up chimneys to mingle with the scent of fresh rain and mud, but he saw no people. Even the dogs and pigs had been brought in out of the freezing rain. Antonio could have stopped and asked for something warm to drink, maybe even a corner to sleep in, but he wouldn't stop until he reached Jesusa, finally returning to his love. *Why had he gone looking for riches when he had such treasures at home?*

The rain wouldn't let up and the road was so mud-bogged and slick, that Candida was exhausted, pushed to the very edge of her strength. Snot made icicles that dangled from both her nostrils and the sides of her mouth. Antonio lay draped over her back with his head against her mane and the two warmed each other on the relentless march.

When at last they neared Dorado, the baleful gray clouds remained, but this time what fell was snow. Antonio had seen snow only once, and he remembered how surprised he'd been at how wet and cold it was in his boots. He'd been expecting something more like fallen ash. There were only a few flakes at first making tight pirouettes in the air and melting as soon as they touched the brittle grass. Then more snow came, a little and a little, until all the air was falling, dancing, drifting eddies of white, until Antonio couldn't see far in front of him. In half an hour the ground had a light dusting like powdered sugar over a cake; in an hour the mare's feet left brown hoofprints behind her as she plodded. Children burst out of houses wearing their fathers' boots on their feet and their mothers' shawls wrapped around their heads. And what a strange spectacle he imagined he must be: a man riding atop what looked like an albino bull.

Antonio kicked Candida to go faster. They galloped across the wooden bridge into Dorado, passed under the shadow of the church bell tower, and barreled south. He'd waited so long to cast his eyes again over his village, but everything was strange under its snowy covering, nothing matching his memory exactly. He found the road home, and tore away down past the graveyard, past the last house on the last cobblestone street, and onto land that had belonged to the Sonoros since King Felipe V signed the papers with his own royal hand. He thundered past the big white house in which he'd been born. He counted the hives, eight, nine, ten, and the orange trees that looked dipped in icing. He was home.

The snow was still falling when he saw his gate. It was late afternoon and the sky was rust red. He slowed the horse and then stopped altogether. There was no snowman outside his front door, no smoke spiraling up out of his kitchen roof, no flickering candle at the window, no footprints in the snow. The latch on the gate had been broken and he pushed it open with one trembling finger. He looked around the yard, hoping to see Jesusa's coffee eyes, see Nicolás's lanky frame, Aura's round cheeks, but all there was, was gray.

The jacal was empty, the goat pen was empty, the chickens, the mule, the dog, everything was gone and any trace now lay under a foot of snow. Antonio tried to calm himself with practical thoughts. Jesusa's sister, Beatríz, lived across the river in Roma, Texas. They could have gone for a visit. The animals could have gotten spooked by the snow and fled. A lot of things could have happened; he told himself the worst things in life tended to be the least likely.

He turned in slow circles in his yard trying to think what to do next, when something red caught his eye, Jesusa's rebozo, waving from a little depression on the other side of the cornfield. She must be there with the children making snowmen. He ran. He slipped once, twice. The red shawl beckoned to him through the winter haze and he grinned as he ran, wanting to surprise them. And when he came upon the rebozo at last, he saw it was not wrapped around his wife, draped across her elegant shoulders, but a wooden cross, one of three that formed a neat row before an expanse of thorny, black mesquites.

He fell to his knees in front of the crosses and the names scratched into them swam in his eyes. They looked like runic symbols, lines and curves—for how could the name, Jesusa Guajardo de Sonoro, carved into a piece of wood, possibly represent the person contained below? How could words account for life, body, spirit, sacrifice, fear, and love? He wouldn't look at the other two graves, he kept his eyes on Jesusa's red shawl billowing in the wind, because he knew if he let his eyes fall on the others he'd start digging, that he'd dig them out of the ground with his hands until his fingers were only bones and bring them up into the light, because no child should be left somewhere so cold and dark.

He stood up and staggered to one of the mesquites as the wind blew in gusts. Gray splotches appeared around him like when he'd dangled at the end of Casoose's rope, and his heart was a lead claw, crashing and scratching its way out through his ribs. He wished for the pistol he'd left back in the cave. Pulled the knife out of his belt. He held it in his good hand, which was shaking so hard that he had to use his broken arm to level it against his throat.

He pushed the blade to his tender skin.

Begged Jesusa for forgiveness.

Told his children he was sorry.

Said a prayer for Hugo.

Pushed the knife in.

"Don't."

Antonio opened his eyes, and there was his shadow beside him, pulling the knife out of his hand. The man turned the knife over in his hands as though he hadn't seen one before, peering down the blade and running his finger over the carvings on the handle. He gave a brief smile to Antonio and handed it back to him and he was repaid for this mistake when Antonio rushed him and pinned him against a tree with the knife pointed at his stomach.

"Did you kill them?" Antonio demanded. "I saw at you Espantosa. Is that why you're following me? Speak fast, you son of a bitch."

If the man was bothered by having a knife aimed at him, he didn't show it. "It was the man's order," he said calmly. "He was called Fish. He sent the one he called Casoose. And I cannot bear false witness." He paused before he added, "They suffered."

"Oh God," Antonio moaned, covering his face with his hand. He brought his hand down and then slapped it over his face again, harder, so that he saw white pinpoints open up. He did this again and again, wanting to hurt himself, until the man put one soft, warm hand over Antonio's.

"You can't stop me," Antonio said. "I don't deserve to live."

"Deserve? You suppose life is the gift?"

"I'll throw myself off the bell tower. I'll light myself on fire. I can stop eating. You don't decide when I die." Antonio was pacing in circles. There was nowhere for his eyes to fall that wasn't a grave and so he looked up into the darkening sky, now streaked with long gray clouds that he'd once been told were the dreams of a long-dead tribe of Indians. "Everything is dead," he said, and he clutched at his throat, for he couldn't breathe. "I killed them. I might as well have pulled the trigger myself."

Remedio stared at Antonio and puzzled at the man who'd been ready to kill himself over murders he hadn't directly committed, but was untroubled by the deaths he himself had inflicted.

"I never should have gone," Antonio said. "I just thought, if I could make things right . . ." He grabbed Remedio's jacket, but immediately let go, feeling how warm it was even in the cold. He blinked at Remedio as if seeing him for the first time. "Who are you?"

"I am Remedio."

"Why are you following me?"

"I'm interested in your outcome."

"What does that— What outcome?"

"That's for you to decide."

Antonio shook his head and turned away. "Speak your piece or leave me alone."

Remedio cleared his throat. It was difficult to perform the imprecise translation of what he knew into words. "You will not die today," he said, "nor tomorrow, or the day after that. You will live until you reach one hundred years, on which day I will speak to you again and require your decision."

"What decision?"

"Whether you pay what is owed, or transfer the debt." Antonio only stared at this and Remedio looked around him for something he could use to explain himself. "This is a beautiful place," he said, watching a buck tread carefully through the mesquite thicket. "I like to watch the sunset. It's always surprised me how little people grieve when darkness overtakes light. It is a beautiful place, but it's difficult to farm, is it not? The corncobs are mealy. The pigs never fatten. I know you never met your grandfather, but know that he traded in cruelties as much as he traded in gold, and he enriched himself mightily with both. The Sonoros have always had a talent for profit through wickedness—your grandfather was not the first to use his particular gifts. And I will not attempt to guess at the machinations of the universe, as it is not my role to do so, but I will simply say that payment is due from the Sonoros and it will be collected. When you reach one hundred years I will return and you must tell me on that day whether you intend to satisfy the debt, or not."

"What happens if I don't?"

"It will be transferred."

"To who?"

"Your son, and his son, and his son. The line is long. There are many who could pay."

Antonio pursed his lips together. "I'll go now, then. I'll pay the debt. Take me, I'm ready."

Remedio frowned at this, having anticipated the man would try to bargain. "You cannot come now. It is not your time to be taken."

"You took Peter, didn't you? I saw you both."

Remedio looked at Antonio for a minute before he nodded. "I should tell you that coming with me forgoes your opportunity for . . ." He paused, searching for the right word. "Reunion. If I take you, you will be alone." Antonio followed Remedio's gaze to the three graves in the snow.

"And know, too, that nothing can hasten your decision. You can come to no harm until you've reached one hundred years. It's an opportunity to think about your choice without distraction."

"How could I hope for reunion?" But even as he said the words the temptation grew inside him. To hold Jesusa again, to hear Nicolás and Aura laughing—how could he choose anything else?

Remedio watched Antonio and he could see the thoughts firing across his mind in little bursts of electricity that were mesmerizing and beautiful, like lacy arabesques etched onto glass. "You can see it is not a decision to be made lightly." He straightened his tie and pushed his hat down on his head. "I will go now. I hope that you spend this time wisely and without regret." He regarded the trees, purpling in the creeping night. "Even the bitterest frosts come to an end," he said. "There is always a thaw." And he started off toward the gate. He was almost across the cornfield when Antonio called out to him and told him to wait.

"My son," Antonio said, breathless for having run across the field. "You said the debt would be transferred to my son . . . Do I have a son still . . ." And his voice trailed off as he turned back to Nicolás's grave.

"There was another boy born just last month." Remedio looked to the gate, where a woman was tying up a mule and holding a basket. "He comes now."

Antonio looked at the gate, and when he turned back to ask Remedio how, he was already some distance away, walking north through the trees.

It was Jesusa's younger sister, Beatríz, who was coming through the gate. She'd married a widowed farmer at fourteen and had been living in Roma, Texas, the last five years, raising his children. She saw Antonio and pointed at the house. When he got to the door she'd already started a fire and had a pot of coffee on the stove.

Always a brittle, acid-tongued little waif, Beatríz now seemed to melt upon seeing Antonio. She fell against him as soon as he'd closed the door and her narrow shoulders shook with silent cries as he held her. He let her stay there until the coffee bubbled over the pot and then she told him to sit down next to the fire.

"I've been staying at my cousin's house waiting for you. He said he saw you tear through town like the devil was behind you and I came right over." She sniffed and whimpered, but caught herself and mixed sugar into the coffee and set it in front of Antonio. When he put it to his lips it tasted like nothing. "I wish I could have caught you before you got here," she said. The logs hissed and crackled in the fire. "What we think happened is that there were five of them, maybe six, and they rode across the river in the middle of the day and, and . . ." She stopped talking and pursed her lips together and looked out the window. Everything was dark. "You should know that Nicolás tried to save Jesusa. He was lying on top of her, I think, to shield her."

Antonio listened without speaking or moving. His coffee sat undrunk on the table.

Beatríz took in a long, shuddery breath. "But the Lord granted us one miracle." She reached inside a basket and picked up a mound of blankets and brought it to show Antonio. Inside was a sleeping baby, a thin child with Jesusa's solemn face. To Antonio it seemed the boy already wore an expression of fatigue, as if he already knew the troubles of the world. Antonio looked away and put his hand over his mouth so he would not cry out and disturb the child, and Beatríz quietly put the baby back in the basket. "He was asleep in the drawer there," she said, indicating a little bureau in the corner. "I don't know how, but he slept through everything and the men never saw him." She crossed herself before she spoke again. "She didn't know she was pregnant, you know. She was afraid you'd be angry when you got home, but I promise you she would never hide something like that from you. They were in Roma visiting me. My husband had taken the boys turkey hunting. When she arrived she was sweating all over and saying her stomach hurt. As soon as I got her into bed she started screaming from the pain and I said, 'My God, you idiot, you're in labor!' Then she started crying and I asked her, was she sad to have another baby and she said no, she was crying because he was going to be a Texan." She laughed a little at the recollection, but then stopped and apologized.

"I want you to know I don't blame you," Beatríz said. "Jesusa never really believed in the curse and I don't either. Those children are with the blessed Mother now. Their troubles are over, no matter what people say."

Beatríz got up and started preparing dough for tortillas. Antonio looked at his house, one room he'd built himself using boards he'd pried off the white mansion. It had been cramped for five people but now felt cavernous and hollow and dark as a tomb. The baby woke with a whimper that soon became a howl. Beatríz began wiping the flour from her hands, but Antonio stood up and went to the baby, who was crying with a red face and convulsively flailing his legs and arms as though he hoped to touch something warm and alive, seeking assurance that someone was out there. Antonio picked him up and the baby briefly stopped crying, searching his face for anything recognizable, but finding nothing, he began crying again, angrier this time that his wails had not conjured the right person.

"I can take him," Beatríz offered, but Antonio shook his head and asked her if she had any milk. She gave him a glass bottle—"My cousin's goat," she said, "fresh this morning"—and Antonio sat awkwardly down with the child in his arms. He'd never fed a baby and he spilled some of the milk down the boy's shirt and onto his cheeks, but he was able to get the rubber nipple near enough to his son's mouth, and the baby, knowing well the routine of the last week, stopped crying, opened wide, and ate greedily, smacking and slurping.

"What's his name?"

"Juan Antonio," Beatríz said with a slight smile.

Beatríz spent the night. Antonio gave her and the baby the bed, while he sat at the table and listened to their gentle breathing, to the wind snapping branches outside, to the fire turning charcoal into ash. He had nothing. He'd been given the white mansion and he'd refused it. He could have studied to be a doctor or a judge and he'd refused it. He married Jesusa and promised her he would stop fighting and stealing and within a year of taking their vows he was robbing steamboat passengers at gunpoint in Rio Grande City. By the time Aura was born he no longer bothered to lie, telling Jesusa he would be back when it pleased him. His entire life he'd been handed beautiful things, which he only crumpled and dropped on the ground, and now finally he would be handed nothing more. He saw the rest of his life in the accumulating pile of gray ash in the stove.

He thought about the night at Espantosa Lake, how Fish had grabbed his shirt and demanded again and again to know why. He hadn't understood it at the time, for he'd closed himself to everything except revenge, but Fish had wanted to know why Antonio had forced his hand and he'd been asking him, in his final minutes, for forgiveness. But what was contrition? It was only words, nothing more than an insurance policy. He thought he understood then why Remedio had refused to take him that afternoon, and how it was at once a cruel and benevolent gesture. Remedio had left him there to suffer in his grief, to slowly draw out and drink all the poison water from the well polluted by his misdeeds. But he'd also left him there to prove his repentance. True contrition had to be more than words. Remedio was expecting him to somehow mend the world he himself had thoughtlessly fractured. He couldn't ask Jesusa and Hugo and the children for forgiveness. He had to earn it with his every breath for the next sixty-nine years. It was a gift and a punishment, making Antonio wholly unsure of which side he believed Remedio served in the cosmic balance.

The baby sighed in his sleep and Antonio winced, for in his grief he'd forgotten he had been handed one final, beautiful thing.

TWENTY-SIX

"This has nothing to do with us," Jaime said, trying to bring some reason back into the discussion. "You can't seriously suggest we're going to be punished for all eternity because of something that happened years before either of us were even born."

Juan Antonio only looked down at the ground.

"Why give us the ability to be evil in the first place?" Jaime asked, his voice rising and his throat tightening. "Why give us the choice? Surely God's sitting up there brokenhearted every time some drunk asshole beats his kids, or some dictator has all his enemies disappeared. Why make us all go through it?"

"I don't know."

"It's bullshit, though. Look at the world. Look at how fucked things are. What's the point? What's the point of any of it?"

"I don't know," Juan Antonio said, wiping a tear from his eye. How inadequate was love when it couldn't stop suffering?

"And we're getting scapegoated—we're getting all the evil in the world piled up on us and we just have to bear it off into the wilderness and you don't want to fight it. You just want to stand there and say, 'I don't know, I don't know.'" And then Jaime stopped talking because the expression on Juan Antonio's face said that there was nothing Jaime could say that his father hadn't already thought, no bargain he could propose that Juan Antonio hadn't already tried to strike. He understood his father had been fighting it his whole life. Juan Antonio, for all of his faults, woke up every morning and tried to be better. And maybe that was all there was and all there ever would be: a daily dedication to the light.

"I'm sorry," Jaime said, and he wrapped his arms around his father and hugged him close, feeling the strength in the old man as he returned the embrace. "And I forgive you."

"I'm sorry, too, míjo. I wasn't a good father, but I tried my best. I tried to learn. In five thousand years, I don't know if the Sonoros ever tried to learn."

"But how do you know all this?"

"My father—who do you think?"

And Jaime had to take a second to let this sink in, that Tragabalas was both real and invented, a man and a character, a remembrance, a myth, a misunderstood story. But being himself both Jaime and the Rooster, he supposed it was, after all, not that hard to grasp.

"I think he thought that by telling me, he was keeping me safe, too. But what he did was put a fear in me I can't outrun."

Jaime was trying to put something together. "But in the song it says Antonio died on his way back to Texas."

"He probably put that rumor out there himself. He likes people to think he's dead."

Jaime blinked. "He likes people to think he's dead? *Likes*, as in, present tense?"

Juan Antonio sank down to the curb and lit a cigarette and indicated that Jaime should sit down as well. "When I was a baby Antonio tried to raise me, despite that he knew nothing about taking care of a child. I was sickly, I had trouble eating, I cried all the time. And he had no one to help him. I have to imagine those first few months were very, very hard. He never said this outright, but I think some nights he was tempted to throw me in the river, believing I might be better off. Finally, one day he'd had enough and he wrapped me up and took me back across the water to my mother's sister in Roma. That's how I ended up living there.

"Antonio would visit me occasionally, though he never took me back to Dorado to live with him. We'd go out looking for wild honey or we'd catch and release the little turtles that live in the river up there. He told me once it was hard to look at me, for how much I looked like my mother. And he didn't own a gun—I thought that was the strangest thing. I always wanted to go hunting and he'd never take me, saying he didn't have it in him anymore to kill.

"So when I was about sixteen he came by the house and said he had something to tell me. We went to a café in Roma, and I remember being more preoccupied with holding my cigarette the right way in front of a couple of girls there than I was about whatever Antonio had to say.

"He told me everything, though. All of it. His grandfather, his mother, his brother, my mother, their first children who were dead—he told me the whole story stretching as far back and as wide out as he could remember. He told me about going to Texas, how the Rangers shot him, meeting a bruja named Cielita and an Englishman named Peter, and how he came to get his horse, Candida. It was like he'd breached a dam—everything just kept coming out."

Jaime listened to his father's recitation of Antonio's story with a mix of horror and relief, for it was exactly as he had imagined, the story somehow passed down through his blood so that when he heard it, it was as familiar as seeing his own features in the photograph of an ancestor.

"He finally seemed like he'd gotten everything off his chest, and by God, what more could he have to say after that? But then he looked over his shoulder. *A shadow*, he kept saying. *Watch out for a shadow*. I thought maybe he'd finally gone crazy, that living alone all those years had done him in. When he was finished he shook my hand and wished me good luck, and I walked away in such a daze that I wondered over the years if I didn't dream the whole conversation."

He lit another cigarette and offered one to Jaime, who took it with gratitude. "I never saw him again," Juan Antonio said. "I had the feeling that he was saying goodbye that day, and I always believed it was for my own protection that he stayed away. I never begrudged him that."

"The shadow—you think that's Remedio?"

Juan Antonio nodded.

Maria Rocha's words came to Jaime, how the iniquity of parents was visited upon the third and fourth generation, and it was like a last puzzle piece sliding into place, the horrifying picture all too clear. And yet, if it was true, if he was damned and had been so from birth, this only made him feel rededicated to life—to Elena, the children, his father, his fans. He wouldn't follow the example of the Sonoros, taking what he could when he could. He'd shine all the brighter, all the way down.

"Okay, but why do you think Antonio's still alive?" Jaime asked.

Juan Antonio sat quietly smoking a minute before he answered. "I think a person knows when their parents are gone for good, when the people that brought them into existence have gone out. I think the air gets heavier or the light changes, something like that. I haven't seen the sun get dimmer yet."

Jaime looked up the street, north, toward Dorado. "I like thinking of him out there," he said. "On that big white mare." Jaime looked at his father, at his raisin skin and Coke-bottle glasses, at his enormous hands that had commandeered mules across Northern Mexico even after the highways were built, and after trucks could haul more for less. Juan Antonio kept his team going for the Indians and the farmers too poor and out of the way for the twentieth century to bother with them. And Jaime thought how miraculous it was that his father was alive at all, and how it was an even greater miracle that he'd been blessed with a richness of spirit so teeming that he could pass it on to Jaime and Jaime's children, a candle that could light others and then others, so that the light could conquer any darkness.

"Maybe he's still protecting you," Jaime said.

Juan Antonio looked up the street as well, to a jacaranda shedding a few purple petals in a warm breeze, and nodded.

TWENTY-SEVEN

Winter howled through Dorado and Antonio left the gate unfixed, the fields untended. At night he cried silently for Jesusa, his tears falling into the exact spot on the mattress that her tears had watered for years. He cried not for how she died but for how she'd lived, and the tears formed a stain the shape of a flower, a multiflora blossom of elegance and regret. He'd piled everything onto her: raising the children, keeping the house, cooking his food, tending the crops, and he despised himself for the hours he'd spent playing cards, chasing women, drinking until he woke up on the back of his horse not knowing where he was. He was cursed, yes, but through no one's actions but his own.

Candida was fortunately still quite attached to Antonio even though he neglected to brush her or clean her stall for days at a time. She learned to let herself in and out of her enclosure by tugging at the handle with her teeth. She grazed in the Sonoro fields all day and returned home every night. Antonio apologized to her one evening when he saw her plodding across the cornfield with burrs stuck all over her matted hair. She bowed her head and closed her eyes under her long lashes and seemed to say, "I understand."

He ate little. He had no money, nothing to trade, and no one to trade with, and so he ate once a day, consuming what little was left in the house and foraging for the rest in the fields.

One evening in February Antonio saw the mare trotting home chewing an apple and it was as though a warm breeze blew through him.

At the beginning of March, Antonio was relieved to see green buds poking up out of his fields, blossoms on the orange trees. The food stores in the house were gone. He was eating wild carrots and grapes, chickweed, and a few pecans overlooked by the birds, and he suffered dizzy spells that forced him to squat on the floor until the gray splotches went away and he could see again.

One night, after catching bluegill in the dusk-pink river, it began to rain. The water churned as a wind kicked up and the little boat in which Antonio sat started to rock. He tried to steady it and row himself back to the bank, where Candida watched him impassively. But the boat overturned as he tried to steer it and he sank into the cold water. When he surfaced his teeth chattered with anger.

It was all too much, to have the weight of so much malign history sitting on his shoulders. How could God expect one man to bear it? Antonio thrashed there, his fury growing as the water seethed and rose around him. "Explain yourself!" he shouted at the sky. "You set loose an avalanche and expect me to stand against it. How? You bastard! How?"

Antonio could not be sure if God heard him, but the mountains heard, and the streams heard, and the spring rains heard, and the snowpack heard, and with a rumble the river was overwhelmed with a tide of water that seemed to contain all six years of withheld rain. Antonio watched the towering flood with equal parts hope and dread: hope that he would die, and dread that he would now be forced to make his choice.

He was engulfed and tossed about, battered and dragged far downstream. When he could finally make his way to the bank and out of the water, after he trudged slow and waterlogged back north to Dorado, he expected to find the island underwater, believing that his fury had somehow brought mountains to their knees, that he'd remapped the earth. But everything was there, the jacal, the orange trees, Candida quietly grazing near the goat pen. The island had survived his anger, survived the flood, and seeing this caused something in him to open, like his eyes were fresh and brand-new, like some obscuring force had finally dislodged.

Jesusa's red rebozo was still wrapped around the wooden cross marking her grave, and the ends flapped in the wind with urgency. He untied it and held it to his face, breathing in her scent one last time before he let it fall from his hands. It caught a gust that took it away and into the sky, where it became a red and rare bird of long feathers. He would see it sometimes throughout the years, silhouetted against the rising sun, preening and waving at the top of a tall tree.

He couldn't return to the jacal, too full of whispers and memories. He found an old surveyor's shack forgotten among the reeds that fronted the water, and there he and Candida settled. It had a table, a chair, a mouse-bitten mattress on the dirt floor.

He was versed in foraging now; he could sustain himself fishing and gathering what he found nearby and he and Candida lived together undisturbed in the brasada. They were there the day the Spanish exited Cuba, ending four hundred years of Iberian rule in the Americas. They didn't hear about the start of the Mexican Revolution, when Francisco Madero successfully deposed Porfirio Díaz, though the name Pancho Villa reached even Antonio's little shack when Mexican bodies began to float downstream. He dragged the fallen soldiers out of the water and buried them near the riverbank, saying a special blessing for each.

He planted fruit trees and pecans. He missed the taste of corn tortillas and so he planted a few rows of corn. He revived the quince trees, grew squash and beans. The soil ripened and yielded fat harvests in a garden that was slowly coming to resemble paradise.

Once, when Antonio returned home from foraging, he heard someone sneeze inside his shack. He opened the door and discovered two priests and two nuns inside, chased out of Saltillo by anti-Catholic extremists. They'd been told that the Río Bravo was fickle and treacherous, and they were too frightened to cross. Antonio told them to wait until late that night. He quickly built a little barge and floated them across, receiving a profusion of blessings in return. Word traveled that a benevolent man lived next to the river and for months Antonio would discover clergymen and women wandering through the brush searching for his little shack, and he escorted them all across the river to Texas, where they could take refuge, his payment a growing cache of prayer cards and medallions. When the Catholic persecutions finished, however, people continued to come.

The brush began to be cleared on the Texas side, and what was once an ocean of live oaks turned into endless fields of onions, cotton, sorghum, and corn. It was the Magic Valley now, stripped, flattened, and irrigated. First it was only men who appeared on Antonio's property looking for safe passage. They came in twos and threes in stained denim and worn shoes and asked if he knew of a good place to cross. They asked this with one hand on the back of their necks, looking down, and Antonio understood that they were hoping he would not extort them for the threadbare shoes on their feet. After a while, whole families appeared. Ever since he'd started taking the Catholics across the river his young fruit trees tripled their yield, and blue and yellow corn shot out of the ground almost as soon as it was planted, and Antonio fed it all to the people who came to him, dropping them off in Texas with wishes of good luck and bags filled with oranges, corn, and pecans.

He was an old man before long. His brown hair silvered, and he grew a long mustache that mostly hid his scar. He spent so much time shuttling people across the river, he soon knew the movements of everyone and everything along both banks. He warned young Mexican men smuggling tequila into the United States when the police were likely to come by. He warned young American men smuggling radios into Mexico that rain was coming and they'd better get their cargo secured. It wasn't only the land that was changing, but the river as well. So many farms were pulling water from it upstream that it had developed rapids and his ferrying became less a kindness than a necessity. One dramatic night when the river was violent after a storm, he heard screaming and he caught a little Anglo girl clinging to a log. He took her across and walked with her in his arms to the church in Fronton, though he left as soon as he heard the priest unlocking the front door.

Candida aged with him. She lost much of her muscle, and she slowed and stooped as the years went on. She was already white, so when her hair silvered it was quite subtle, and Antonio could only see the difference on a bright, sunny day. Every morning for years he went outside expecting to find her keeled over on her side, and every morning she was right where she'd been the night before, standing next to the little shack chewing buffalo grass. It was as though she were waiting for him, that she preferred they go together into the unknown. So he eventually stopped expecting her to die and instead felt only gratitude each morning when he opened the door and she was still there.

The day the young American president was killed, when airplanes thundered and crisscrossed the sky from Dallas to Mexico City and back again, Antonio used his knife one last time to split open an early squash and scrape the flesh into a pot to cook. He wiped the blade clean on his shirt, closed the knife, and then pitched it into the river to be carried down to the Gulf, the Atlantic, away, away, a story closed, the violence of the blade a song he no longer wished to remember, the circular swoop of time finally straightened and vanishing into the far distance.

Antonio was surprised when he opened his eyes on his hundredth birthday. As he'd gone to sleep the night before, he figured he'd wake up to find himself in some sort of purgatory lacking gravity or color. But he woke up in the same place he'd laid down, under a fat-bellied mesquite outside his shack, and beside him was Candida, her old teeth working over some purslane. It was late morning and the sun was bright and high. The dew still clinging to the grass held sunlight inside like little orbs of gold. Antonio looked around expecting to see Remedio, but he and the horse were alone, and so he got up with a little difficulty and began his day.

He'd expected to be in more discomfort as an old man, but in general he felt good. He felt better, in fact, than he had many days when he was young, a change he attributed to a diet high in foraged weeds, as well as a heart that had unburdened itself gradually, shedding hatred and resentment, greed, anger, fear. He carried other things—grief mostly, and regret—but they were different weights. He wondered daily what Jesusa would have looked like as an old woman, wondered whether her hard face could have softened like butter. And his lost children. Who would they have become? And Juan Antonio, now likely with children and grandchildren of his own. What lives would they inhabit, how far through time would the branches of his tree extend?

Antonio stretched and listened to the noisy starlings in the trees. The Sonoro lands had grown Edenic in the last forty years, the Catholics having blessed the land so that the pecan trees sagged under the weight of their bounty every fall, and the sweet fragrance of orange blossoms was carried as far away as Laredo. He'd spent the last few weeks picking what there was and putting it into baskets and setting these along the well-worn path the braceros and their families took when they crossed into Texas to work the fields. The river was low now and there was no need for his ferry, but people were used to crossing at this spot and so they came anyway, and Antonio wanted them to have something to eat.

On this, his last day on earth, he decided he would go and clean the graves one last time. He climbed slowly onto the mare's back—it was not so easy for him to swing his leg up over her anymore—and together they trudged across the property.

He spent a long time gathering armloads of flowers of every hue and he laid them in front of each grave. He cleaned the area of dead leaves and twigs, shook cinnamon on any ant mounds that were near, and then he knelt down and said a prayer for each of his children, asking God to tell them he was sorry. "Give them a kiss from their papá," he whispered, "because I won't be seeing them again." When he got to Jesusa's grave he laid down on the warm soil and cried, for though it had been almost seventy years, he could still feel her thin hand in his. He could still hear the sound of her quiet tears in the night, could still see the light of love in her smile. "I want to come to you," he whispered. "More than anything I want to hold you and tell you that you are my life. But God forgive me, I cannot join you. My love for you will never extinguish. It will live in me for always. For always."

And when he opened his eyes and wiped the tears from his face, he was surprised to see that the sun was setting. Candida nickered and nudged him with her muzzle. Someone cleared their throat and Antonio turned around to see Remedio standing there, his hat in his hands.

"I expected you this morning," Antonio said, slowly getting to his feet.

"You wanted to say goodbye."

"Then you know what my decision is."

Remedio nodded.

"What about my faithful companion?" Candida stopped chewing clover for a second to look up but, finding nothing of interest, returned to her dinner.

"The journey is long," Remedio said. "It would be better for you to ride."

Antonio fed the mare one last apple from his pocket and climbed onto her back. He'd long ago accepted that just about everyone he'd ever known was dead, but he'd always drawn comfort from the fact that the trees would outlast him. Taking one last look at the fruit trees, the shack, the cornfield, and everything beyond sinking into purple night, it was so strange to think he wouldn't see it again. But perhaps Juan Antonio would, and his grandchildren and great-grandchildren. In the morning their eyes would open and would continue to open every day in the bright certainty that they lived beyond any shadow, that this particular darkness was no longer at their heels.

Between cloud banks Antonio could see the stars, and they seemed as bright and numerous as they'd been when he was a young man, when he'd sat with Cielita and laughed about the hungry scorpion in the sky.

Remedio walked in front with Antonio plodding gently behind on the mare. In Texas, lightning illuminated the flat landscape.

"Where are we going?" Antonio asked, for he understood where he was going in a cosmic sense, but he hadn't realized that the journey also included a terrestrial leg.

"Espantosa Lake."

Antonio laughed at this. "I knew it," he said. "Hell *is* in Texas."

Remedio said nothing, for he was thinking. Had it all been for nothing, then? Should he have taken the baby? When he'd offered the man redemption and a lifetime to consider the alternative, he was sure that he would spend the years atoning for his mistakes in preparation to rejoin his family. He'd been right about the atonement. By Remedio's count the man had saved six dozen lives and rerouted, for the better, many more. His goodness was a rising tide that spread beyond the border, eventually lapping both shores of the continent. He'd purged himself of every vice, let go of every impulse that had once stained his soul, and still he chose to go with Remedio. He understood why the man wished to sacrifice himself, and he suspected there was an impulse toward martyrdom as well, but still, he hadn't expected that through it all the man would choose for himself the very path that had been given him at birth. It seemed too neat.

When the scorpion stung him at Jaime's house it had sent Remedio into a terror. He'd wandered the city for days, the insect following him at every turn. He kept thinking about those stone pillars in the desert, how the men who'd carved scorpion likenesses into them were trying to control what they feared by worshipping it. They believed that by sacrificing to their goddess, they could choose where her favor and disfavor fell. But it was all folly; misfortune was not for them to direct. And after Remedio worked this out, he left the city and returned to the place where the river split, to the green jays and the red-eared turtles.

And as he thought about it now, Remedio came to the startling and uncomfortable conclusion that it was not the man's intentions Remedio had misunderstood, but his own. He'd selfishly wanted to redirect the man's fate just to know that it could be done. He'd dangled a prize out to him and was frustrated when the man did not take the bait, though he should not be surprised. It was not his role to rearrange the fates of men, as arbitrary and unfair as they often seemed to be. He straightened his tie and fixed his gaze on the yellow lightning streaking down ahead of them. Of course it hadn't been for nothing, he told himself. He had redirected the man's fate, if only for a little while, and in doing so altered many lives. He'd been right to leave him in his mother's arms. That the man had chosen the same fate only affirmed Remedio's choice. He turned back and looked at Antonio, now whistling a little tune in the face of the approaching storm. Remedio used to wish he could be human for a day, to have inside him the capacity for randomness. Now he satisfied himself by trying to whistle, and it sounded exactly like the green jays.

"Will my son know what I've decided?"

"In time."

They walked north some ways until Remedio chose a spot where it was good to cross. Before they stepped in the water, Antonio stopped and looked back at Dorado, at Mexico. After they emerged in Texas he heard a sound from the other side like the very ground was moving, like the island was sewing itself back to the mainland. Like the land could, at long last, close the circle, heal the breach, make itself whole.

THE SONORO FAMILY

from Antiquity to Present Day

BY MARIA GASPAR ROCHA DE QUIROGA

Published 1783

Sevilla, España

My pen is still, my room quiet, the dark of evening reaching my mind. What folly of men to believe they may learn the trade of the gods, and what folly of this simple woman to believe she may complete a treatise on the source of all human affliction. I fear my ambitions have outstripped my abilities, my fancy outshining reality. May our descendants live free of the shadow of our sins? May the future hold brighter promise than these dark days? I stare into the candle flame and see only the infinite bend of the arc of time—a rise, a peak, a fall—no more and no less afforded anyone, not even a Sonoro. And wherefore are we made to suffer, always suffer, inside the space of this insignificant flame?

EPILOGUE

The rain had stopped and the damp, twilight city glittered in reds and golds. A white limousine waited outside on the street, and Jaime in his tuxedo, Elena in her pink satin gown, and Juan Antonio in a pair of rumpled tan pants and a guayabera went downtown to el Cine Ópera.

"It'll be good if the rain holds off," Elena said, and Jaime agreed, though secretly, silently, he prayed the clouds would open back up, the sewers would overflow, that on this night of all nights a biblical shower would rage, trap everyone at home, and occupy the journalists for the next few days. But the windows of the limousine remained clear and the sidewalks outside cafés began to fill. Jaime crossed his arms and ran one thumb over and over his lip, the cold, smooth skin of his thumb against the barest opening between his lips triggering a sensorial disjunction so that his lips felt large and his body small, an inversion he leaned into the longer they drove, hoping somehow to become small enough to swallow himself, to completely disappear.

Elena squealed when the limousine turned the corner and they could see the throngs outside the cinema, what looked like hundreds of reporters and fans holding colorful umbrellas. From up high they must have looked like a field of nylon poppies. Elena opened and closed her compact three times to check her face. Even Juan Antonio was affected. He asked

Jaime if he could borrow his comb, and he regretted aloud that he had no lapel upon which to pin a flower.

Into the cold ocean Jaime plunged. Flashes and flashes and shouts for him to turn here, turn here, smile, wave, hug your wife, hug your costars, blow us a kiss, look up there, you look fantastic, she looks fantastic, isn't it all fantastic, Rooster we love you, we love you, we love you! By the time he was permitted to cross the red carpet into the theater his cheeks and jaw were cramped from the effort of holding his smile in place for so long. And inside—more photographers, well-wishers, kisses, and handshakes. "Something to be proud of" was said again and again. But no words could undo the certainty knotted up in Jaime's belly that he did not want to walk into that theater, that he could not, with his whole being, be proud of the movie about to premiere.

The lights flickered and a tone sounded, signaling everyone to take their seats. Jaime excused himself, found Elena and his father, and together they walked up the gold-carpeted stairs.

Inside, the pit orchestra was playing a lively western waltz. Jaime allowed himself to be led to his seat, making sure his face was strong and placid, making sure everyone in the room saw him as a man who'd accomplished exactly what he'd set out to do. Perhaps if he could fool them, they'd never notice the holes in the construction, the absences, everything he wished to say and couldn't say and lacked the imagination and strength and talent to build.

"I'm so nervous," Juan Antonio said, mopping his face with a handkerchief. "I don't know how you sit there so calm."

Perhaps he should have written the story about his father, Jaime thought. Perhaps the Sonoros' new chapter really began with him. Had he said enough in his story, followed the thread through enough time? Because Jaime had seen it—what was twisted could be set straight . . . eventually.

". . . a continuance of a grand tradition," the producer was saying into a microphone, standing in front of the giant, white screen. ". . . a complicated antihero for our complicated times."

The lights went off, the Estudios Churubusco logo blazed across the big screen, and the opening credits rolled, followed by a quotation:

"It is a hard thing to be a good man."

—Maria Gaspar Rocha de Quiroga,
*The Ignominious History of the Sonoro Family
from Antiquity to Present Day*

His father was a good man, Jaime thought. And he himself tried to be good. Transcendence wasn't a plot device; it was real.

The film opened, the first act began, and as Jaime liked to do at movie premieres, he quietly turned in his seat and watched his wife watching him on-screen, her face lit blue and purple, the soft colors ebbing and flowing over her tender features like the ocean mirroring a sunset. He watched his father, too, and enjoyed how the old man's face softened at the likeness of Antonio, kissing his on-screen son and telling him to be the man of the house before he set off for Texas.

In the second act, an old woman rescued Tragabalas and healed him. After she saved Jaime, as Tragabalas, she blessed him before he set off in search of the Rangers, and as Jaime watched, he swore he could see a man riding a white mare far in the background of the shot. He blinked his eyes and looked again, but the man was gone.

In another scene, Tragabalas and the Englishman were riding through the desert in dire straits, in need of water. There was a wide pan of the flat, unforgiving landscape and, yes!—there he was again, clearer now, a young man with wild brown hair on a massive white mare that looked more bull than horse.

Jaime sat forward in his seat and forgot to breathe. Sometimes he was far off in the distance and other times he was mixed in with the crowd. He was handsome and full of vigor, his bright green eyes shining with a luminousness that could have made him a movie star himself if he'd been born in the right century. He had his scar, but it was not so gruesome as Jaime had been led to believe. It was a ropy pink line that ran from his right ear to the corner of his mouth, disappearing inside a dimple, so that it looked like someone had simply folded over two pieces of his face and pinched them together like dough. During dramatic scenes he would make his face fearsome or brave, according to the mood, and likewise during funny scenes he would pull comic faces that looked quite a bit like the ones that had made Jaime an icon. This wasn't a gunslinging macho; this was a man who was enjoying himself, and who wouldn't have given a damn whether other men trembled when he entered a room.

"You should be proud, míjo," Juan Antonio whispered, gripping Jaime's arm. "Very proud," and Jaime's heart filled to bursting.

At the end of the movie, Tragabalas was finally reunited with his family in a tearful embrace, and the man was there as well. He emerged from the dark shadows of the jacal and stepped into the left-hand side of the screen. He kept coming forward until he took up over half the screen, until he blocked most of the parting shot. Jaime looked over at his father and the old man's face was tear-streaked and frozen in wonder, and Jaime knew Antonio was visible only to the two of them, perhaps only during this viewing.

Antonio looked into Jaime's eyes, Juan Antonio's. He pushed his hat a little farther down on his head, and he smiled.

Author's Note

Everything in this book is true except for the stuff I made up.

My great-grandfather Antonio Gonzalez was a bandido in the late-1800s. At some point he was put in jail in Houston, escaped, was chased down by the Texas Rangers, shot in the face, and left for dead. Except that he lived, hid out in Texas for a year (supposedly in an encampment of former slaves), and then made his way back to his family in Mier, Mexico. After that people started calling him "El Tragabalas," or the Bullet Swallower, and for a while I believe he enjoyed some notoriety in South Texas and Northern Mexico, becoming a minor local legend. Texas folklorist Jovita González (no relation) even wrote a short story ("The Bullet-Swallower") about him, which was published in the 1935 anthology *Puro Mexicano*, compiled by J. Frank Dobie. Antonio was embarrassed by the scar the bullet left across his face and he grew an enormous mustache to cover it. I have his Alien's Identification Card from 1928 that mentions a "scar on right side of face."

Other elements in the novel are true: the dead cattle along the Nueces River and the riot in Little Mexico in Corpus Christi were both recorded in *Maria von Blücher's Corpus Christi*, the diary of a German woman who was an early inhabitant of the town. Jesus "Casoose" Sandoval was a Texas Ranger and member of Leander H. McNelly's Frontier Battalion, and he did indeed torture people by stringing them up and suspending them repeatedly until they confessed or died. And thanks to the late journalist and historian Murphy Givens, I learned about the reef road that connected Corpus Christi and the neighboring town of Portland. It must have looked like a miracle to watch wagons cross the water like that.

I first started researching *The Bullet Swallower* in 2015, knowing that it was going to be a difficult task. I wanted to write a magical realism Western about a Mexican bandido and his movie-star grandson despite knowing nothing about magical realism, Westerns, bandidos, Mexican movie stars, life along the Texas-Mexico border in 1895, nor life in Mexico City in the 1960s. It would not have been possible to write this book without the incredible resources available to me through the Oakland Public Library and interlibrary loan. Among the dozens of books used in the writing of this novel were: *Views Across the Border* by Stanley R. Ross; *Riding Lucifer's Line* by Bob Alexander; *With His Pistol in His Hand* by Américo Paredes; *Taming the Nueces Strip* by George Durham; *A Private in the Texas Rangers* by John Miller Morris; *Mexican Postcards* by Carlos Monsiváis; *Life Along the Border* by Jovita González; *Borderlands/La Frontera* by Gloria Anzaldúa; *Adios to the Brushlands* by Arturo Longoria; *Mexican Cinema* by Carl J. Mora; *They Called Them Greasers* by Arnoldo De León; *The Labyrinth of Solitude* by Octavio Paz; *Where the Air Is Clear* by Carlos Fuentes; *Pedro Páramo* by Juan Rulfo; *Blood Meridian* by Cormac McCarthy; and *Autobiografjúa y Anecdotaconario* by Eulalio Gonzalez.

This last book is of particular note. Eulalio, or Lalo, Gonzalez, widely known in Mexico as "El Piporro," was a cousin of mine. Throughout his long career he was a beloved comedian, actor, singer, and dancer. And in 1964, at the height of his career, he wrote and starred in a comedy called *El Tragabalas*.

Here is the story I heard growing up: In the early 1960s Lalo visited my grandfather Antonio Gonzalez at his home in Detroit and asked his permission to write and star in a movie about Antonio's father, the actual Bullet Swallower. My grandfather absolutely refused. He was horrified at the idea of the family's history being used in this way, didn't want his father turned into a film character, and was apparently disdainful of Lalo's entire career, thinking he was somewhat of a singing buffoon. Clearly undeterred, Lalo wrote and filmed the movie anyway, and my grand-father was furious and reportedly never spoke to him again.

It was originally my intention to write a fictionalized account of ex-actly this story, using real names. There was only one problem: I couldn't corroborate this account anywhere. In Lalo's own autobiography there is scant mention of the film, and no mention whatsoever of his having any family connection to the real Bullet Swallower. Furthermore, the actual film, *El Tragabalas*, has nothing whatsoever to do with the story of my great-grandfather. In the film Tragabalas (who has no scar, by the way) is a roaming do-gooder who helps an old man escape from jail, saves a bank-er's daughter from being carried off by a violent card sharp, and then frees a rural town from the evil clutches of a wealthy brother and sister. Did he intend to write a movie about my great-grandfather and then change his mind and wrote this instead? And if so, why keep the title? I don't know. And sadly, as Lalo passed away in 2003, I could not ask him.

The other problem with using Lalo Gonzalez in my book was that, by all accounts—his autobiography, newspaper and journal articles, documentaries, and an interview I conducted with film historian David Wilt—"El Piporro" was a really nice guy who was adored by both fans and colleagues. In other words, he made for a lousy protagonist. I couldn't make him do anything bad, and I like to make my characters do bad things. And so I made the decision to change not only his name but his character as well. In the end, the only similarities between Lalo Gonzalez and Jaime Sonoro are: (1) they were both the highest-grossing film stars in Mexico in 1964, and (2) they both starred in a film called *El Tragabalas*. Everything else is made up. But Lalo was a brilliant comedian and, luck-ily for us, many of his films and songs are available on YouTube. I highly recommend watching them.

Love and abrazos,
(Tonia) Elizabeth
Gonzalez James
September 2022

Acknowledgments

Thanks to my agent, Peter Steinberg, for seeing the potential in my manuscript, for patiently answering my thousands of questions, and for being brilliant in general and hilarious in specific.

Thanks to my editor, Tim O'Connell, for wringing the best possible story out of me and for giving *The Bullet Swallower* an enormous pair of wings. I cannot thank you enough.

Thanks to early readers including Joey Garcia, Emily Cooke, Jenny Fosket, Jenelle Lindsay, Jacqueline Hampton, Carrie La Seur, Monee Fields-White, Anita Felicelli, Denny S. Bryce, Stacia Brown, Brad Felver, Cleyvis Natera, Amanda McTigue, Ezzy Languzzi, Anne Falkowski, Tamar Shapiro, Annalisa Garofalo, Tess Weitzner, Katie Aspell, Ricardo Bandrich, and Mary Pauline Lowry, and a special thanks to my incredible writers group: Noah Sanders, Kurt Wallace Martin, Celine Piser, DB Finnegan, Sarah Bardeen, and Galadrielle Allman. Viva las Lady Riders!

Thanks to Elizabeth Facteau for answering my very random horse questions (i.e., What would happen if you rode a horse naked??).

A special thanks to Judith Flores for help with translating and for your friendship.

Thanks to Janis Cooke Newman, Mat Johnson, and Cristina García for your guidance and your masterful edits.

And finally thank you, as always, to Larry, for everything.

About the Type

This book is set in Tiempos Text, which was created by New Zealand designer Kris Sowersby. It draws on the style of Times New Roman and was originally designed as part of the Galaxie Copernicus family, but it eventually evolved into its own family. Due to its clean-lettering design, Tiempos Text is an elegant and classic font.

About the Author

ELIZABETH GONZALEZ JAMES is the author of the novel *Mona at Sea*, as well as the chapbook *Five Conversations About Peter Sellers*. Her stories and essays have appeared in *The Idaho Review*, *Southern Humanities Review*, *The Rumpus*, *StorySouth*, *PANK*, and elsewhere, and have received numerous Pushcart Prize and Best of the Net nominations. Originally from South Texas, Elizabeth now lives with her family in Massachusetts.